MW01420772

# Spiritus Ex Machina: Dark Tales of Creation

LC von Hessen

# Spiritus Ex Machina:
## Dark Tales of Creation

LC von Hessen

GRIMSCRIBE PRESS

NEW ORLEANS, LOUISIANA

Published by

**Grimscribe Press**
**New Orleans, LA**
**USA**

**grimscribepress.com**

# CONTENTS

Dedicated to my familiar, Gregor Severin Montresor (a/k/a Monty): erudite gentlebeast, champion snuggler, tiny tiger in my home.

# Introduction: Machines Spectral and Infernal

Michael Cisco

AT ONE POINT in the story "The Contagion," the main character cries: "... the past *makes* us!" – and this could serve as a motto for this entire collection. These stories invoke the past, but in opposition to an official history; the past that makes these characters is a repressed and/or overlooked past that has been hidden or lost. LC von Hessen's protagonists often find themselves caught in a kind of ordeal of self-discovery prompted by the recovery of the past from behind the curtain of history. They do not seem to be at one with the world they find themselves in, but are, in a way, vindicated by an encounter that demonstrates all too plainly that they are the ones who are at one with the world as it actually is – it's the crowd who are out of step. In their superficiality, their conformity, their incuriosity, ignorance, obliviousness, or downright stupidity, the general public in these stories are deluding themselves when it comes to reality. This is where von Hessen's work intersects with Lovecraft, in the notion that the common run of mankind lives on, in a now familiar turn of phrase, an island of ignorance surrounded by an infinite sea of horrors. However, where Lovecraft expresses a conservative yearning to maintain simple, straightforward categories of identity, fixed ways of life and canons of value, that is to say, where he imagines that island of ignorance as a kind of lost paradise, for the narrators of these stories, that island was never anywhere they wanted to be, that vision is part of the horror, not its respite.

The past makes us, but it doesn't make us happy, and finding the hidden past, while it may deepen our understanding, will also traumatize and threaten us. So, these stories tend to revolve around a conflict between desire and those limits that are commonly imposed on it, and/or around a conflict within desire. The object of desire in these stories is almost always a kind of simulacrum: a doll, a mannequin, a figurine, an automaton, a mummy. In this nightmarish vision, desire acquires a secret potency to reduce living people to images, and often the protagonists of these stories find themselves, like the multi-valent main character of "Heirloom," trapped and paralyzed in a sort of living death that is the work of desire. It's as if desire here were a secret Medusa, transforming whatever it gazes steadily upon into an effigy of itself. As what might be a necessary counterpart to this, often the innately inanimate will take on a nervous sensitivity, becoming quasi-living fetishes.

The style of these stories also partakes of this nervousness and this connection to the past. There is, in von Hessen's style, an attention to detail, a deliberate insistence on a vocabulary that's slightly antique, a moderation of pace and a care for description that clearly reach back to early twentieth century and nineteenth century models, so that even the desired language is placed before us like a museum piece. Both the form and the content partake of the same erotics of museum. This gives most of the stories a timeless quality but moreover, they make it possible for von Hessen to invoke the possibility of shock and impropriety without having to write up to a louder volume or more gruesomely demonstrative spectacle. The advantage of writing somewhat more formally is it makes it possible to shock the audience with a falling away from formality, discretion. It empowers implication, and meshes nicely with the theme of the dreamer, since the dreamer feels something hidden moving behind the veil of formal niceties, middle class proprieties, churchical pieties, and so on.

The result is a blend of the carnal and the oneiric which often creates a productive tension in the stories, notably in "The Patent-

Master." That story is perhaps the clearest, but not the only, example of the way that tension can be mapped onto the past and the present, particularly through a generational disharmony. Something of the sort also happens in "The Spectral Golem," which seems to invoke E.T.A. Hoffmann as much as Lovecraft, resulting in an Expressionistic, intermittently absurd or mocking affect to the story. Here the characters are like cartoons, so the element of the simulacrum is introduced via stylization rather than concretized in a figure like a dummy, a puppet, or mannequin. In story after story, von Hessen exploits the more frightening aspects of desire by representing it as the transfiguration of someone into a marker or a passive double of themselves. The characters don't really relate to each other, or at least not to the protagonists, except via an intermediary shadow that reflects more of what they want to see than what the protagonist expresses or struggles to express. In many of these stories, notably "This Night I Will Have My Revenge on the Cold Clay in Which We Lie," there is a surplus of desire without any outlet, which seems to founder in these shadows, and being engulfed by them at a nightmarish party or similar get-together is one of the ways in which these protagonists meet their endings, if they are endings.

The way that art mediates desire and self-awareness is explored in a more reciprocal way between two artists in "The Medium and The Message," and then again in "The Obscurantist," which takes this concept into more direct realization.

Ready yourself now for a lengthy rumination on these dark themes, on guilt, on fantasy, on the body and its relationship to itself and other bodies, on dreams, on the past, and on those various techniques, artistic, entrepreneurial, and technological, that have been developed to prolong, extend, and deepen what, in the end, is an unconscious and often painful ambivalence.

# I

# The Archon's Factory

# An Infernal Machine

THE YOUNG LADY dropped her parasol onto the hay bed and giggled nervously as she arranged her skirts over the wooden stool. The machine-keeper—a slim, youthful man barely older than herself, with childlike eyes as blue as seawater—gently fitted the iron band around her skull and instructed her to keep her head still for the moment.

Her husband, a middle-aged gentleman with a broad moustache and an interest in phrenology, coughed with impatience.

"Now what did you say this contraption was meant for?" he asked brusquely.

"Well . . . its purpose is to reveal and display one's greatest desires," replied the machine-keeper in a soft-spoken voice, lowering the bowl over the young lady's head. "Now lean forward a bit," he whispered to her. "Rest your chin on the bar and look into the eyepiece."

The machine-keeper stood back and turned a great crank at the side of the device, flipping a pair of large, gilded switches with a show of effort, leaning forward and cautiously spinning dials to meet precise settings under glass displays. The machine began to rumble with grand and repetitive factory sounds of metal parts meeting, churning, pumping, sliding against one another inside the polished steel frame as curls of smoke emitted from a flue set into its roof.

The lady's husband checked his pocket watch and stared with skepticism at the banner for this exhibition, which depicted a flat, cartoonish version of the machine-keeper gesturing toward his apparatus below a typically hyperbolic description of the act. The machine-keeper himself plucked stalks of hay from his black frock coat, annoyed that the hay could not be restricted to live attractions as he feared it would enter the machine and clog its workings. He did not notice the lady's husband examining him until he was addressed by the man.

"Why," said the gentleman, "by any chance, was your father an aristocrat?"

"Pardon?"

"I refer to your bone structure." The man sniffed as if his observations displeased him. "You have a wide, triangular face with refined cheekbones, and your facial angle approximates eighty degrees. What the devil are you doing here?"

Before the machine-keeper could think of a response, the lady let out a clear, high laugh, like a young girl who has never known hardship. Her hands rose to caress something that was not there, and her husband's hirsute eyebrows met in wrinkles above his nose.

"Darling!" the gentleman called, with a stern edge. "Would you do me the honor of revealing what it is that so enchants you?"

She did not answer, at least not in words, and her husband growled into the machine-keeper's ear that he ought to shut down the device now.

The machine-keeper gave the lady a soft tap on the shoulder. "I do apologize for disturbing you, but I am afraid your session must end soon," he whispered. She nodded a disappointed assent, and the machine-keeper began to manipulate the controls, with less fanfare this time.

"Put me into that thing," the gentleman ordered once his wife was disengaged from the machine. He was dutifully seated and plugged in, arms crossed with doubt, and within a minute or two he began muttering displeased notions under his breath, which grew louder until he was shouting for the machine-keeper to shut it off and release him.

Detached, he immediately grabbed the machine-keeper by the shoulders and shook him. "Great heavens, man! What sort of an infernal machine do you think you're operating?!" he bellowed. "Such things can turn decent women into hysterics! And to think, at a family attraction!"

"I can't help what you see—"

"Hogwash! I won't stand such corrupting influences in my own community. I shall report you to the proper authorities at once!" With that said, he grabbed the young lady's arm and stormed off. She threw a blushing glance at the machine-keeper before disappearing behind a flapping tent wall.

When the constable of police arrived the next morning, he found nothing. The carnival had moved on during the night.

* * *

Most who experienced the machine were, however, not so outraged as that particular gentleman. Most were delighted.

The carnival posted its bills in many landscapes over the years, from rolling shores with wind full of sand-grit to mountainsides with mist coating the tents and cages, from flat plains with awestruck country folk to crowded cities with chattering sophisticates. There was a carousel full of mythical beasts carved out in grotesque detail, a double-headed fetus preserved in a jar, a booth with flying wooden pigs one could shoot to win a fancy doll, a prowling tiger captured in the wilds of the East, a dragon-woman who had serrated scales notching her skin and had learned to spit fire from petrol, and a marvelous mechanical contraption that revealed its spectators' desires to themselves. This last machine proved quite popular in most towns, with small crowds sometimes clotting its entryway to watch the icily elegant machine-keeper softly explain in vague, lay terms what it was meant to do.

This explanation was naturally never enough for the visitors and there was much speculation amongst themselves as to how the machine operated. A typical explanation involved a mesmerist wedged inside who would hypnotize the sitter through the peephole; others believed the device released certain herbs into the sitter's lungs to produce temporary delusions. The superstitious sensed a foray into deviltry while the more scientifically-minded believed the metal ring placed over the sitter's skull transmitted thoughts as energy into some sensational translation apparatus. Skeptics, of course, only saw quackery, concluding that nebulous images of what people wanted were placed in the viewfinder according to the sitter's perceived type, or that patrons only saw things in the machine because they believed they would.

No matter how it worked, the machine drew constant marvel and joy throughout the years. Children saw the gratification of simple desires or the realization of great futures as adults, depending on their ages, and their grandparents witnessed a peaceful end of life and a glorious beyond. The poor viewed comfortable prosperity; the wealthy saw satisfied self-fulfillment. Blushing brides and nervous grooms beheld a happy, secure, passionate marriage. Young soldiers about to ship out to war saw anything from a safe return home to glory and decoration on the battlefield, and their later widows would leave the machine with moistened cheeks, having witnessed a warm and loving reunion with their husbands' ghosts. Due to the nature of some people's visions, the machine was thought at times to be connected with fortune-telling or conjuring of the dead, though the machine-keeper was quick to deny this.

The machine-keeper himself was subject to gossip and supposition, as well as adoring looks from ladies in the audience and appreciative winks from certain gentlemen, to all of which he seemed rather oblivious. Did he build the machine himself? If not, who had? Was it his father; was it a family occupation? Where did he come from and how did he come to join the carnival? Did he have a wife, a sweetheart, children? Most importantly, what did the machine-keeper *himself* see in his fantastic device? To this last question, he would only smile slightly, avert his eyes, and almost seem to blush, saying that it did not matter.

The machine-keeper took great pride in his machine. Each night, after the visitors had gone home, he would unscrew the back panel and clean out the internal mechanisms. He picked out bits of straw, sand, insect corpses, and other detritus; he lovingly oiled the turning gears and cylinders, the pipe flue, all the minuscule bolts and levers hooked together like a skeleton. He would polish it all by hand, the golden brass and silver steel, until it shone like a pharaoh's tomb, although he knew no one but himself would ever see it. He was worried to the point of paranoia about the outer shell becoming dented or scuffed, all the more since it took two of the carnival's strongmen to lift it into the wagon, though after a few years the machine was fitted with wheels for easier transport. In cold seasons he would keep the machine running through the night, sleeping on a woolen blanket spread over the hay, taking comfort in the warm, rhythmic vibrations against his bare cheek and stomach.

* * *

The owner and manager of the carnival had run the place for more than three decades, having started in the business as a teenage boy driving tent spikes into the dirt. Now he was getting on in years. He came upon the machine-keeper sitting in a corner with his sleeves rolled up, delicately rubbing grease into the notches of a gear the size of one of the exaggerated lollipops for sale on the midway. The manager tapped the ground with his cane and the machine-keeper looked up at him.

"My boy," the manager began, "I do wish you'd enjoy your youth while it lasts. You're in your early, middle thirties now? That's still young yet. And all I've ever seen you do is work on that gadget of yours. You don't go off with the other men and play cards or drink and carouse or chase the local women." He let out a chuckle that sounded more like a wheeze.

"Why . . . it simply doesn't interest me, sir," the machine-keeper replied softly, turning the gear in his hands and examining the spokes.

"A bit of a pious sort, are you? No shame in that, I would say."

The machine-keeper shrugged without lifting his head. "No, sir. Not particularly."

"An odd fellow you are." The manager gave him a hearty pat on the shoulder, provoking a slight wince.

"You know, I fear I won't be around much longer. So many changes have gone on in this past decade alone, so much upheaval, and a man can only stay in this sort of business for so long. You ought to find yourself a good, steady job while you can, perhaps in the civil service, where there isn't much danger and you can work your way upward; hand over the care of this machine to some young lad in need of work. And get a nice, pleasant young girl to be your wife: you're still handsome and youthful enough to get women on your looks alone, I should say. A wife could bring you out of your shell a bit, I think; they always have to go and talk and gossip with their women friends. And then, babies! Just think how delighted you'll be to watch your wife suckling and singing to the little one, dancing about the nursery with Baby cooing in her arms. Then, to watch your son grow up to look just like his father, and perhaps inherit his position in business someday, while your little girl stays cute as a bug, playing innocently with her dolls and later gifting you with grandchildren and caring for you as you begin ailing . . . how wondrous that Nature has given men someone to care for us in all stages of life: in youth, our mothers; in maturity, our wives; and in dotage, our children! Why, doesn't that sound like a marvelous life?"

"Frankly, I . . . no, I don't think so. Not for myself, no."

"But it's what one *does*!" the manager sputtered. He blinked rapidly behind foggy, round-lensed spectacles and scratched a bald pate sparsely covered by a few slicked-down strands of snowy hair. "Women are a pleasure, and children are a *joy*!"

"Not for me," the machine-keeper repeated. "I wouldn't care for that life. No."

The old man squinted and shook his head. "Yes, quite an odd fellow you are, my boy," he muttered.

* * *

The manager was dead within a year, expiring limply in the bed of a local hospital. He was succeeded by his eldest son, a rowdy, listless man who favored cigars and loose women. With his booming voice and large physical presence, the new manager had previously served as the carnival's pitchman, standing at a podium near the entrance and announcing the attractions in grandiose terms.

During these years, the carnival lost some of its popularity as many preferred to flock to the cinema or local nightclub. Those who did show up often went with their noses in the air and their lips twitching in cynical smiles: what quaint old pastimes our parents had! Every bite of doughnut was laced with irony.

To help drum up business, the new manager began to arrange a special section of the carnival in which, for an extra fee, one could view an array of adult-oriented attractions. This included a burlesque revue that occasionally featured some of the freaks, and a penny arcade peepshow. Now the main customers of the carnival were groups of overfed businessmen with laughing, drunken mistresses clinging to their arms in shapeless dresses, and boisterous ruddy-cheeked college men accompanied by shy, naïve girlfriends putting on a pose of jaded sophistication. The new manager wanted to add the machine to the penny arcade, but the machine-keeper insisted that it did not fit that classification and warned that viewers would feel taken if they didn't see what they had expected. The manager shrugged; he felt the marks deserved what they got and it was no problem of his.

Around this time, the machine-keeper, who had kept his youthful looks longer than most, began to age. His full, dark hair developed iron blotches at the temples and grew a bit lanker as the faint lines around his eyes and upper lip deepened and hardened. The veins in his hands began to protrude like plump worms and the joints of his fingers turned knobby as the flesh around them receded. He was not as limber as he used to be: his tendons were growing stiff and inflexible, marrow scraping together rigidly. He felt his joints could use a good oiling if only he could take out his bones.

* * *

One late edition to the burlesque show was a gorgeous hermaphrodite of about 25, who looked outwardly female but was said to have near-full sets of both parts—of course, only those who saw the revue, or were among the many men she was reputed to have had, could know for certain.

She visited the machine-keeper one night after a show, still in the heavy, garish stage makeup meant to make her face less angular, with an imitation-silk robe loosely tied over her sequined bustier. He had been inspecting the machine for dents and loose bolts, and almost jumped when she tapped him on the shoulder with a lacquered nail.

"What're *you* up to, mister?" she said with lowered eyelids. Her voice was simultaneously soft, heavy, and oddly rich: hearing it was like stepping into a dense fog.

"Busy," he replied, turning back to his work.

"Oh, but I don't think you're *too* busy." She slid a wrench out of his hand and ran her nails around its outline. "I think you're entitled to a break sometimes."

The machine-keeper did not spread gossip, but he was not immune to it. "Now, look here. I'm far too old for you. My fiftieth birthday is a stone's throw away: I'm nearly twice your age."

She smirked. "Oh, don't be silly. I think I know what I like."

He gently pulled the wrench from her fingers and stared down into the hay. "But I'm, I've never . . . I'm just too old for that now. I'm too old to start. You've known so many, and I've had nothing. I could never compete; I could never hope to. It wouldn't be fair."

The burlesque dancer's lips pulled back bittersweetly. "Times aren't so easy now," she said, placing a kind hand on his shoulder. "We all just want to be happy."

He shook his head with screwed-shut eyes. "No, I couldn't. You're quite attractive, but I couldn't. I couldn't. Find yourself a young man who's had many lovers."

"Poor fellow . . . you really don't know, do you?"

The machine-keeper was only concerned about his device. It didn't run so smoothly now and needed extra care, and he found himself having to squint and lean closer to objects in order to inspect them. Some of the parts inside were beginning to rust and grow blunt: the glass of the peephole was replaced recently after the old one, long cultivating scratches, dull spots, and tiny nicks, sprouted a lengthy vertical rift after the wagon hit a nasty bump in the road. Replacement parts were already difficult to find, and he feared the day when they would become totally obsolete.

The dancer noticed him staring at the machine after a stretch of silence.

"Does it work?" she whispered, with the restrained excitement of a child about to hear a secret. "Does it *really* work?"

"Of *course* it does," the machine-keeper snapped, sounding ruder than he had intended.

❊ ❊ ❊

The dancer never came to visit him again. Within a month, she was shot and killed by a soldier she had taken to bed: a young man who had not been aware of, and could not have appreciated, what she was. The incident caused a scandal, and the carnival was forced out of that town overnight, the dancer hastily buried and inadequately mourned. The manager only featured typical sorts of women in his revue from then on.

This change did not bring in customers, however. The idea of a carnival seemed vaguely droll in light of all the fanfare and anticipation in the real world, with its new leaders and pristine promises. The general mindset was run through with an ambiguous shudder: the future could bring glory and bliss, or it could bring destruction and decay. It was best not to guess openly.

When war broke out, the carnival's touring schedule was limited: there were other priorities. The manager drew on patriotic fervor for hasty reinventions of existing attractions, adding more game booths in that vein with caricatures of enemy soldiers one could shoot for prizes. He pasted recruitment posters up next to banners advertising amazing mesmerists, ferocious performing lions, and live men with lobster hands. Of course, the manager's personal misadventures had often landed him before the law, and he was only trying to conjure a Good Citizen version of himself for security in this new atmosphere.

Although nowadays, it was not the manager who was harassed so much as the carnival itself.

* * *

"You there!" barked the officer of the law. "Old man!"

The carnival was nearly deserted at the time. The machine-keeper sat hunched over on a second stool next to the device: he could no longer stand there for hours at a stretch each day. He blinked and faced the officer, a youngish, officious man with scowl-lines dug into his forehead.

"Yes, I'm speaking to *you,* old man! Do you see any other old men around?" Flecks of spittle flew from the officer's mouth. "I need to know what this *thing* of yours does, and I don't mean that overdrawn hogwash on that musty old sign. What is it, some sort of parlor-trick scheme? You get people to think you're doing magic; you're promoting the supernatural? You should know that's not allowed, but there are bigger problems for you here. Fact is, that old metal box of yours isn't registered with us, and so you obviously don't have a license to operate it. Do you even have a permit to work? You know you're not *too* old. Sitting on your rear and pressing buttons on some overgrown tinkertoy does nothing to help the war effort or your country."

"But I've had it for years, so many years," the machine-keeper quavered. "What does this mean?"

The officer sneered. "How in the hell are we supposed to know what you're *really* using that thing for? For all we know, you've got something in those smokestacks there transmitting messages to the enemy as we speak. Perhaps it's even rigged-up to launch little missiles."

"Oh, but it's *not,*" he pleaded. "All it does is show people what they want. That's all. That's all it does. I could show you—"

The officer lowered his eyes at the machine, observing the antiquated design, the glossy panels and dials and switches that had been lovingly hand-polished over the decades but were inevitably losing their luster. "What *I* think about this thing . . ." He suddenly drove his boot into the side of the machine, causing a great metallic clang followed by an echoing clamor. The machine-keeper reeled back with the air pushed out of his lungs, as if he himself had been struck in the stomach. "I think it's a fine heap of junk and ought to be *scrapped.*"

"No, no!" the machine-keeper cried, his eyes gleaming with water. "I'll show you! It works, I'll show you, right now I'll show you and you'll see!"

The officer stood back with his arms folded derisively. "I'll see? What, old man, I look like a sucker to you?"

"Oh, no, no, of course not. But you'll *see*; let me show you and you'll see!"

The officer chuckled and shook his head. "Well, old man. (Pathetic old man.) If it would humor you so much, let's see how good a game you're pulling before I have to take you in."

He allowed the machine-keeper to lead him to the stool at the front of the machine, remove his cap in place of the flimsy metal ring, and go through the same calm spiel the machine-keeper had repeated each day for more than half his life. It took more effort now to turn the crank and flip the levers, but the machine-keeper did not mind: he had no audience to perform for now.

After just a few seconds, the officer said, "All right, you've had your fun. I don't see anything."

"You have to *wait,*" urged the machine-keeper. Part of the device had begun rattling inside.

The officer was silent throughout the rest of his session with the machine.

Once back on his feet, adjusting the cap on his head, he stared at the machine-keeper as if the man had sprouted a pair of antlers.

"*How*?" he rasped. "How did you know . . . ? There must be a catch—who have you been speaking to?! I demand to know . . . but that's just not possible . . ." At once he caught himself, realizing that an officer must not show such incredulity, especially in that sort of public arena. "You're a good patriot, old man," he said with forced sternness and a quick, manly nod. "You won't be bothered again."

* * *

The machine-keeper wasn't bothered by the government again. War ended soon enough and so did the manager's life, of a heart attack during a heated argument in a bar. The manager's only living relative was a grown daughter, the product of an encounter with a showgirl, who had been raised a ward of the state and was now quite formal and self-disciplined, with no use for the frivolity of show business—including the carnival she had inherited.

Nonetheless, it brought in more money than the monotonous factory job she had held down during the war. Unlike her father and grandfather, who both owned and ran the carnival but preferred to call themselves "managers," she referred to herself as the proprietress, which earned a good deal of secret grumbling and mockery from her new employees. Her first order of business was to abandon the strip show and any other acts of questionable taste, including the entire freak show, which she considered degrading. She began a lengthy process of transforming the carnival into a bland, but profitable, funfair: after complaints from parents that their small children were frightened of the old carousel's mythical beasts, it was traded in for a new one with innocuous ponies.

The machine-keeper was relegated to a far corner of the fairground. He couldn't walk long distances now without the aid of a cane and his skin was becoming unmoored from its structure, especially in pouches beneath his eyes and the webbing between his fingers. Those who found their way to his machine were often shocked enough that it still ran on clockwork and a crank shaft, not bothering to sit and look inside it for themselves.

The proprietress, with her strict, businesslike nature, was still concerned for the machine-keeper and often urged him to sell his machine to a museum: maybe he could also get work there as a guard so that he could still be near it, and perhaps improve his health as well, since he would be able spend his days indoors and not have to travel so much. He listened to her suggestions while staring at the ground, and she often found herself repeating what she had said, unsure if he understood her. In truth he just didn't know how to tell her the idea was not suited to him, not at all.

And so he stayed for a few years, sitting in the corner with both hands resting on his cane, head bowed slightly beneath his hat, sometimes dozing off before a shrieking child ran up with its mother behind and he would have to scold it meekly against touching anything. The machine grew increasingly slow, now taking almost ten minutes to work with a sitter in position, and most people naturally didn't want to wait so long with so many other, more novel, more exciting attractions to see. There were a number of scratches and scuffs he could not shine away and some of the interior parts looked incurably soiled and tender with rust.

He was examining this interior one day when it occurred to him that, in the half-century he had cared for the machine, reaching inside to clean and tighten and manipulate, he had never truly felt what it was like to actually *be* inside. There was a space just wide enough for him to sit back with his legs curled up. He set aside his cane, his grease rag, his wrench and screwdriver, and crawled into the space. At first the teeth of cogs and sharp edges of assorted angular parts bit painfully into his sagging flesh, but he adjusted soon enough and took in the rich scent of oil and ash detritus, the cool smoothness of iron, brass, and steel cradling his body. He yawned: he usually went to bed around that time of night and now he felt too tired to unbend himself. He reached out to replace the back panel, rested his cheek against a belted wheel, and fell asleep. Only a few tiny dots of light from the covered eyepiece made it inside, like a constellation with a long-forgotten name.

* * *

The proprietress sold the machine to an antique dealer after the machine-keeper had gone missing for a few days. Nobody else knew how to run the thing and it was a nonexistent draw anyway. She replaced it with a haunted house for children, full of friendly skeletons and white-sheet ghosts with broad black spots for eyes.

"I can't use this thing," the antique dealer muttered to his assistant after less than a week. "It was a mistake, pure and simple. Spare parts? I don't even know how to open that contraption." He glanced over at the machine, which was pressed into a corner of his warehouse, and grimaced. "I want you to get that thing out of here; take it to a junkyard, I don't care. It's starting to *smell*."

The assistant took a whiff herself. "Oh, I see. Maybe a dead animal got in there somehow."

"Maybe."

The machine-keeper's husk shifted as the assistant wheeled the machine out of the warehouse. That soft sound made the antique dealer's skin prickle as he examined a new acquisition: a spyglass in a fitted box with delicate prints of songbirds around its borders, which could be extended to ludicrous lengths and set up, pointing downwards, to stare into purgatory.

# The Patent-Master

My mother never spoke to me about her life as an exotic dancer in the island coastal town. I knew that she had lived there, of course, having fled from the mainland after earning her Bachelor's degree, in order to prove she would not marry a dental hygienist or auto parts salesman and bow her head each Sunday. This, needless to say, was before her career as an itinerant lecturer, before my birth, and certainly before my long-recurrent dreams of jade seas and endless rooms and faceless folk.

My mother, with her plastic-lensed glasses and burgundy blazers, a black silk scarf knotted about her neck. Dark hair cut in a sharply-parted pageboy, lips slashed with midcentury crimson when she bothered to wear makeup at all. Moderately tall, she nonetheless loomed above me in her sensible heels, through a cloud of cigarette smoke that clung to her clothes in a grey halo. She liked to have a *thing* in her hand with which to gesticulate: a glass of red wine, say, or a cigarette. The latter habit had worn a velvety, authoritative burr into her voice; later, all too predictably, it brought cancer, though she had seemed so imperious as to be rendered immortal. The act of taking a drink or a drag would temporarily sharpen her cheekbones into a pair of meathooks. She was, by all accounts, a formidable person.

My mother spent the bulk of her time lecturing around the country and the world. Thus I knew her mainly from recordings: in front of podiums, mostly, or theatrically pacing onstage, or issuing sardonic chuckles on academic panels shot by student videographers.

She did not, as far as I know, ever lecture in the island coastal town. I inferred over the years that some formative experience had happened in that town, which she would not discuss on those rare occasions when the subject arose. She would issue a terse *hm!* and we knew the matter was closed.

I did not accompany her on these lecture tours but was raised at home by a string of nannies and clueless, kindly stepfathers who were content to let me alone to read and tinker and draw. To everyone's relief, I'm sure, I was not the type of child to run around and scream at all hours like the pair of toddlers in the apartment above mine back in the city, reverberations of their stubby limbs thumping like blows through the century-old layers of wood and plaster above my head. No, my youthful nights were spent drifting to sleep alone with the hum and drone of the washing machine and central air and the great metal box with its grey-painted chassis bolted down in the basement, fueling the churning guts of the house. At these times the dreams began.

*Caligari angles, jagged and steep. Sharply-carved gleaming obsidian. Uneven blocks of top-heavy tenements poised to judge and devour any passersby. Sickly coils of mist writhing at wrists and waists and ankles. Narrowing alleyways that recede tautly enough to scrape skin from bone. Black-jade sea dotted with narrow boats, cresting along on black poles under perpetual night, ferrying silent passengers with heads huddled beneath roiling skies in shades of emerald and arsenic. Faceless folk, bodies like twigs with twine ligaments wrapped in crude oil and tar, white heads featureless but for two dime-sized pinpricks approximately where eyes should be, yet too widely-spaced for a true human face: perhaps a vitreous gleam inside, had I ever dared to look so closely.*

Weird dreams are not in themselves unusual—is there even such a thing as a "normal" dream? Forgetting to take one's final exams, perhaps? Or a carnal encounter with a minor celebrity?—but it so happens that I return to the same place every night I sleep long and well enough to dream at all, traversing recognizable landmarks I know better than the buildings of my own street in the city where I've spent my entire adult life.

*The* Musée des Monstres *with its crowded tiers of gape-eyed dolls and arcane medical curios, waiting for endless perusal. The abandoned shopping mall, grey storefronts colonized by faceless folk, drawing their blank heads back into shadow at my approach. The pallid manse of many rooms where time never advanced through months, through years, through decades, where I am pressed into endless journeys without thought, as though all has been plotted out for me in advance.*

During my mother's rare visits home, she would bring me a heavy coffee-table book from some city she'd visited, typically on the subject of visual art, which was the only thing she consistently knew I liked—yet rest assured that, however surreal their subject matter, my recurring dreams were not derived from these books. At eight years old, I once presented her upon arrival with a crude, malformed clay ashtray I'd fashioned in art class—which seemed to offend or embarrass her somehow, to my utter mortification. We would take in various galleries, followed by dinner out with my current stepfather in which they would share terse household news and veiled allusions to private grown-up matters, periodically interrupted by waitstaff handing over a phone with news from her agent or publicist. There was, in retrospect, an exhausted if restless quality to these visits, like slouching on a battered green room sofa before yet another night's performance.

Her presence inspired anticipation and awe but her recordings frankly bored me, as they would bore any child who lacked an exceptionally precocious level of pretension. After her premature death, her will ordered all records of her intellectual property—dot-matrix printouts of unfinished treatises stacked in shoeboxes in her office closet, tidy rows of hand-labeled cassette tapes, video clips suspended through airwaves and ethernet—destroyed by her attorneys, unfortunately right around the time I neared my 30th year and finally began to develop some curiosity about her life's work. I was, and am, perplexed and frustrated at her motives for eradicating everything.

Occasionally, both before and after her death, my mother's fans would seek me out, or stumble across me in the course of their obsessive researches, and attempt to discuss her ideas with me; but, inevitably, my eyes would glaze over at the concepts they could not summarize without slathering in a dense layer of adolescent nihilist pablum. They were the sort to sneer at anyone who had the utter temerity to *enjoy things*, asserting that a mindset heavily pessimized by chronic mental illness represented a valid and clear-headed philosophy of life: naturally, they reserved most of their scorn for fellow disciples who didn't appreciate my mother's work in precisely the same manner they did themselves. Those who were not affronted by my lack of encyclopedic knowledge of her philosophical oeuvre—as though I were expected to pick this up by osmosis—expressed a disappointment verging on disgust that I stood before them at all, as if my mere existence had driven a red pen through their Master's thesis. Thus I was repeatedly thrust into the awkward position of having to feel apologetic for the fact that my birth had unwittingly violated a vital tenet of some complex dogma that was utterly foreign to me. I would find no answers from *them*.

True, my mother was not conventionally maternal in the least—though much to the consternation of armchair Freudian commentators, I didn't and don't feel I was missing anything by having a Mother instead of a *mommy*. I couldn't picture her pregnant, her svelte body swollen with sacs of blood and fluid meant to cushion an expanding zygote. Or cooing over knitted booties and duckling-embroidered burp cloths. Or clapping along with televised puppets singing the alphabet in comic falsetto.

I could not even picture my mother as *young*. I could recall no photos of her without crow's-feet behind her lenses and regal silver-grey streaks in her hair: none, at least, until a certain shiftless night at the old house.

After a lull of some years during my tenure in the city, the dreams intensified following my mother's death, especially after my return to that house to help settle her affairs; and having awoken at 3 AM, physically and mentally exhausted from what felt like endless hours of rambling through the black streets of jagged angles, I tried to distract myself by sifting through a box of loose photographs from the closet below the stairs. Photos that were never posted on the household walls beside her stern professional portraits, doubtless because they were so deeply out of character.

My mother as a little girl with pigtails and frilly ankle socks, squinting up at the sun. My mother, perhaps 20, with heavy bangs and a green turtleneck and an acoustic guitar, *smiling* with *teeth exposed* alongside a handsome young man on whose lap she appeared to be sitting. And most bizarrely: my mother onstage, a small circular stage extending from a catwalk in roughly the shape of a keyhole, in a black room surrounded by low seats, entwined around three spotlit silver poles, long hair teased wavy and big with bangs in a Hokusai crest, wrapped in nothing but strategically-placed white bandages like a brazenly sexualized mummy.

A printed label on the back denoted this as a promotional image for a gentlemen's club in the island coastal town.

* * *

Now I have drained my meagre savings to travel to the island coastal town. I've rented a modest bungalow held up on stilts within walking distance of the shore and spend much of my time sitting in local cafés, attempting to draw in my notebook the way I used to do before the rigors of adult life drained the impulse from me. I cannot afford to return to the mainland—to the city—until my grant comes through, so I suppose I'm to reside in the island coastal town indefinitely.

What, beyond scraps of my mother's hidden past, had I expected to find here, in the island coastal town? A landscape conforming, in precise detail, to the constant dreams of my life? Yes, I admit it. Much, I'm sure, to the embarrassment of my mother's starkly rationalist disciples, that hope had very much crossed my mind; it would have fulfilled a certain kind of logic to step off the boat onto a black glass pathway below a turquoise sky, greeted by the lidless stares of the faceless folk—and thus, instantly, an answer uncovered, a purpose to my life conveniently achieved.

In fact, the landscape of the island coastal town has the quality of a dreary watercolor: sky and coastline rendered in various shades of grey, edge of the world shrouded in a perpetual haze of mist. Grit-filled winds whipping against bare skin preclude any true seaside leisure, as does a painful glare off the sand at midday. The town itself is built around low hills with wobbling, meandering pathways paved in mottled cobblestones: when I'm feeling uncharitable, which is often, I liken them to molars wrenched from giants' gums and crammed into the street. These pathways wind around tightly-packed blocks of buildings painted once-bright colors, their inhabitants wearing no masks and normal human skins. Local guides testify on street corners in colorful garb from two-and-a-half centuries ago to entice tourists to learn of the island coastal town's supposed history, indicating with flailing fingers that the infamous Ms. So-and-So was conceived *here* and the acclaimed Mr. Such-and-Such was murdered *there*. Had it changed much in the three decades or more since my mother had lived here?

I consider the photo of my mother, which seems to have been taken underground: this is unusual in itself since buildings in the island coastal town are not, as a rule, built with subterranean floors, given the risk of flooding. Now, the café I prefer has outdoor tables set in a loose rectangular U around a staircase descending into the ground, from which a low mechanical drone arises, probably a generator powering the kitchen appliances and weak electric fans: I believe the gentlemen's club is or was located here, but have yet to ask around. I am not the sort to strike up conversations with strangers. Beyond those money-starved locals who haven't yet fled to the mainland, the island coastal town is populated by gawking tourists and self-imposed exiles. Prices are raised for foreigners, presumed to be easy marks. This, as it happens, poses a serious problem for me.

My mother's career never brought great riches to our household, despite her fame, and her estate is currently being legally squabbled-over by her two most recent ex-husbands. My own career in the arts has not accrued much in the way of wealth: thus, for now, I must control my finances with an iron hand. And while I sit at umbrella-shielded circular tables nibbling at the local fare, meat or starchy root vegetables in a fried crust of dough, I spend far more time filling my stomach with hot liquids in order to trick it into a false sense of satiation. Tormenting my nostrils with foods I cannot afford, not until my grant comes through.

I find myself rationing money by rationing calories: I can spend *this* much on *this* amount of food before, by *this* time of day, I develop a headache or feel my limbs droop and my hands shake and a siphoning feeling in my stomach like a living, suckling creature clinging to my organs, and I have to waste daylight by sleeping to rest my nervous system. At times the beginnings of Panic will start to well up at the base of my skull and snake their tendrils gently but firmly through the crevices of my brain, apropos of nothing but an empty gut. When a masticated ball of mush at long last enters my stomach, the nutrients are leached out in a mad rush of gastric acid, causing my body to be utterly drained. And when it isn't enough, the next day my body will take its revenge by setting my mind adrift from its functions, slogging about in a bowl of grey slurry chained to a seeking void inside my torso. How inefficient, this overly-complex meat network; how easily it breaks down when one part fails. Easier to be a set of twigs and twine covered in tar . . .

My elderly grandmother went mad from malnourishment, so I'm told: a crash diet in which her weakened body cannibalized both brain cells and fat cells and brought forth dementia. Will I follow suit and lose my mind because of food, because of money? How very stupid and sad, to lose one's mind alone in the island coastal town. Did my mother ever have to live like this? Is that why she took up smoking?

In this near-trance state of struggle to retain both energy and consciousness, thoughts of the dreams well up in my brain without any particular catalyst. A warm fascination seeps in, *surges* in, a hunger-drive almost sexual in nature. Almost like love. What I once imagined love to be.

For a long time in my life, I avoided contemplating my dreams at all for fear they would become a daytime obsession. An obsession lurking dormant in my subconscious, patiently awaiting the right time. And the right time, it seems, has come.

And so in this state, every day, I sit in the shade, attempting to draw and waiting to hear back about the status of my grant.

* * *

Today, however, I find a man hobbling over to my table: a fellow expatriate, from the looks of him. He's dressed unseasonably in a lumpy maroon cardigan with a gently-inflated rubber pouch dangling over his belt, which I soon realize is a colostomy bag. In his sixties or thereabouts, he wears his age like a battle wound, shielded by a set of aviator glasses that sink into pouches beneath his eyes. His haircut appears some 30 or 40 years outmoded, probably unchanged since he first came to the island coastal town. He looks like a former lawyer: not in the sense that he'd retired from the law, but rather had walked away from the profession for some obscure personal reason.

The man plugs his four-footed metal cane into gaps between the cobblestones and pulls himself forward with care. He smiles, which seems to take pained effort.

"Ah! You must be Erminia's child."

Erminia was not my mother's name. I can only assume it was her pseudonym considering its vaguely aristocratic pretensions.

I tell him yes, and he nods. "I knew her well. You're welcome to visit my house tonight if you wish to—to discuss the matter."

He scrawls an address on a crumpled napkin from my table and stuffs it awkwardly into my hands as though this were a secret, as though anyone cared, before hobbling back down the lane.

*"Knew her well,"* did he? My mother favored soft-spoken librarian types: she had married (and divorced) four of them during my lifetime, all more conventionally handsome than this man. His features, I noticed, fit together somewhat oddly: too much space between his abbreviated beak of a nose and his upper lip, which was oddly flat, as though it had been sliced off and scabbed over in a shiny weal of scar tissue. His watery eyes were the dull grey of well-handled dimes, a trait they shared with the local seashore. He struck me as the human embodiment of a prolonged sigh.

Nonetheless, I've taken up his invitation, as I have little else to do. After sunset I follow the serpent-coil sidestreets past row-houses with identical façades but for their outward coat of paint, their few inhabitants giving me a single flat-faced nod of acknowledgment before returning briskly to their business. The man who knew my mother likewise greets me with a nod at his door, followed by a prickly attempt at a smile.

Inside, it's quite dim and sparsely outfitted, lit by a single lamp with a tilted shade perched on a side table. The walls of the living room are painted in some dark, antiquated hue I find difficult to decipher, burnt orange or olive green. A small, yellowed newspaper photo of a woman's face has been shellacked to the wall by the fireplace; above this photo, a crooked nail holds up a loop of piano wire or fishing line with wooden sticks at either end, like a device for slicing lumps of clay.

I have not eaten for hours. This was the normal time I would have eaten dinner and my body is thus calibrated to expect food, a fresh jolt of nutrients. Sitting down too quickly makes me dizzy, a cascade of starry static temporarily obscuring my vision. He does not offer food or drink.

The man drops his cane into an umbrella stand by the door and eases himself into a wheelchair near the fireplace with a grunt. I notice the matted carpet is coated with a layer of dust in which twin wheelchair lines have been carved through in precise routes like the tracks of a carnival dark ride. I notice an oddly familiar smell of smoke.

"I wasn't always a pathetic old man, you know," he says. "I used to be a pathetic younger man. And before that a pathetic child, but she didn't know me back then."

It occurs to me after a few moments that he is joking.

"And your mother: what's she doing nowadays? Or, pardon me, what *was* she doing?"

"She was a professor of philosophy."

"Ah! Professor Erminia," he muses, with a dreamy smile.

Again, this was not her real name. I don't bother to correct him.

"And you, what do you do?"

"I used to draw, mostly, but now I make collages and assemblages."

"Of course you do."

Somehow this feels like a slight.

"I've applied for a grant recently," I tell him. "I should hear back any day now."

"Hm," he considers.

I realize the couch I'm sitting on is also filmy with dust. As is the fireplace. As is the small ottoman at the man's feet, printed with sepia-toned 19th-century world maps.

"I'm often inspired by dreams," I say, to fill the air. "I find I often have . . . very vivid dreams."

"Yes, I expect you do."

I'm conscious of a faint, almost subliminal mechanical hum at the back of the room, behind me, distracting me from his rather presumptuous statement. He fumbles in the side table drawer for a pack of cigarettes, letting loose an irritating cellophane crackle.

"I was an inventor in my younger years. A master of patents." He shakes his head. "I know, an arrogant title. It was given to me. 'Patent-Master.'" A dry chuckle. He flicks a plastic lighter. "'Patent-Master' I may be, but in truth I'm only a vessel for greater things. I myself am nothing. A total nothing."

It's apparent to me that this man is an obvious crank. Not surprising: my mother attracted that type. And that "title," good lord. My immediate mental image of a Patent-Master sports a kettledrum belly straining the spangled suspenders he's hooked his thumbs beneath, grinning ruddy-cheeked around a fat cigar below a battered top hat at a cocked angle. This Patent-Master has none of those things.

"You don't need a physical prototype to file a patent," he continues. "Only schematics, only an abstract. Most people don't realize that. And they let the ideas slip away." A gesture of dismissal in smoke. "I had a modest supply of family money, but I made a minor living from the sale of my patents. The schematics, rather. She—Erminia, your mother—she convinced me to sell most of my patent schematics as art objects. Collectors have them, now. Galleries. I don't know." He sighs.

"Only one of my patents was ever built: by me, at least. Just the one." He holds up one dust-colored finger for emphasis. "Well, three copies of the one. Only three in the whole world. That's all. That's the one I *kept*."

I realize he's talking about something specific: that a copy of this one patented invention sits in the back of the room, a few yards behind me. A large, roughly rectangular object dominating the back wall, covered by a dusty drop cloth. Undoubtedly the source of that constant machine drone.

"You know," he says, "there's a local funereal custom. Perhaps you've heard of it. The dead are each burned on a pyre in a coffin made of dough, with root vegetables packed in beside them. Which are then plucked out of the flames, you know, with tongs. And they're eaten by the heirs and executors." He smokes his cigarette. A long, awkward silence ensues.

I notice a record player in the corner with a furry pelt of dust obscuring its glass cover. I imagine any record inside would skip in an infinite loop. I feel the need for a ticking grandfather clock or stray faucet drip to break the tension.

There's a straining ball of air inside my stomach, a red pulse in my head. I am sinking from the inside. I need to eat. I need to drink. I need to go back to my bungalow and lie down for awhile. I need to take care of this faulty meat contraption I'm sealed inside. I need him to answer me so I can leave.

"Why did my mother come to the island coastal town?" I ask him. "What was she escaping?"

He smiles, indulgently. "How much do you know?"

"I only know that she was a—a dancer here."

"More than that." A long drag and exhalation. "Your mother and I had an *arrangement*." He chuckles. "You see, I knew her as *Mistress* Erminia."

Oh.

I see.

Few things truly shock me anymore. I am too exhausted to be shocked now, to feel anything too strongly except a bodily-induced Panic I hope will not come. My mother, the imperious, sharp-witted, diamond-hard stalker-upon-stages. Yes, I suppose it makes a certain type of sense.

"I wasn't her only client—tourists, you know—but I was her only regular."

"That you know of," I blurt.

He shakes his head. "I was her only regular. This island is small. There aren't many people to talk to in this town. Now, I don't kid myself she loved me or anything, but she was lonely. A smart woman, and lonely. After a session, we'd talk a little, or watch TV. Right . . . there." He points at a dusty rectangular outline on the wall which I hadn't noticed before. "And even among the tourists, you know, there wasn't much demand for a specialist of her calibre. I could always tell the difference between a prostitute who was just getting paid to enact an unfamiliar fantasy and someone who *knew* what she was doing and *enjoyed* it." A reverence has crept into his tone. "She gave me the most wonderful welts."

I let out a nervous cough.

"Oh, we're all adults here." He stubs his burnt filter and lights another with shaking hands. "She'd make me wear costumes, all the time, in case she dropped by, and I would have to wear them under my clothes. After these 30 years I still do, just-just in case." He undoes the top button of his cardigan and pulls out the serrated green point of what appears to be a jester's collar.

"Or a dunce cap, like the penitents would wear d-dur-during the Inquisition. Sh-she called me her patent puppet boy, w-when I was good." He grins, the jester's-collar flap drooping from his neck like a peeled fruit. "'Y-you're pathetic! You're a *bad* inventor! You're a Master of *None!* I could invent this f-foolishness in my sleep!'" A forgotten clump of ash drops into the dust at his feet.

"It's true," he says, quietly. "My patents don't serve a grander purpose. They're not even good at making money. Not for me, not on their own. In my life's work, I have failed." He stares into the empty fireplace for several moments, then looks back at me. And smiles. "Now you're here, you can end it all."

Frankly, I would prefer to leave now.

"She . . . *used* me, sometimes. As a reward," he yammers on. "And made me wear a mask. Would you like to see it?"

No, I do not especially want to see whatever leather appendage my mother fastened around his neck to conceal his homely features during sexual congress. This is already more than I ever cared to know about my mother's intimate life. Yet he bends forward to crack open the sepia-toned ottoman and rummage around inside.

The man pulls out a short brass cylinder: "Do you remember the kaleidoscope?" He almost pronounces it *kaleidy-scope,* like a child. Does he mean this specific kaleidoscope or merely the general concept of kaleidoscopes as youthful diversions? I immediately recognize this as a very silly question, automatically taking the thing in my hand. I peer at the dim light of the side table lamp, refracted through emerald and turquoise and red-black slivers of glass.

When I lower the kaleidoscope, I see him wearing the mask.

The mask is blank white, featureless, with two dime-sized, wide-spaced holes for eyes. A familiar mask I have seen for years at night.

A wave of anxiety courses through me, cold nausea constricting my throat.

"All right, that's quite enough. Take it off now."

"First," says the Patent-Master, "*why don't you take off yours?*"

Guided by supernal marionette strings, my hands lift up, under my chin, under my jawbone, and pull off my face.

I cannot see the edges of my nose or the rise of my cheeks. I am afraid to reach up and touch in case I feel bone, or eyeballs floating in air, or a void concavity where a face should be.

The thing in my hands slips onto the carpet. I don't dare glance down to retrieve it.

"You aren't going to win that grant," the Patent-Master's hidden mouth continues, his eyes a vivid gleam. "You've been outbid. You must let this hope die.

"Do you know what it really means, to be out of hope? Oh, it isn't that you *want* to die, but that you simply don't care about living, about maintaining life: that it honestly *does not matter*, in your mind, what happens to you. You could be set upon by mad anatomists and vivisected alive, and would only watch the whole process dispassionately while strapped to the table until your consciousness shut off from shock or blood loss. Utter, utter indifference.

"It was my last hope, your mother's and mine, that you should earn this knowledge. To be understood was the last hope we had left."

The Patent-Master reaches up with his thin hands and fashions a wide, round leech-mouth in the white material of his mask. He beckons me to reach inside the black pit. I fumble past the jutting lumps of teeth and sluglike tongue until I find the lever.

His head drops off cleanly onto the carpet, a fresh indent in the dust.

The body remains still, a cigarette moldering between the fingers. I turn to his machine before the air starts to fill with singed flesh.

My head throbs inwardly, near the point of explosion. Yet I pull back the drop cloth to reveal a grey-painted metal chassis with a familiar row of switches and dials and potentiometers, better-maintained than those my mother's basement, above a clouded glass tank where, after wiping away the condensation, I see my dreams move in miniature.

I shift the knobs to uncover different landscapes, the black-jade sea, the narrow alleyways, the pallid manse, until the levels in my body return to a flat line, until all need is gone: not sated, not deficient, but simply no longer there.

* * *

In the underground cabaret at the foot of the café steps, with my unface cloaked and my heels crushing broken shards of glass, the third patented machine stands forgotten: where, in a churning tank of dreams, my mother dances, forever, whether she wanted this or not.

# The Spectral Golem

SAMUEL WINGATE CURSED his neurasthenic temperament and lack of proper summer attire as he daubed a slimy sheen of humidity from his forehead, squirming at the rings of sweat pooling in the armpits of his waistcoat. His left-hand palm still throbbed beneath his glove thanks to the slash of a dagger concluding his Order initiation, with a sample of his blood duly collected and sent ahead for the Great Unveiling.

Wingate was, at the time, earning his graduate degree in biology at Miskatonic University, meanwhile teaching life science at a local boys' school to make ends meet. Every night he returned to a humble rented room overlooking a quaint Puritan churchyard in which the names of the deceased were largely obscured by time and lichen. During his free hours, he would stroll through the graves, seeking out his ancestors' names and studying the pithy epitaphs. Later he might peer through his microscope at a sample of grave-mould he had scraped away, as if some secret of the Tomb lurked within its squamous tissue, nourished on the collapsed bones of his forebears. And as if (he sometimes thought bitterly) some essence of those dead forebears might reveal to him the key to some greater position in society—or at least the means to rent a room in a boarding-house that did not befoul his sensitive nostrils with the lingering odor of mildew.

Wingate led an uneventful life of relative solitude, yet this was ultimately his preference. He would often lose track of time while engrossed in studies of the quiet workings of the organism and its cells. The self-contained microcosmic spheres of organelles, the kinetic thrum of electrons, all these unseen cogs that keep the world turning through sheer metaphysical force: this was all vastly preferable to the modish clattering mania of the dance hall and skating rink, flocked with local young ladies whose unspoken entreaties conjured up forbidden thoughts of paths he dared not tread.

He had been invited to the Great Unveiling in lieu of his mentor, Professor Hanwell. The professor was recently bedridden after contracting some mysterious ailment following an ill-advised field excursion through a certain quarantined acreage west of Arkham. "Hang on to your health if you aim for tenure, lad," Hanwell had told Wingate with characteristic geniality before emitting a phlegmy cough into his fist.

It was, Wingate knew, a true honor to be selected to join the Order, let alone attend the Great Unveiling, and it could serve as an excellent advance for his career. Of course, Wingate was not a genuine occultist, considering himself an inherently rational-minded fellow devoted only to quantifiable reality rather than the favor of some esoteric devil or deity, yet he was filled with the speculative curiosity regarding the unknown which seemed to mark all true men of science.

Wingate had never traveled so far from Arkham before, never in the span of his 23 years. With a modestly-sized, newly-purchased suitcase dangling from his undamaged hand, he had boarded his solitary train car without farewell from either his parents (deceased) or his sweetheart (nonexistent). He stared out the window lost in thought for hours as the locomotive churned its wheels through mountains and plains, ever further from the lapping seashore and tangled forests and gabled cottages of his youth, a massive silver snake wending through the American landscape to creep inside its pulsing industrial heart.

Somewhere in Pennsylvania, his eye caught a decaying barn with its planks discolored and its ceiling caved in, its sole remaining double door yawning widely below a rusted metal pentagram set into the frame. His initial sense of sorrow at such a rustic historical structure being allowed to collapse into decrepitude quickly gave way to a certain smugness that the aged symbol inset by the barn's former owners had not managed to save their fortunes. *Fie!* he thought. *An end to superstition!*

The city of his destination, once host to the fabled World's Fair, was said to run with a sleek clockwork efficiency thus far unknown to Modernity: its buildings resembling a slew of swords and rapiers piercing the fabric of the sky; its factory smokestacks fitted with colored dyes to churn out vapor in various fanciful shades hitherto unrecorded by the human eye; its moguls and working-men alike all galvanized with pride of craftsmanship, nation, and purpose, elevated to religious heights; its radiant electric lights visible for miles in all directions in a convolution of vibrantly beckoning stars, forming an array of man-made constellations.

Yet the gleaming White City of which Wingate's nursemaid had spun gushing tales in his boyhood had long since devolved into a land of outsized filing cabinets towering above his head in grime-encrusted heaps of brick, its streets cramped with defecating horses, soot-belching automobiles, braying newspaper vendors, hawkers of shoddy merchandise, daytime drunkards, and undifferentiated rabblerousers from every corner of this adolescent nation. There was no true Progress visible here beyond the baseness and mire of textile mills and slaughterhouses: even the latest art on exhibit appeared to consist of little more than exploded shingles and mangled knives.

Wingate bristled instinctively at any incidental brush of a strange body on sidewalk or streetcar, convinced some rapscallion was about to lift his watch or wallet—or, worse yet, pluck the Order badge straight from his lapel, not that they would have known what it represented. En route to his lodgings, a panhandler wearing a battered sailor's cap and several days of stubble requested change in an accent that sounded, to Wingate's horror, roughly Scandinavian, and he nearly lapsed into a paroxysm of hysteria on the urine-sodden pavement—though he later conceded that this melodramatic reaction was hardly a sign of good breeding. Even after retiring to his assigned hotel, his ears were assailed through glass and asbestos and sumptuous wallpaper by car horns and domestic discord, the mingled chatter of a thousand illiterate tongues. Clearly, he thought with vague disgust, not a single person in this city could boast of any ancestors who owned more than a hectare of land! He wished in that moment to barricade himself behind a pile of eugenics treatises on the link between chronic poverty and inherited degeneracy before dimly recalling that his own family's fortunes had peaked around the year 1066.

Wingate was struck with a hard strain of nostalgia for his hometown: if a fellow wanted to hop in the Miskatonic and drown himself on some deserted stretch of picturesque shoreline where his colonial forefathers once took leisurely strolls, why, he could be sure to do so without witness or interference! Yet here, in the city . . . one could not feel *alone* here. Even within the confines of his hotel room with the door locked and curtains drawn, lying on the bed in an attempt to regain his composure, his quiet reverie was distracted by the maddening gnawing of rodent incisors within the room's wooden framework and an unseemly moaning emerging from the nearby bridal suite. Perhaps worst of all was the repeated, uneven shuffling of mysterious steps on the hallway carpet, causing him to fancy he could sense an ear pressed to the doorframe and an eye peering through the keyhole: perhaps next, an unseen hand would try to turn the knob. Wingate felt as subject to the incidental scrutiny of strangers as a madhouse inmate—and this only made him retreat further inward.

When he had managed to rouse himself sufficiently from his failed attempt at relaxation, Wingate arranged for transport to the automotive plant of Thaddeus Greensward-Krenwinkel, a highly-placed Order member who was to host the Great Unveiling. Viewed through a tall row of cast-iron pikes that served as the plant's security fence, this towering structure stood as a grand plateau of seamless, reinforced granite, a single block of stone purloined from a quarry of giants. Its flat rooftop was capped by a cluster of smokestacks emitting silver-white steam, its walls bordered high on each side with glittering panels of windows that caught the gleam of the sun like fish scales. The sight commanded in Wingate a certain quiet majesty, bringing to mind the preserved ruins of a long-lost civilization.

Upon displaying his badge and awkwardly attempting to enact the secret handshake with the stiff-backed, hawk-nosed Order sentry posted at the front gate—who, upon casting a quick but forceful glance at Wingate's person, was thoroughly annoyed with him for not having taken the discreet side entrance reserved for servants and tradesmen—Wingate was hastily ushered through the length of the factory, its foundations laid as bare to the naked eye as the clean-picked skeletal innards of the giant whale gathering dust in Miskatonic's specimen department. A clipboard holding a stack of generic inventory forms was shoved into his left hand, knocking against the fresh wound under his glove and causing him to suppress a wince: he was sharply instructed by the sentry to pretend he was merely a safety inspector, should anyone inquire about the purpose of his visit.

Wingate vastly preferred this vision of modernity to the filth and chaos of the streets outside. As he followed the brisk steps of his guide, he found himself nodding with approval at the nimble hands and focused actions of the well-scrubbed factory denizens: clearly, he thought, of a higher calibre of breeding than one might expect in such a workplace, though there was something oddly unsettling about their uniform features, cold expressions, and vaguely ashen complexions. He craned his neck in wonderment at the vaulted ceiling that loomed above him with the height and acoustic echo of a cathedral, drowning out all other sound but that of the machine dominating the facility's vast interior.

This immense machine, the factory's centerpiece, the nucleus of all automations within, appeared to Wingate as a colossal arachnid, the Edison Age descendant of a clockwork automaton created for the amusement of royalty. (As a boy in Arkham, he had seen one of these in person at the University's museum: limbs and jaws moving with smooth lassitude only to jerk abruptly to a halt or new direction, leaving a profoundly uncanny effect on his young mind.) The machine's exterior casing—its exoskeleton—shone with the forthright gleam of steel, etched with decorative curlicues in a near-cuneiform script. A network of brass pneumatic tubes outfitted with transparent glass panels conveyed metal ingots throughout the processes of the body in a series of improbable angles and curves: these ingots entered the machine by way of a six-pronged set of interlocked mandibles at its front, each ingot hoisted by three strong men and launched into the gaping mouth as the mandibles clammed shut with the booming metallic resonance of a church bell. As the wound of his left palm itched beneath its gauze wrapping, Wingate idly wondered how many men had lost hands between the shining jaws.

Passing through the center of the room, Wingate watched as a team of workers steadily, laboriously cranked the handle of a pulley bearing the clanking links of a great chain emerging from a long rectangular pit set into the concrete floor. Soon a massive cauldron was hauled up to the surface, brimming with a roiling, brackish fluid alive with whorls of intermingled colors and emitting a strong, oddly masculine scent. The ascending cauldron briefly dinged against the huge exhaust duct impaling the machine's abdomen from above before being carefully tilted at such an angle that a steady stream of fluid poured from its spout into a funnel set atop the body, sliding into a concealed furnace. A great hiss of gaseous smoke immediately followed, an array of dials at the machine's thorax began to twitch insistently, and the gilded hemisphere poised above its mandibles glowed with an inner light, as if some unseen intelligence had suddenly taken notice of the callow youth standing below.

Meanwhile a set of conveyor belts jutting from the back of the machine shuttled half-formed parts to other, unseen chambers of the factory. A line of grey-faced women with hard-set lips stared blankly into space as their hands moved with seeming muscle memory, plugging brass appendages into corresponding apertures. Two other lines of workers monotonously fanned huge bellows set into the sides of the machine; on either side of them, eight sharply-bent piston-legs churned forth in a slogging percussive pattern while a staccato rhythm emitted almost hypnotically from the great machine's confines, creating a symphony of industry that spoke to Wingate of the highest standards of Progress. Though deeply intimidated and nearly overwhelmed by it all, he felt a swelling of pride in his surroundings: his only true complaint was the heavy degree of humidity within the plant, which had settled a layer of sweat over his slim frame as soon as he walked through the doors.

The sentry ushered Wingate past this display without comment. He was led into an unlit corner of the factory, up to a dingy metal door marked HAZARDOUS MATERIAL—and here the guard fumbled with the heavy ring of keys dangling from his belt.

The door opened onto an elevator shaft. Wingate cautiously peered into its murky depths, attempting to see where the car's dangling cables ended, and was roughly pulled back by the sentry, who admonished him with a stern shake of the head. A pair of keys, turned simultaneously in their respective locks, set the elevator to life. Wingate lost track of the many minutes he spent waiting for its arrival.

The guard retracted the elevator's latticed bronze gate and bade Wingate to join him inside. The elevator operator on duty was another well-built, stone-faced worker. Wingate noted that his uniform and visible skin were curiously free of perspiration, and the white-gloved hand loosely gripping the control lever was marked with a deep indentation, as if lightly bitten by some giant beast.

The great machinery's rhythmic vibrations aboveground slowly faded to ghostly echoes during the elevator's descent. The sentry let out a sigh, his dark eyes narrowed to reveal premature crow's feet.

A dim, tapering tunnel awaited Wingate and his guide after the elevator slowed to a halt. Gently illuminated by glass-globed sconces full of gaslight mounted high on the rough-hewn rock walls to either side of him, the tunnel impressed upon Wingate a strong sense of claustrophobia: he could neither see its ending nor sense the extent of its height. The pair's footsteps sounded far too conspicuous clanking along the cast-iron pathway: the acoustics of the tunnel seemed somehow incorrect for its apparent dimensions. Wingate could not help but consider unseen ears hidden within the bedrock, or the crescent-shaped blade of the dreaded pendulum swinging ever closer in the darkness above.

Passing through the doorway at the tunnel's merciful end, Wingate was escorted down a circular staircase resembling an enlarged spring, coiled in readiness for some ominous subterranean design. Its high railings, extending far above his own height, ensured that he could see nothing of the surrounding foundations. The residual heat of the factory's workings made these railings warm and slick to the touch, like the belly of a snake that had lain in the sun.

At the landing, he stepped into what appeared, absurdly, to be a brief reception lobby. Behind a polished mahogany desk stood a small pinch-mouthed girl about Wingate's own age with the sickly complexion of a recovering consumptive. The brooch at her collarbone indicated her to be a member of the Order's female auxiliary.

She cleared her throat audibly as Wingate passed by.

"Pardon me? Sir?"

Wingate turned to look at her impatient stare.

"I'll be taking your hat and your timepiece before you proceed any further, sir."

He patted the golden chain of his late grandfather's intricately engraved watch, presently dangling from his waistcoat pocket. "I beg your pardon?"

"It's the regulation, sir." She held out a petite lace-gloved hand with some impatience.

The guard lightly elbowed Wingate's ribcage and rolled his eyes.

Wingate freely surrendered the hat in his hand, its brim slowly growing misshapen from the sweat of his palm, yet he detached the pocket watch from his buttonhole with some reluctance. His thumb traced the family crest imprinted on its cover.

"Please, miss, do take care. That watch is a family heirloom—"

"I'm sure it is, sir."

He wanted to stay and observe where exactly this glorified coat-check girl was stowing his belongings, but was urged into the next room by the sentry.

Another long hallway stood before him, this one significantly better-lit. Its walls were lined with large banners and tapestries depicting images and tableaux out of the Order's symbology, much of which was still a mystery to Wingate. Here was a reproduction of some Egyptian relief perhaps recovered from a dusty tomb. Here was a black goat with yellow eyes and horns gnarled into curlicues, raising a single hoof as if in greeting. Here was a late Medieval sorcerer who appeared to be fashioning the binding of a book from the flayed skin of a captured devil. Here was a squatting, muscular creature with a pair of webbed wings folded across its back and a malformed face with a set of dangling appendages in place of a mouth. Here was the darkened silhouette of an *ancién regime* gentleman flanked by a series of overlapping spheres. Here, on a field the color of bile, was a strange icon depicted with such unsettling geometry that he felt the immediate urge to look away. Here was an image that—but no, it could not possibly depict—

Wingate wished to observe certain of these banners in greater detail, but was pressed ever onward by the sentry.

In time their own echoes intermingled with a faint muttering ahead, growing louder until they stood before a great circular doorway. The following chamber was sealed shut by an intimidating barrier recalling that of a bank vault, yet somehow more complex: it resembled a trio of brazen ship's wheels set within one another in descending order of size, yet the position of each wheel's spokes clearly held some significance. This portal, Wingate realized, was essentially an enlarged combination lock: and in confirmation, his guide deftly rotated each wheel into its correct position, upon which it slowly slid open on well-oiled hinges.

The guard, clearly relieved to be through with Wingate, offered him a perfunctory bow and wave of the hand to invite him into the

Exposition Chamber. As Wingate gingerly stepped inside, he was startled when the metal door clanged loudly into place behind him, instantly drawing the room's attention to the unstudied newcomer.

He, Samuel Perkins Wingate, the mere son of an Arkham hosiery salesman, stood among the storied guests of the Great Unveiling, who had journeyed from crumbling turrets and luxury suites all around the globe to attend. And he immediately began to worry about the potentially unkempt state of his dress in the wake of the heat upstairs—the inadequate tailoring of his suit, the increasingly dingy and poorly-starched quality of his cuffs and collar, the degree of frizz that had crept into his carefully combed hair—all while surrounded by Order members of spotless lineage who scrutinized this youthful interloper in muttered asides. He silently reached up to straighten his tie.

The Exposition Chamber, he noted, was designed with the approximate dimensions of an opera house. Wider than it was long, its high vaulted ceiling encouraged the muffled whispers of a churchgoer. A quincunx of crystal chandeliers dangled from the ceiling, wired with electric lights that mimicked candle flame through onion-domed glass bulbs. The chamber's marble floor, outfitted in a chessboard pattern, was partly concealed by a wide Persian carpet which extended all the way to the stage and podium at the back of the room.

The back of the stage was concealed by a velvet curtain some thirty feet high, emblazoned with a massive Order emblem that continually warped and wrinkled in on itself with every idle motion of the fabric. The proscenium arch surrounding the stage was composed of a series of painted wooden panels: they were imported, it was whispered, from the court of a decadent 18th-century Empress, who had commissioned a private theatre in which to witness political prisoners' executions through the cruelly inventive means devised by her various lovers. Some of the paintings depicted genteel Rococo scenes typical of their era: pastoral landscapes in which culotte-clad youths cavorted with rosy-cheeked maidens in the seclusion of Provençal woodlands. Others held compositions of such immense depravity that Wingate instantly blanched and turned his back to the stage, trying desperately to maintain his composure.

He glanced around at the rest of the chamber. Its dour bedrock walls were enlivened by tall crimson curtains and a smattering of armchairs at its perimeter, occupied mainly by the elderly and infirm. He didn't notice any sort of discreet exit through which one might find the water closet and sincerely hoped he would not have to answer the call of nature during the ceremony. A grand piano had been positioned near the eastern wall: here a lithe blindfolded man in a crisp tailcoat hunched over the keys, performing a simple, monotonous, yet mournfully evocative tune that cycled back into itself again and again in a sea of dreamlike reverberations that buoyed Wingate along like a draught of laudanum.

Wingate politely elbowed his way through the crowd, seeking the attention of a certain broad-shouldered man at the base of the stage steps who could only be Mr. Thaddeus Greensward-Krenwinkel: a robust fellow clad in a pair of jodhpurs and equestrian boots (for "riding his iron horses," as the automotive mogul was known to say), bearing drooping sideburns and a connected moustache that formed a pair of uneven scythe-hooks over his jawline. Greensward-Krenwinkel had, according to Professor Hanwell, devoted a private wing of his factory to the mysterious contraption that was to be unveiled here at this gathering. He had hired separate contractors to fashion each mechanism within the device in total anonymity, never allowing any of them to become acquainted with each other—and those who asked too many questions were sent away to complete a specialty project on the Pacific Rim, or so their families and business associates were told. With a forehead creased in uncertainty, the great industrialist briefly studied Wingate from a safe distance, squinting down at the timid novitiate through his pince-nez.

Meanwhile, Wingate observed the rest of the crowd, strangers all. Here was a notable East Coast doctor with an articulated false arm made of brass, perhaps the work of the same craftsman who had fashioned the prosthetic silver nose of a certain syphilitic factory scion in Europe. Here, with both hands clutching a gilt-headed walking stick and shoulders stooped beneath an opera cape lined in a sickly shade of mustard, was a known head of a local organized crime syndicate. Here was a beetle-browed Czarist smoking an ivory pipe carved in the shape of a man's head, half of which was flayed to the skull. Here, in animated conversation, were a trio of Brahmins from Boston to Bombay to Berlin, each sporting a moustache that drooped low over the bearer's upper lip in oddly identical fashion. Here was the lone woman in attendance: pallid, aloof, and severe, with the top half of her face veiled by a delicate net of black below the saucerlike brim of her hat (he assumed the girl at the reception desk hadn't the temerity to request its removal), and her Order badge affixed as a curious brooch at the collar of her fitted widows' weeds. As Wingate recalled, she was the Viennese Baroness Friede von Tepesch, the esteemed translator of a recent corrected edition of *Von Unaussprechlichen Kulten*.

And at the very back of the room, here was a man whose presence seemed rather dubious: a tall and sinewy fellow in his middle thirties, clad in the rubber gloves and leather apron of a welder or boiler-master, with a pair of wide-lensed goggles perched above his eyebrows (which, to Wingate, brought to mind sinister recollections of the fabled Innsmouth look). The man caught his glance and offered him a wide, congenial smile that Wingate found deeply, absurdly unsettling, as if a figure in a wax museum were attempting to strain its features into a crude approximation of humanity.

The ostensible boiler-master stood before a set of controls mounted beside the stage, partly concealed by a drop cloth which, like the stage curtain, also bore the Order's emblem. A convoluted series of metal pipes snaked out of the control panel and across a visible section of the wall to take root somewhere within the vast contraption waiting behind the gentle sway of the theatrical curtain. Wingate knew this to be the central purpose of the Great Unveiling.

The fellow in the leather apron approached Wingate and flicked a gloved finger at the Order badge pinned above the younger man's breast pocket.

"It's good to have friends, isn't it?" he said dryly, before emitting a strange, hoarse peal of laughter.

Wingate, flustered, could not manage a reply. The man scrutinized Wingate's appearance while theatrically stroking his chin.

"I haven't seen you since . . . mm, last century ago. Do they still make that toffee you like?"

Wingate had no idea what this man was talking about. Perhaps he had been mistaken for someone else.

"I-I don't, er, believe we've been introduced, sir . . . ?"

"I'm the Conductor!" said the man in a startling burst of enthusiasm. Wingate shook a bony hand encased in slick rubber. "Boy, you've got a lot to learn." That unnerving hoarse laugh again, like a pair of grinding-stones caught in his throat.

The Conductor gave him a hard slap on the back. "Don't worry. You're gonna live," he whispered, with conspiratorial relish. Wingate felt the rise of gooseflesh under his shirtsleeves.

"Why, you must be Hanwell's protégé!" proclaimed Mr. Greensward-Krenwinkel, reclaiming Wingate's attentions from the Conductor. His recognition came as a profound relief, and Wingate felt less of a rank impostor.

"Welcome, welcome!" The man shook Wingate's hand with a vigor belying his advanced years. "I hope your journey has been a pleasant one. Have you been enjoying your stay in our fair city?"

Wingate offered the polite lie expected of him.

"Dreadful news about old Hanwell. Just dreadful. I know he would have loved to be here, today of all days . . ."

"Oh, certainly, sir! He spoke of it often during my initiation proceedings."

"You'll give him my regards once he recovers, won't you?"

"Why, of course!"

With a paternal smile from the automotive mogul, Wingate was invited to mingle with the other guests: it was, after all, his apparent duty to become acquainted with his new brethren in the Order.

"I hear you're at Miskatonic: is that correct?" inquired an elderly, red-nosed man in a clipped English accent. He had introduced himself as Lord Arthur Gurney.

"Why, yes, sir. I hope to become a professor once I complete my studies."

"Ah! Splendid course of action: splendid, dear boy. My own grandson here . . . Oh, Reginald!"—he beckoned to a small, feverish youth with bloodshot eyes and a rumpled ascot—"Was recently sent down from Cambridge. It seems the lad was neglecting his studies in favor of building a—what was it, then?"

"A perpetual motion machine," the boy muttered. He glared at Wingate with arms folded.

"Speak up, Reggie! You know my hearing hasn't been the same since the Crimea!"

"A *perpetual motion* machine."

"A clockwork thingamabob!" cried Lord Gurney with a laugh. "Oh, the follies of youth!"

His grandson was not amused.

A blindfolded footman paused beside the trio, silently proffering a tray of champagne flutes. A pair of wide, bright eyes had been painted atop the pale leather of the blindfold's fabric: a disconcerting sight. Another footman nearby carried a plate of hors d'oeuvres: thin wafers topped by strips of shining iron-colored meat that was most likely eel. He, too, wore a painted blindfold.

"Pardon me for asking, sir, but . . . why do all the servants have their eyes covered? Doesn't that make their tasks rather difficult?" Wingate's own eyes had begun to water from the heavy smoke exuded by Lord Gurney's cigar. A wonder that the old fellow's gold-rimmed monocle had not fogged up in the subterranean humidity.

"Odd, isn't it? They *used* to wear theatrical masks with the eyes blotted out! How jolly it was! Cheers!" The lord lifted his flute and clinked the rim of the glass against those of the two younger men.

Wingate, never much of a drinking man, took a sip of his champagne. The bubbling fluid left a bitter undertaste as it slid past his tongue. He held the glass up to the light and noted the liquid inside was tinged a faint, sickly green—which, unstudied as he was in the realm of spirits, he deemed to be not quite normal.

"On-on the subject of Miskatonic," Wingate began, intending to keep up his end of the conversation, "A second cousin of mine is-is actually a professor of economics there. H-he recently recovered from a long illness, and—"

"Oh . . . I see." His interest queerly, abruptly dropped, the lord puttered off to speak with the brass-armed doctor, trailed by a haze of grey cigar smoke and his sullen progeny.

Attempting to blink the water out of his eyes, Wingate accidentally stumbled backward a bit and knocked into the brooding man in the mustard cape.

"Watch your step, kid," the man muttered in threat, his lower lip quivering.

Nerves and residual heat were conspiring to give Wingate a fresh outbreak of perspiration, which dripped down through his cuffs onto the undoubtedly expensive carpet. His own handkerchief proving inadequate, he dared to approach the Baroness.

"Er, pardon me, ma'am, may I trouble you . . ."

Her head snapped back, cobra-like, at the sound of Wingate's plea. He was instantly silenced by the hard, fiery stare through her veil, a faint question mark rising from the ebony cigarette stem protruding from the stern cut of her lips.

Wingate discerned that he was not faring very well.

A tap on his shoulder brought his attention back to the odd man in the leather apron, who caught his gaze with sharp, focused intent—and held it firmly. Wingate was surprised not to have noticed before, but the whites of the Conductor's eyes had an iridescent quality made all the more distinct by the opaque blackness of his pupils and irises. A pair of polished onyx discs set into twin orbs of gypsum within the chiseled face of an ancient deity that shared the Conductor's aristocratic features, a statue bricked up within its temple upon the unmourned death of an apostate pharaoh, a temple buried beneath centuries of sand and discord until the Lost God's name emerged only as a nonsense word in the liminal state of consciousness immediately before the mind shuttered itself in sleep. Wingate saw all of this in his mind's eye with the sudden clarity of a long-forgotten childhood remembrance and wanted very much to escape this man's attentions.

"Did you pack your parasol? The summer air will be full of gas." The Conductor formed his hand into a rough approximation of a pistol and aimed an imaginary bullet at a visiting Hungarian noble. "*Psssshw,*" he emitted, pulling the trigger.

"N-now that's not a thing to-to joke about," Wingate said, his voice barely above a whisper.

The Conductor laughed, far more loudly than was appropriate. No one turned to look at him.

"Grab a playbill, Sammy! The mountebank is about to wave his wand." He backed away slowly, his eyes locked on Wingate's like a mentalist's, whistling a tune that Wingate recognized with a start as belonging to the accursed symphony that had driven rational gentlemen into fits of violent madness on an infamous night in Paris only a few months prior.

Wingate screwed his face into his best semblance of a polite smile in an attempt to remain composed and dignified. Yes, he would nod and bow as long as was necessary and then take a long bath in his hotel room and board the train back to Arkham and give Professor Hanwell his full report and prepare a lecture on photosynthesis for a classroom of bored, squirming 13-year-olds.

Still avoiding the mocking gaze of the Conductor, Wingate found himself cornered by a wispy-haired big game hunter delivering a rambling drone about basalt blocks found on an Egyptian expedition when Greensward-Krenwinkel finally mounted the podium, cleared his throat, and bade the room to remain silent.

At last, the Great Unveiling was about to begin.

"Gentlemen . . . and lady," he began, with a deferent aside to the Baroness, "We here, as members of the Order, are about to bear witness to the lone true spiritual experience left to our era. Yes: Christ the Carpenter has found his profession quashed beneath the wheels of the locomotive bearing a fresh load of materials to the factory, his cross torn down and coated in iron to build the underpinning of an aeroplane. One cannot stand still amid the inescapable march of Progress!" (He thrust his index finger upwards at the ceiling—and presumably, by extension, at the uncharted heavens.)

"Do we not live in an age of alchemy made flesh? Great lungs propelling us into the skies; wheeled wagons puttering along of their own accord; the power of the Sun harnessed"—(And here he flicked the chamber's conspicuously-placed electric light switch in a show of effect)—"for our merest conveniences? Why, the eminent Herr Wolfgang Halperin is even now financing his own airship voyage to the Moon, in order to wrest its grand stores of silver from the savages above!" (Gasps and cries of astonishment broke out through the audience.)

"And yet—now, calm down, if you will—and yet . . . we must not forget our Elders." (Nods of approval and mutterings of assent. The Conductor gave Wingate an unseemly wink.) "Yes: throughout all the millennia of human knowledge, it is only now that They have deemed us worthy of gaining the means to contact Them in direct fashion. I aim far beyond the stereoscopic phantasies of Mr. Edison, suitable for little more than the infernal jangling of 'rag-time' and licentious dancing pictures fit only for those who have grown mad from self-pollution and poor moral hygiene. And the trick photographs and gauze prosthetics employed by those fraudulent folk who call themselves 'spiritualists?' *Humbug!*

"No wonder the vast majority of prior attempts to communicate with the Gods have failed: our civilized human tongues attempting to pronounce the words of evocation—even their very names!—must sound to the Elders as little more than the ceaseless yapping of mongrel dogs. Even the most studied elocutionist and master of languages performing such a rite in his most adept diction could no more summon the attention of the Gods than a daguerreotype of the deceased would revive an inert corpse!" (An array of chuckles, some more nervous than others. The Conductor elbowed Wingate in the ribs and ground his teeth in annoyance: "*You* try having such fun with an old clay cadaver.")

"Yes: only contemporary technology could enable it to be so. Even if one could dredge up a phonograph recording of Abd-al-Hazred cackling antediluvian formulae in the dark of his cell, would the wax not simply crack and boil into a horrid, scorched sigil of Doom from the maddening strength of Their power?

"But we are modern men, my Order brethren, and we now have access to modern methods.

"Thus, the Great Unveiling here today refers not merely to the revelation of this grand design you have all been anticipating, but to the dropping of barriers between our own dimension and . . . those *beyond*." (Murmurs of curiosity.)

"Gentlemen, I bring you . . . *The Spectral Golem!*"

Mr. Greensward-Krenwinkel swept his arm backwards, pointing his walking stick towards the concealed mechanical mass occupying the length of the stage. In the same instant, the Conductor grasped and tugged a vertical cord which whisked the curtain back in a triumphant motion. The electric lights overhead glinted off his rubber accoutrements and the glass of his goggles.

What stood before Wingate was a sort of Olmec head, roughly square in shape, with the edges rounded off. At least twenty feet tall in height, its outer casing was fashioned from stainless steel panels welded flush and firm as the reinforced body of a warship. Two looming sockets were set high on the Golem's forehead, each inset with a glass globe appraising the Order members with a cold, unblinking stare. Below these eyes was a skeletal nub of a nose that appeared purely decorative; and above them, its forehead was deeply etched with a set of inscriptions in a peculiar archaic hieroglyph unknown to Wingate, centered around what appeared to be a conducting rod. A phonographic trumpet jutted from each side of its head in approximation of ears, and a pair of cupped hands hovered below the creature's chin. An open grille was inset between the palms: as Greensward-Krenwinkel explained, this was in order to collect offerings of liquid and ash.

By far the machine's most dominant, awe-inspiring aspect was its mouth. Encompassing fully two-thirds of the Golem's face, this consisted of a massive aperture shuttered with a circular diaphragm in the manner of a camera. Wingate stared at the fitted blades' polished brass and thought of whirlpools, of leech-mouths, of the spinning wheels of charlatan mesmerists.

Judging from the various pipes extending upward, outward, and beyond, Wingate presumed that an engine of some sort must be hidden from view; and he noted that a small generator and automated bellows flanked the Conductor's rubber boots, alongside a now-revealed array of unmarked controls set into the wall at approximately chest-height.

Wingate's eyes traced and re-traced each curve, line, and angle of the Spectral Golem as Greensward-Krenwinkel continued.

"... powered by an ingenious mechanism of Prussian design and manufactured from the finest Evzenek steel, the Transversal Expiator combines steam and electricity—our own man-made thunder and lightning!—with the essential salts of the Borellus method, and private contributions from the mad Serbian out in New York ..."

Wingate found he could pay little mind to the man's intricate technical explanations and let his gaze discreetly wander among the expressions of the guests: the childlike awe of Lord Gurney, the stony glare of the Baroness, the constant smirk of the Conductor beside him.

Perhaps it was only his imagination, but the heat of the room had begun to increase.

"A man must wind his watch in the correct manner," whispered the Conductor, his breath reeking vaguely of sulfur. Wingate shivered.

Mr. Greensward-Krenwinkel doffed his jacket, strode across the stage, and bent down on one knee to deliver a solemn offering into the Spectral Golem's waiting hands. No words of evocation were spoken: for, as he had explained, this would have been a mere ritual for the fancies of men, not the true language of the Gods. He uncapped a glass bottle full of intermingled powders—including, Wingate recalled, a recent sample of the new initiate's own blood, and presumably that of all others present in the chamber—and tapped the dry mixture into the open grille. He then retrieved another bottle from his waistcoat pocket and poured a viscous liquid on top of the powder, faintly glowing in the manner of a radium dial.

Standing aside, Greensward-Krenwinkel gave his signal to the waiting Conductor, who, with a forceful throw of a lever and eager crank of a wheel, set the Spectral Golem into life.

The contraption's palms clamped shut, as if in prayer, trapping all remnants of powder and fluid inside. A sharp, forceful burst of steam pummeled its way through the pipes, passing between the Golem's metal hands with such intensity that they pulsed and shook as if with arthritic tremors.

Abruptly enough that nearly all guests present were knocked backwards with a start, a spark of violet lightning shot out from each of the Golem's eyes, writhing and quivering and twining together into the rod standing firm on the machine's forehead. The blazing orbs seemed to focus their diabolical judgment upon Wingate's unworthy presence in the room, casting peculiar angular shadows over metal and marble and polished stage boards. He was reminded of the bare autumn branches of backyard elms knocking against his window as a small boy, which had caused him to dream of spindly-limbed ghouls eager to claw through planks and plaster to crack open his spine and pull out his viscera.

Wingate was conscious of a stirring in the air, an unseen pulsing-outwards from the Spectral Golem that went far beyond the mere vibrations of an outsized factory machine, combined with a peculiar feverish heat that gave way to a sudden chill and back again, nearly pushing him to the brink of nausea. Among the other guests, there was some quiet applause. The Baroness idly fanned herself.

With a somber nod from his employer, the Conductor threw another lever. The heat had caused some of his pomade to melt and loose dark strands hung madly over his goggles, which had now been set into place to shield his uncomfortably piercing eyes. And he grinned with a perverse excitement that seemed to border on lust-mania as the diaphragm in the mouth of the Spectral Golem slid open.

Wingate caught only a glimpse of the pure blackness within before the Edison bulbs of the chamber burst their filaments from the inside, shattering glass shards onto the assembled crowd below. A great electrical sighing-out resounded overhead as power seemed to halt over the entire plant, perhaps even the city far above. And yet the bellows blew, the steam coursed through its pipes, the violet lightning shot out and crackled before him, now the sole source of light in the room. Soon it was joined by a third, far denser strand emitting from some transistor inside the Golem's mouth, flickering over its great looming visage like some unholy amphibian tongue, almost seeming to form patterns and glyphs that . . . perhaps . . . Wingate could *just* make out . . .

The Conductor threw a surprisingly strong arm around Wingate's shoulder in a manner that might seem comradely in other circumstances, and he shuddered heavily at the doubling of cold sweat. Yet the man only clutched more sharply, turning to grin at Wingate with a set of teeth that appeared, in the flashings of lightning, to elongate at the ends, dreadful little points like the waiting jaws of the piranha.

"The mask is off," he hissed. "Don't look away from *the Face*." Wingate lacked the will to disobey.

A new sound began to arise above the spark of lightning and hiss of steam: a collective murmur trickling out of the phonographic ears and slowly increasing in volume. These were not the voices of human beings, nor indeed of any living thing that had ever walked upon the earth during Wingate's short lifetime. These rumblings of horror so stirred Wingate's stomach and bowels that he felt his bones cringe and writhe inward, away from the inner systems of flesh, and he thought absurdly of roast chicken, its dried skin and drained musculature on his supper table with Mother and Father at the house on Aylesbury Street, beside a dollop of potato and a serving of peas . . . he never liked to eat the peas . . . a tendon was still attached to the bird's dead wing, and to his delight he could make the wing flap, which left Mother aghast . . . he had plucked out the heart and giblets, and wanted to preserve them in ethyl alcohol, like the men in the high tower . . .

And the world wavered. Wingate would have collapsed if not for the Conductor's vise grip. The darkness within the aperture was no longer an absence of light, but a tangible *presence of void,* a heaviness of the sort felt by one who cannot see or hear an enemy's waiting body, yet can sense his silent breathing in the dark.

The residual fog of tobacco smoke over the heads of the Order members now mingled with a writhing black mist. The void within the Golem's mouth had developed, if not quite a surface, then a tangible manifestation of itself.

Wingate was no longer sure whether the otherworldly sounds were indeed emitting from the Spectral Golem or were merely the hidden language of his own bodily workings, speaking of how they detested him. Sheer madness, he knew, as the Conductor's rubber claw clenched his shoulder, such that Wingate could almost feel their bones meld through the marrow, yellow-white and fibrous . . .

From the dark of the Golem's mouth, tendrils had begun to form in place of teeth and tongue. At least, that was the most accurate point of reference Wingate was able to grasp in attempting to describe the scene before him. Tendrils . . . gnarled roots of an ancient tree . . .

prehensile tails stripped of flesh . . . drippings of ink . . . writhing appendages of the Kraken . . . tangles of spider-silk under the unsettling enlargement of the microscope . . . ropes of congealed ectoplasm . . . all crept and squirmed and slithered their way out of the great dark maw in order to meet the evening's esteemed guests.

The Conductor's smile was one of absolute triumph, standing rigid and proud as a decorated general when the nearest tendril passed over his form. As *it* caressed his rubber gloves, his leather apron, his exposed flesh, he wore a face of indescribable, nearly obscene bliss. Of course, Wingate knew, he was an utter madman, if *man* he still was, or indeed ever had been. Oh yes, *he* had known what would happen: he must have. Surely he was an agent of Theirs, a true one, not a mere Order devotee. Why hadn't they all run out of the chamber, screaming in terror, as Wingate would have done long ago were he not rooted to the spot in fear, and . . . and something else? Had the Conductor sabotaged the mechanics of the door, locking them all within a glorious tomb? Oh, too bad, too bad . . .

The tendril moved on to Wingate, looming a few feet above his head like a monstrous monk with head darkly robed, stooping down to prod his face and body—

And in that moment, all conscious sensation came to a halt. For all of his senses had been fully enveloped, *invaded*, covered and filled both inside and out with perversely-mingled extremes of pain and prurience, with such intensity that his civilized mind could do nothing but detach and attempt to drift away to someplace safe. Wingate was taken back to a schoolboy nightmare, when an unseen figure of Death had come to claim him in the night, looming over his bed in silence, reaching out a hand to his prone, motionless body—and he had felt himself fall, screaming, into darkness, until he awoke twisted in his bedsheets, feverish, heart pounding, too terrified to let himself slip back into the dream-world where only pure Fear awaited him.

Vaguely in control of a few timid thoughts again, Wingate stood paralyzed beside the Conductor, witnessing further events with an odd detachment. Across the room, a tendril enveloped Lord Gurney and abruptly withdrew, leaving only a skeleton, viscous and red and steaming, with a monocle shattered at what remained of its feet. The doctor with the brass arm had, it seemed, already been explored, for his once-sturdy form had been reduced to a molten lump of metal. Mr. Greensward-Krenwinkel attempted to back against the wall, yet *it* coiled around him like a gelatinous boa constrictor, his false teeth spat out, his eyes and tongue bursting from his skull at the extreme pressure, blood and organs and adipose tissue forced out of his pitiful corpse through every available orifice. The Baroness was the last of them all: her own tendril formed a veinlike black webbing over the pallor of her face, much like the patterns of the marble beneath her feet; imprinting itself within her flesh until her body cracked along the fault lines, bone-dry and bloodless, as if she had been nothing more than a plaster model.

In the last movement Wingate was permitted, he glanced over at the Spectral Golem, the Transversal Expiator, Summoner of Demons, Genius of Modern Man, Missionary of its own Madness: its eyes scorching, nostrils flaring, teeth gnashing as its great tongue spoke with Wingate's own dimension.

This was the final moment of consciousness Wingate knew before awakening in the city's nearest madhouse.

At least, such was the incredible story related by Samuel Perkins Wingate upon his admission to the asylum. No such chamber was ever discovered in the factory following Mr. Greensward-Krenwinkel's disappearance, nor was any "Conductor" located matching the description given. Following an investigation, the city-wide electrical outage was officially described as the product of a blown furnace; the young man's own condition was deemed a case of acute nervosism. Over two decades later, the truth of that afternoon's events and Samuel Wingate's role therein have never been fully determined, although perhaps the modern methods of insulin and electroshock may finally endeavor to bring him out of his fancies.

And in his cell, with its frayed padding and stink of antiseptic, so far from Arkham's quiet cobblestone alleys and low-keening whip-poorwills and the kind tutelage of the long-dead Professor Hanwell, Samuel Wingate felt the presence of unearthly miasma surrounding his meagre frame at all times. It had always been there, he knew; it was only during the Great Unveiling that the Truth had been revealed to him. Samuel Wingate was never alone, nor had he ever been in his life.

Patient Wingate was known to fall into a state of abject panic at the presence of an overly conspicuous metal tube, and he could not look upon a pattern of interlocking lines or serpentine figures without seeing them squirm in their setting and unfurl themselves towards him, groping at any uncovered orifice, to slither in and siphon all fluids from his body and brain. He often had to be restrained or else would claw and bite at his own flesh to uncover the presence of any infiltration: he once stole a sharpened spoon from the day room, attempting to slice open his belly and carve out his traitorous intestines. "They-they tell me they're going to strangle me," he had muttered nonsensically, scratching at the wound with bitten fingernails.

Wingate knew—as he told his most trusted psychiatrist—that he could hear the bacteria inside his body, speaking in tandem as emissaries of Great Ones below the earth and beyond the stars, teaching him the hidden names of all things, the glyphic names that he picked out endlessly, on every surface, with every available liquid. In his dreams, he could hear the call of the Spectral Golem hidden belowground, sending its tendrils up from the bowels of the Earth to search for him.

When he was well-behaved—when he was calm, and did not ramble of supernatural things, or deface the sanitarium's property, or injure himself (a long-standing habit judging by the healed slash on his left-hand palm)—he might be allowed access to his prized possession: the heirloom pocket watch he had lost on the factory grounds. It was badly damaged and no longer functioned properly, yet Wingate could sit for hours staring into its cracked face, into the eye which glimmered intently back at him, a polished onyx disc set into an orb of gypsum.

# II

# The Dollmaker's Studio

# This Night I Will Have My Revenge on the Cold Clay in Which We Lie

*THIS NIGHT MY tendons and fingernails shall root below the earth, wrenching aside cracks in pavement and plaster, tapping the strength of lost foundations and forgotten bones.*

*I shall take my revenge on the barbers and fishmongers, on the crest of the Fourth Horseman, on the planted flag. The black web that chokes and constricts. The liminal hymn of possession.*

*This night I will have my revenge on the little man and let neither flesh nor fae constrain me.*

* * *

In the wake of the epidemic, certain small businesses within the city were known to host clandestine gatherings after hours. This was meant to help recompense the revenues lost when their shop windows gathered dust, their entryways were boarded up, their coffers lay fallow, by official decree. For the guests, this served as a tentative return to social debauch after so long hiding from Pestilence. Among these festivities was a secret sex party held in the lower level of a discount department store.

She was invited to this party by the little man.

Now, he didn't have any iteration of genetic dwarfism: he was not that sort of little man. Nor was this a slight on his endowment, which she had neither seen nor experienced. He was indeed short, but simple shortness would not have earned him the sobriquet of *little,* and he did not rightly strike her as a *small* man. He had the mien of a sinister doll, with his hair parted just so, his wax-pale complexion, his dress shirts and waistcoats, an unblinking witness in a doll-sized chair on an old woman's white shag carpet. He was handsome, at least by her standards: the gently Byronic air of a man with dark secrets of eros slinking around in his cranial folds, yet scaled down a bit, so his head ended at the tip of her nose—though as her own height was slightly above average by ladies' standards, he was not *as* little as one might assume. He did not know she thought of him as *the little man,* though he wouldn't mind being called such, at least not by her. A sly smile of delight that she, Celestine, had a private name for him at all.

But yes, the little man. He might even have been hosting this party: she hadn't dared ask, as the mere prospect of attending, let alone *touching* another person, perhaps even her acquaintance, *the little man,* was thrilling enough.

The pair of them slipped into the discount department store some time after dusk, a quiet retreat into a side entrance, down the stairs to the lower level. She was not sure whether this party was sanctioned by the higher-ups, a pock-faced CEO waving an indifferent assent to young people's diversions in a fog of cigar smoke, or perhaps an enterprising floor manager or cashier who had finagled the keys after dark.

She, Celestine, wore a pale blue sundress, the better to blend in with the diffuse blue-grey shadows cast by after-hours floodlights across the cheap linens and linoleum tiles. A silver pendant, a token of her patron goddess, glimmered through sheaves of strawberry-blonde hair wafting about her sternum.

He, the little man, wore his black velvet waistcoat. The white sleeves of his dress shirt were ruched up to the elbow, revealing the scattered lines of dark hair on his forearms, the insistent blue snaking of his veins. He clasped his hands together and peered about for a proper place to speak with Celestine in relative privacy.

A company of milk-pale mannequins, their heads lopped off clean and bloodless, patrolled the floor as hip-cocked Templars of Commerce with sales tags dangling from their mushroom-stalk necks like announcements of stockaded criminals' misdeeds. Pairs and thirds, a few in costume, huddled in dim corners, conversing in museum whispers. A man spoke of his return to the factory where, at the cafeteria table, his fellow workers silently passed a cake from hand to hand: literally, with bits of cake scooped out by one's bare hands, ungloved, unwashed, unsanitized, frosting beneath one's nails, crumbs brushed away from unguarded lips. A woman recalled the ambulance sirens that had passed so frequently outside her windows that the sound was often caught in her head like an advertisement jingle. A woman said she'd thought of working as a glass machine girl in a pachinko parlor, sitting in a box like a mechanical fortune teller and seeing only her reflection in the mirror as anonymous hands and various organs probed her legs and apertures for as long as their tokens could buy, and could imagine whomever she wanted without breathing the same foul air. A man had left his office shortly before the shutdown to see a derelict on the sidewalk with diseased organs spread out on the pavement before her, perhaps or perhaps not her own, as a High Denialist sermon blared in the nearby park. A woman had heard of that sermon, seen the photographs of its patrons fallen down dead as they stood.

Celestine wrenched her attentions back to her host. The little man, so he explained, derived from a line of impoverished chandlers. In time, they had tried to increase their fortunes with a line of wax candles fashioned into intricate shapes. Perhaps she knew of that ingenious mold of the Virgin Mary with eyes that wept waxen tears the further the candle burnt.

"Oh," she said, "did your people make that?"

"No," he said, "but it did inspire them."

Perhaps, he intimated, he could sell models of anatomical hearts and Hands of Glory to the occult supply shop at which she worked as a stockist, a job she had been fortunate enough to keep since the shop had been operating mail-order during quarantine. But, she tried to explain, Hand of Glory, *main-de-gloire*, was just a corruption of *mandragore*, the mandrake root, and did not mean an actual hand. At any rate, the shop was already well-stocked with veneficia.

One branch of his people, the little man continued, had broken from the family trade and partaken in a certain hubristic voyage to the Antarctic, had perished on a southerly island and been disinterred some 200 years later displaying well-preserved breeches and wig and hard-gritted teeth, an expression the little man now demonstrated for her. He had first seen the infamous photograph as a child, in a book about mummies, paired with a paragraph questioning whether hair and nails continued to grow after death, all without knowing this cadaver was his distantly-great grandfather.

Celestine, who knew more of maritime history than the little man assumed, considered that if the man in question were truly an impoverished chandler without prior sailing experience, he could not have advanced to an officer's rank by the time of his premature death and thus would not have been buried in an officer's trappings. Some obscure joke, perhaps, at the ancestral little man's expense, at his bravado and vainglory.

Furthermore, she recalled a great admiral who had died at sea and was preserved in a cask of rum for the voyage home; an emperor-general whose body was immersed in honey for the long procession back to his domain. Yet the ancestral little man did not come home. Like a noosed, bound, repeatedly-stabbed mummy tossed into the bog as a leathery sacrifice, a warning to the curious.

"It does," he said, "get very cold in the ground." The little man's pale knuckles brushed hers and his lips twitched upward. A rosy bloom spread through her skull and veins.

*Ah yes,* she thought. This *is why I'm here.*

An impatient knock on glass meant he had, unfortunately, to depart from her side for a bit so he could let someone else in. A strain of communal lust in the quiet air was beginning to stir. A nipple pinched behind three layers of cloth. Sluglike glistening of engorged tongues. A hand cupping and squeezing a denim bulge. The vibratory hum of a nearby throat. Anticipatory arousal.

Celestine was encouraged by the prospect of impending coitus *with the little man,* yet bothered by the tiny pricklings at the very top of her inner thighs. She ducked behind a pallet of earth-toned tablecloths and retrieved a razor from her bag. With a slick of spittle on her palm serving as lather, she lifted her skirt and hurriedly began to shave. She had last shaved yesterday morning and the little chopped hairs were already pushing through the surface like an obstinate crop of weeds.

This act was mainly to prevent stubble burn, which had indeed happened with another man in her past, a **very bad** man, a varlet in fact, with his irrational rage at being unable to turn her heart and pin down her mind; at any rate, that man's last visit had led to three days straight without shaving, and consequently a raw chewed-out splotch was ground into his frenulum by her pubic stubble during an especially vigorous round. He had shown it to her, lifting up his flaccid cock in the aftermath of the act, with a look of pride in his cocaine saint's eyes. That chafed instrument, she thought now, had been all he was good for. And had she not been inside a discount department store, she would have spat at his memory.

So long it had been, so long, the populace bound up indoors like pupae waiting to unfurl. So long since she had charted a new expanse of living flesh, practically revirginized by extended quarantine. The corporeal experience of sex was a living memory turned to dust, scattered to the winds alongside the agents of Pestilence.

"Come, come," said the little man, and led her by the elbow to a discreet door off the children's aisle. It was here, he explained, that he rented his private workshop.

Like most sculptors' studios, the little man's workshop was beset with an array of orderly clutter. Stray appendages of wax dummies hung on butchers' hooks before the walls to either side, dangling above a cement floor littered with sawdust shavings. Odors of hot metal emitted from lumpy molds for experimental candles. Anvil and vise. Compass and square. Antique wooden chairs busted up for spare parts, spindles splayed like broken ribs. The little man, smiling softly, bid Celestine wait a spell while he tended to a large pot of burbling wax on a cast-iron stove at the back of the room.

She stood, hands folded, beside a large work table in the middle of the studio. One of the little man's creations dominated most of its surface: a crudely human figure, female, its substance resembling not so much beeswax as the sickly yellow of raw fat. The figure's supine frame was propped up by the angles of its disproportionately thick arms, its legs bowed around a child-sized human chair in a sexless U shape. Its lips were pursed and carmine-red, its wax skull bedecked with a shabby dark wig.

Most curiously, the angles and curves of its limbs were inset with hair. Not like a naturalistic growth of human hair, but strung across the gaps like an Aeolian harp. And yes, this was definitely hair, not wire or catgut. Celestine peered closer: strawberry blonde. She involuntarily touched her own hair in that exact same hue, fingers brushing against the body-warmed heat of the silver token of her patron goddess.

And in a flash of insight, she knew.

The little man was controlling her with black magic.

(And just *how many* awful men must have used black magic on her before, those execrable pinpricks lodged in her cerebrum over the years! So many arrows shooting through her daydreams on strings of queerly formidable lust: addictive and wrenching, entirely inexplicable in their sheer intensity. *How*, until now, had she been unable to see the truth?)

Stray strands of her own hair plucked from a restaurant booth, at a café table, on the occult supply shop's counter, (*in the sickroom*) (*at the funeral*) and secreted away to his workshop. And what other personal concerns had he managed to gather? Flakes of dander, used tampons, third-degree relics? All worked into his wax. And parading her before his foul little strings as if she would never know: the absolute *gall*. A cold-burning anger flushed through her body, a tremble of rage in her fingertips.

She yanked the hairs out of the sculpture. The hard wax instantly cracked in their wake.

She looked at the little man, looked and *saw*. The little man with his weak, stubbly chin like a half-descended testicle. His hair, receding unflatteringly at the temples as though a pair of horns were due to sprout. Delicate thin lips now came across as puckered and mealy-mouthed. A very commonplace little man.

And she had thought of— With *him*—!

But the little man, too, saw Celestine. Saw her damage to his puerile totem.

His no-longer-handsome features now twisted with spite, head lowered like a charging bull, hand upraised in a sinistral splay.

"So you've ruined my fun, Celestine," said the little man. "So I can still ruin yours."

And, deepening his voice to an oubliette pitch, he pronounced the incantation.

Celestine ran. She ran past the wax dummies now squirming on their hooks. She ran past the guests of the secret sex party, all their false skins sloughing off, mumbling their orders in her wake. She ran past the line of guests in suits and heels waiting for entry outside below a cage of scaffolding: they were, one and all, plague dead covered in wax. They had come to him, to the little man, for the wax cure, coating their skins to preserve the flesh, to keep soul and body entwined. And now wax veins unfurled from wax skins, wax phalanges emerged from wax torsos, tendrils and tentacles and bristling anemone-fronds probing and stretching and seeking Celestine. Such was his influence, his force in the world.

Yet, for all this, he wanted more.

*How dare you, little man.*

*How* **dare** *you.*

*Mother, my Mother, set me alight.*

And Celestine burned silver-violet. Arms raised and eyes rolled back, she melted the world, melted it all with the force of her rage, with every step on the blacktop, every step under the scythe-hook moon, under the streetlights hoisting security cameras that wobbled in the slightest breeze.

She surveyed stray bones and clots of hair in the tallow that flooded the streets, that poured into the gutters and bashed at the grilles of basement windows. And it occurred to her for the first time that *the little man invited me here knowing I did not survive, that none had survived, the city streets empty since the Pestilence had claimed us all, sitting in our rats' nests with our box fans and air conditioning to forestall the rot, the cold clay in which we burrowed for so long.*

# Heirloom

IN THE LAND of the valley beyond the pines, it was long known that the dead would rise from their graves to cavort and caper after dark. The adults had largely forgotten this truth, their collective memory ground down over the years by quotidian concerns and responsibilities. But the children knew, trading wide-eyed whispers at tilted grave slabs and disrupted patches of earth. They knew that when the thoughts of the living were swept off in dreams, the dead clawed through the dirt and helped each other emerge from the softening wood of old coffins, shrouds flapping like banners, teeth and tongues and ragged tendons bared to the winds, loose eyes popped back into sockets while dangling from their stalks.

A girl of this land, who had grown to be lovely and clever in equal measure, lived by the forest at the foot of the mountains, and forever dreamt of More. Her charms had caught the eye of the local lord for some time until, one day, he had her abducted from the town square and taken to his castle. There she was locked into a wide stone room in his castle's highest tower, its only door replaced by a set of thick convex bars like a clammed-down knight's visor; and there she would stay until she agreed to marry him.

As it happened, this girl already had a lover: a comely young man from the village, a tailor's apprentice, known for the poignance of his singing voice. And not long after her abduction, this young man met his premature death. It wasn't clear by what ends, exactly—perhaps a fit of plague, perhaps marauding bandits, perhaps the ever-thirsting axe of the executioner—but dead he was all the same.

Affixed to the outer window of her room was a pulley system with which the servants of the castle brought the girl food and cleared her chamber pot. And each night after the lord of the castle had retired, the dead suitor crept up the hill and over the moat, removed his head from his shoulders, and set it in the basket, hoisting it up to her window to come and sing to her at night. His body would then wheel the basket back down, whereupon he would stitch his head back onto its proper place before returning to the grave. And the next night he would rise from the dirt, loosen the heavy threads at the base of his neck, and begin again.

In this manner, the girl and her suitor lived, and defied the lord; and in this way, for months, for years, for time uncertain, the wicked lord was refused a bride.

* * *

*She couldn't remember a time before—the boat house—or was it the greenhouse?*

*At night she had slipped out, candle in hand, hoping the stink of the tallow would not give her away. Pursued by men with cloaks and masks and stilettos, actors in a Venetian drama—but whence had she conjured these figures?*

*It was so bright then—a ball of mirrors on fire—*

* * *

"I really don't think so," she said, finally. A softness in her voice that betrayed a fear of sounding firm and true. Predictably, he interpreted this as indecision.

"But Linda—"

But-Linda's fingers twitched for a cigarette. She had given up the habit more than a decade ago, for the sake of the Boy. And now, for the Boy, she was shunted into the role of mealy-mouthed, hand-wringing, no-fun Mommy, a tendency she had hated in her own mother, pursing her lips and whinging about how—sigh—*expensive* it was, that doll she wanted. She stared into the dusty box, at the woman's unblinking glass eyes, and hated herself a little.

"Where would we even put it, Frank?" she said. "I mean . . ." She sighed.

He smiled. "I always wondered what my uncle did with the rest of his collection. Always regretted he sold off Thurston's trick sarcophagus. And Hardeen's straitjacket. She's a family heirloom, hon!" He squeezed her shoulder.

*Just like tugging a string, to make a doll talk,* she thought, eking out the uncertain smile he wanted.

The house predated central air, and in that summer's excessive humidity, an expanse of century-old paint and plaster on the ceiling had come unmoored from the wooden slats of the foundation: from hairline cracks to drooping flaps to an array of large chunks abruptly kicking up dust and dead larvae on the living room carpet. Yet this revealed the hidden hatch to the other half of the attic, to Uncle Silas's collection, to the woman in the box, the girl behind glass. Deliberately spackled over some time ago.

Linda picked up a chunk from the floor, balancing its heft in her gardening glove. Could she read the history of the house, as though examining the rings of a tree trunk? A layer of pale putty covering sickly midcentury green covering jaundiced off-white covering grey clumps that looked like cement, but with bristling brown hairs inside. A split-second fear of asbestos gave way to the realization: this was horsehair. Horsehair plaster. The ceilings and floors were full of horsehair.

She pictured herself, her family, living for years inside a giant horse with wooden slats for bones.

She thought of the girl behind glass, her husband's late uncle's folly, slowly digesting inside.

* * *

The toymaker's grandest commission was revealed in the bright air of the garden to sighs and gasps of approval from the court.

Eyes wide and round, pupils dark and trusting, and knowing. A keeper of secrets. Perfectly coiffed coils of wig-hair curving around her neck to rest gently at her collarbone. Her dainty waist, pinched wasp-like and correct.

Her feet dangled slack at the ankles, one slipper nearly fallen onto the grass. Her hands hung lank and loose like a strangler's.

"Remarkable," cried the youth in the black tricorne. "She looks absolutely alive! The eyes, are they opal? Mother-of-pearl? And her skin"—he touched it, gently, with an ungloved hand—"Could it be—oh, not mere wax—gypsum, ivory, alabaster?" He brushed her immaculate cheek with his knuckles. "Why, she is splendid enough to present at Versailles!"

"Is not the Dauphin a bit young to take on a mistress?" quipped the Comte de Curval.

"Not if he takes after his father," whispered Madame des Volanges.

"You are a genius of the highest order, *signore!*" the youth insisted.

"Ah, how you flatter me, Signor Mirandola. I am—how do you say?—but a humble *conduttore.*" The toymaker grinned, revealing yellow teeth that appeared all the more discolored from the crackling powder coating his face, and gums that bulged white as if harboring worms. A gilt-rimmed pince-nez had left a pair of ruddy indents at the bridge of his nose as though he had been nipped firmly by a small mammal.

"The clockwork mechanism," he continued, "was assembled by the Atelier Le Marchand. The eyes—alas, not opal, dear *signore*—are a most ingenious contrivance of inset glass and mirrors, designed by a Swiss jeweler, the finest of his canton." The humble conductor chuckled to himself. "His grandfather crafted fresh eyes for the catacomb saints."

He reached a knobby, trembling hand under her chin and pressed upwards. The jaw swung open slightly, just enough to peer inside the gentle parting of the lips.

"The teeth are genuine. Procured from a traveling dental extractor of some repute."

"And does she play and sing? And dance?" asked Mirandola, clasping his hands together in excitement.

"Alas, no. But, you see, she is incapable of yammering on, about commonplaces and fripperies, like a wife." The humble conductor cast a knowing look at the Comte. "She is, I daresay, the only true poetic soul of Womanhood."

The girl's head tilted, first left, then right, and nodded slowly as her eyelids shut and rose in time. Her wide eyes glistened wetly.

"An eminent physician of Salzburg," he said, with lowered voice, "crafted the serum." The worms quavered in his grin.

"Her name is Thérèse. At least, I have named her that: you, of course, may call her whatever you wish." He bowed low, spreading an arm before his creation, inadvertently displaying the piebald patches on the elbows of his green velvet coat.

The youth fell to his knees before her, tears of gratitude gleaming in his eyes. "Signor Castaigne, you have restored joy to my heart! She is—why, she is utterly *priceless!*" He scooped her up in his arms, spinning her about, a merry bridegroom.

* * *

*Skirts clutched in one hand, candle raised above her head—down the stairs, the spiral staircase, a windowless tube, like*

*—the spinal column in his study—*

*She must never, never, never stop running, but from—*

*???*

*Not from—*

*The man with the filmy eye?*

*—No!*
*—a marriage—*
*—No,* no!
*And finally the constricting stone walls opened up into a broad dark room*
*—the oubliette?—*
*where the candle guttered and died.*

* * *

In the land of the valley beyond the pines, it was long known that the dead would rise from their graves to cavort and caper after dark. The adults, minding traditions whose symbolism was long lost to time but were clung to all the more dearly, barricaded their doors against the stink of putrefaction, and clutched their whittled crucifixes in white-knuckled fists at the stroke of midnight.

A girl of this land, who was not born the seventh son of a seventh son, nonetheless dreamt she could throw an enchanted wolfskin about her shoulders and transform into a ravening beast under the scythe-hook moon. Her charms had caught the eye of the local lord for some time until, one day, his most brutal henchman clubbed her over the head and tossed her into a rough homespun sack to be imprisoned in the castle. The bruise of his blow pressed into her skull at each bump of his cart on the cobbles, and he manhandled the muffled hollows of her bound body when he tossed her at the lord's feet.

Now, the wicked lord was also a man of science, and he knew how to ensure she could never escape. She awoke strapped into a chair of his alchymical workshop as he held before her a syringe full of air. He knew that but a single breath in her veins would disrupt the humours and stop her heart. The lord calmly slid his empty needle into the bend of her elbow as she strained against the straps. And she watched herself die.

Yet immediately after he withdrew the syringe, he plunged it into a vial of elixir of his own concoction and injected the girl's body once again. Now, though she would rise at night like all the other dead, she would henceforth only fall into a death-trance during the day and would not rot—but only so long as he gave her a daily dose of elixir. Thus she was bound to him forever.

As it happened, this girl already had a lover: a comely young man from the village, a tailor's apprentice. He was murdered on private orders from the lord, his body dumped into a shallow grave by the path into the pines. The wolves of the forest dug their paws into the loose-packed dirt and gnawed at his limbs.

Each night after the lord of the castle had retired, the dead suitor removed his head from his shoulders and set it in the basket, hoisting it up to her window to come and sing to her at night. Sometimes he would send up other parts he had carefully carved off, with which she could divert herself for a time. And each night, before dawn, he would have to stitch himself back together again.

The suitor had developed blackened holes at the base of his neck from the constant tear of heavy thread through stiffened skin. His cheekbones, once high and fine, threatened to bore through his flesh like a dull pair of knives.

"I am parched, my darling," he rasped, after he sang to her of love. His voice sounded baked in the sun.

A tear unfurled from the corner of his eye, its trail unusually sluggish and meandering. This was not a tear, she realized. A fly had lain eggs in his brain. She could not tell whether he knew.

"I am parched," he repeated. "Please, my love. Some water. Please."

But she had no water, save the cold leavings of her chamber pot.

"Save me from this," she whispered, to no one she could hear or see, as she tipped the pot into his waiting mouth, onto his lolling tongue. "Save me save me save me—"

* * *

The impresario named her Marta after his dead tubercular wife. He dressed her in his dead wife's paste jewelry and told her about his woes after the customers had all gone home with lighter pockets. He had bought her for a song, which he felt rather unfair to her.

That curious Frenchman with the broad moustache had kept her in a grandfather clock for decades. The clockwork ticking bothered him, supposedly.

The impresario crossed the Atlantic, with Marta in a wooden crate, shortly after Versailles. The war had left a drought in his lungs, an iron harvest in his heart.

He installed her in a glass box, decked out in red and purple and gold imitation silk, with a deck of cards spread over the wooden board on her lap. She, Marta, was now a teller of fortunes.

When a coin was inserted into the slot at her knees, she blinked with slow purpose, her head bobbed side to side as if in thought, and her index finger tapped knowingly at the deck before shuffling it rapidly in her hands and repeating the same gestures, in the same order, for several seconds. Finally she lifted a card between thumb and forefinger, turned it face-up, set it before her, and tapped twice at its surface. This was her job.

The impresario joined with a company touring from England. To prevent any abuse over his accent, he claimed to be a native of Prague.

"Come one, come all, ladies and gentlemen, young and old!" cried the barker, his bulk perched on an upended potato crate. "Come witness the legendary capers of Gardyloo and Shivaree, of Canticle and Woad! The Vermiform Counter-Corporal juggles 15 bayonets and swallows a dozen electric eels, live, in person, only, only, only for—"

The impresario winced and covered his ears with his hands while passing by, immediately regretting the stain of pomade on his immaculate white gloves. He winced again.

"Hey, Mac, how much for the dame with the cards?" said a loud man in a pinstripe suit, with his back against a tent-pole and his right foot on a bale of hay.

The impresario was off the clock and exhausted. He pointed silently to the coin slot.

"Man-to-man, fellah," said the loud man, "*You* know what I mean. How *much?*"

The impresario sighed and shook his head, not looking back as he returned to his wagon.

The loud man in the pinstripe suit came back for him that night. This time he carried a jackknife and was quiet as a church mouse.

* * *

The Boy climbed up the rickety folding stairs to the attic. The Boy coughed into his fist at drifting wafts of dust decades older than himself. The Boy listened for a car in the driveway, the rhythmic series of machine clunks that meant the garage door was opening, knowing he would not hear either of these things for hours.

The Boy wiped dust from the glass box with the edge of his shirt.

The Boy peered up at her jewel-green eyes, her faded violet kerchief, her gentle smile. Her deep line of cleavage drawing a trail into perfect artificial breasts.

The Boy unbuttoned his fly.

* * *

*She slipped through the central aperture of the hourglass—*
*—and was caught there, kicking and clawing—*
*Her mouth full of dust—*
*Her eyes full of sand—*

* * *

Two girls, one small and dark, one tall and fair, stepped into the dim-lit sideshow tent.

They were less than sisters. They were more than friends. In the safety of the dark, they entwined their small hands.

Their eyes, adjusting to the light, lit on the pretty woman in the glass box.

"Told you, Neely," said the shorter of the two. She flashed a jagged, mischievous smile. Over the years, this smile had worn a light bracket around the left side of her mouth, and the left side only.

Neely smiled back. The two had shared a bold red tube of Maybelline for the day's outing. The dark-haired girl privately believed it suited her far better than Neely.

Neely leaned forward, examining the details of the fortune-telling machine. The tarot cards had faded after several prior seasons in the sun, and the paint on its exterior was scuffed and chipped from rough handling, but the eyes of the wax (?) woman inside stared back at her vibrantly, intensely.

"Gosh, Rita, would you look at those *teeth*," she muttered, aware that she was making small talk to conceal a vague disquiet.

"The better to eat you with, my dear," Rita said. "Now let's waste a couple of dimes." She fished around in her purse until she found a coin, which she duly inserted into the slot.

Set to life, the fortune teller cocked her head at Neely, nodded once, and blinked slowly, deliberately. Tapped the deck with a slender finger.

From the side of the box, a stream of ticker tape emerged.

Rita snapped the paper out of the machine and squinted down at its contents.

"'In the land of the valley beyond the pines,'" she read, "'it was long known that the dead would rise from their graves to cavort and caper after dark. The adults had largely forgotten this truth, their collective mem—'"

"I don't like this."

Rita looked up from the paper to see Neely standing stiffly, eyes wide, face blanched, clenching her hands so hard the knucklebones protruded yellow-white. She looked absurdly, unmistakably, terrified.

Rita wrinkled her nose. She must be faking it.

"Oh, what's the matter? You love all those Universal pictures! Just last week, you begged me to take you to *Bride of Frankenstein!*"

"Well, I don't like this. I think it's perfectly rotten." Her voice quavered, nerves drawn taut like piano wire.

"And all those detective pulps from the drugstore—"

"I want to go home."

"Neely—"

"I want to go home. Vera was right about you." She stormed out of the tent, practically running.

"Oh, for pete's sake—"

The tent flap closed.

The woman in the box stared.

And stared.

And blinked.

* * *

In the land of the valley beyond the pines, it was long known that the dead would rise from their graves to cavort and caper after dark. The adults, on these nights, would leave out the newborn children who were too sickly to live, or whom they could not afford to feed, in the hope that the dead would take these offerings and spare their families. They painted tree stumps with butchers' gore and knackers' leavings to divert the twisted mouths and rictus claws. They hovered about the beds of the dying, hammer and stake in hand, to impale the dead face-down in their coffins. They wailed hysteric orisons at the scythe-hook moon.

A girl of this land, who was thoroughly tired of it all, had been living by the mountains far too long for her tastes. Her charms had caught the eye of the local lord for some time until, one day, his private militia beat her bloody when she refused to let them ravish her en route to the castle, and she died coughing up clots of tissue at his feet from the many knives that had punctured her organs.

Now, the wicked lord was also a man of science, and he knew how to ensure she could never escape. He injected the dead girl with a serum created in his laboratory in order to revive her and preserve her flesh from decay. He did this every day, for years, until the threat of marriage was forgotten. This was simply their life now.

She thrust her bare arm through the bars. He gave her the shot. Neither of them smiled.

She heard rumors among the servants that he anesthetized peasant girls from the village during the day and had his way with them. She wondered if he would stop doing this if she agreed to lie down for him. This thought was exhausting.

As it happened, this girl already had a lover, or did years ago: a young man from the village, whom she had thought much of, once. He was dead, most of the time. His head had been cut off to prevent his coming back.

It didn't work. Beyond the pines, it never did.

"What if I wore his flesh?" the lord asked once.

"No."

"What if I wore his flesh over my face?" He mimed holding up a mask, then moved his hands lower. "What if I wore his—"

"No."

He dipped the syringe into a vial of serum.

"Please," she said softly. "No more shots. You should just let me die."

The lord reached out a hand to stroke her hair through the bars. "But then I would be killing you."

Each night after the lord of the castle had retired, the dead suitor removed his head from his shoulders and set it in the basket, hoisting it up to her window to come and sing to her at night. And each night, before dawn, he would have to stitch himself back together again. His body had become more thread than flesh, stretched taut over shriveled muscle.

His singing drove her mad. She dreaded it every night, almost more than the lord with his syringe. The ripe stench of rot made her gorge rise even before the basket reached her window. A rain of maggots dribbled out of his slack jaw, along with a barrage of terribly small, sticky, clotted sounds emitting from his swollen tongue which no sane mind would consider *singing*. His nose, long collapsed, eyes fallen away: a set of raw gaps in a skull. By no means could he still be doing this out of love. Nothing more than rigid sense-memory. His body no longer knew what else to do.

*Escape*. Yes: she would break the cycle and escape from all this. She wedged herself between the bars of her window and jumped down to the hill. She wanted oblivion.

But as it was nighttime, her broken body did not die. And in the distance, she could hear the six black horses of Death's carriage descending from the scythe-hook moon to pursue her across the land.

Chased by Death in his ragged black shroud and gilt-wheeled stagecoach, the girl could think of nothing to do but run.

She tried to run through the cornfields; Death sheared them away with his sickle.

She tried to run through the alleys; Death sent his plague-rats to nip at her feet.

She tried to run through the sea; Death cast a blight of ice from his palm.

Death, the master, the hunter, the lover, hooked her by the ribcage on the edge of his blade. This was inevitable. The dead girl, dressed in her rags, curled up on the stagecoach seat, sobbing.

In time she lowered her hands from her face and looked around. The red velvet cushions were illuminated by a hanging lamp sloshing kerosene about its font. Death doffed his stovepipe hat and clasped a meerschaum between his teeth.

*But this is the wrong era,* she realized. *I'm not supposed to be here.*

The smooth puttering of rubber on pavement. Death, grinning, in black pinstripes and spats. A faceless chauffeur at the wheel.

*No, no, this is all wrong—*

A stainless steel-inlaid subway car, packed with ruby-eyed shadows, glaring at her for being very, very late.

*This is all wrong—*

Death grinned and said nothing.

* * *

His great-uncle's greenhouse was always a source of consternation. The belching humidity made him want to strip off his clothes and run, through the glass, to some imagined oasis, hopping in the water and backpaddling with ducks and frogs and no nursemaid. And certainly no great-uncle.

The old man scared him. He always carried with him that stale powdery smell of elderly men's sweat, his breath reeked of tobacco, and he still wore the fusty wig and breeches of the previous century, like a ghost or a barrister or a barrister's ghost in a theatrical production. And he spent a lot of time talking to a man-sized mahogany cabinet.

"Come here, boy!" the old man wheezed from behind a bush.

He lowered his head and obeyed. And was startled to realize his great-uncle had wheeled the cabinet here beside him.

The old man bent his head down very low, to whisper his tobacco rasp into the boy's ear. "Would you like to meet your great-grandmother?"

The boy's brow furrowed. "S-sir?"

The old man laughed, which turned into a cough, which turned into a wad of spittle expectorated into the roots of a fern. He turned around and, with a flourish, opened the doors of the cabinet.

*It's a doll*, thought the boy. A pretty doll, he supposed, with lashes thick and curled: he supposed they were made of horsehair. It wore a stuffy old *ancien régime* costume with stains across the satin. And it was the size of a real adult woman, like the kind artists used as models; but his great-uncle had never expressed any artistic talent, to his admittedly limited knowledge of the man.

"She is Woman, lad!" he roared, and the boy reared back at his unexpected volume. "The vessel of all life!" Abruptly, the old man lifted the doll's right wrist and drew back the lacy flounces of her sleeve.

The boy was not sure, exactly, what he was supposed to be looking at. A collection of felt folds had been sewn quite deliberately into the doll's wrist. They fanned out baroquely on either side, one layer atop another, before meeting together again at the bottom and a bit more heavily at the top, in roughly the shape of an eye turned on its side, but with the socket empty.

The old man's grin made the boy uncomfortable, and he quietly requested to go and play outdoors in the garden.

"The vessel of all life!" the old man cried when he assumed the boy was no longer in earshot. The boy glanced over his shoulder to see the old man collapsed into the doll's lap, ardently pressing his shriveled lips to its felt wrist.

* * *

*He came to retrieve her at night, wearing his sword on the wrong side. She ought to have known even then.*

*"Our ship, my love!" he grinned. "We sail tonight!"*

*"But darling, I thought we were going on horseback?"*

*No matter, that: she took the cloak and domino from his proffered hand.*

*The halls of the castle were like foreign coves in the dark. She had been fitted for a glass eye after the Incident, but he still wore an eyepatch. The darkness cast monsters beneath her lone intact eyelid.*

*Raising his sword to the moon, he cried: "Onward, to the Isle of Death!" And, pressing her hand: "No fear, my darling; that's only the colloquial name!"*

*His arm around her shoulders, bare beneath the thin cape.*

*The moonlight glinted sharp shards off the boatman's pince-nez—*

* * *

Three girls, decked out in sequins and heels. One on the chaise, one leaning on the bench, one sprawled atop the piano. Heads bobbing, lids fluttering, strategically-placed spotlights sparking ripples of glitter through their gowns.

"The Order is gonna love it," the foreman said to himself.

His favorite was the girl in blue, the piano girl. Her head was perched on her palm, the fishtail skirt of her dress fallen back to reveal a shapely set of gams saucily kicking their heels back and forth—but a bit too slowly, as though suspended in aspic. He could only hear the motor when he put his ear right up close to her chest.

A fourth girl sat stiffly upright in the corner, opera gloves up to her armpits. A functionary of the Order frowned down at her.

"Whatsamatter with this 'un?"

"That's the prototype. Little too old-fashioned."

"Mm." He rubbed his chin with thumb and forefinger, considered that he needed a shave. "Back in the box, then. We got an auction comin' up?"

* * *

Linda, alone for once, crossed her arms and stared through the glass.

And stared.

And stared.

Until the woman blinked.

Linda gasped. But surely it hadn't been wound, or refueled, or whatever, since—

The woman tapped her deck of cards with an index finger.

Tapped the cards tapped the cards tapped them taptaptaptaptap*tap*.

From within the eye sockets, a black ichor dripped down her face.

* * *

In a land long ago and beyond the sea, men of means ensured that they and their beloveds would never have to die. They commissioned portraits in marble, in oil, in word, and in song, that would live on long after blood crumbled to powder and bone fell to dust.

A girl of this land, who had grown to be lovely and clever in equal measure, forever dreamt of More. Her charms had caught the eye of the local lord for some time until, one day, he asked for her hand in marriage. She did not share his rank, wealth, and position: thus, the betrothal was made in secret.

As it happened, this girl had long dreamt of him as a lover: a comely young man, he certainly was. And not long after his proposal was accepted, he suggested they run off to a foreign land and elope.

After the pair crept out at night together, the girl realized something was very wrong. They were not heading towards the chapel, but to the workshop of a strange man in a piebald velvet suit. "This won't hurt a bit, *ma jolie*," he grunted, and then she could hear nothing more.

Until—

"The secret," Castaigne whispered to Mirandola when all other guests had departed, "lies within the cranium!"

He pressed a discreet indentation behind her left ear, and the skull swung open on a hidden hinge.

There it lay: pink and red, wetly pulsing, and very much alive.

"Ah!" cried the youth. "Now she shall live on *as I love her*, as that perfect font of Womanhood upon which I prostrate myself; not as she *is*, beset with human flaws and frailty.

"Ah! How marvelous! She shall live on forever."

# The Contagion

ONE SUMMER, WHEN she was seven, Sylvia set the devil free. There, in that stifling room under the gaze of the fading icon. There, in the quiet old house with gingerbread trim. There, in the knotted bruise-black shadow of the mountains.

The day of the crime was quite routine. Sylvia Dreiyer, her older brother Bobby, and their mother had embarked on their annual drive northeast to spend a week at Mom's college friend Auntie Lindy's home on Cape Cod. This was the only time Sylvia ever saw the ocean. It never occurred to her to ask why their father never came along: this was just a trip for Mom and the kids, an unquestioned tradition from time immemorial, inevitable as the Tooth Fairy's payment for lost molars and bicuspids. Incidentally, this was also the last summer before her parents' divorce.

Sealed inside the family sedan for hours at a time, little Sylvia would stare out the window, make up idle stories in her head while listening to cassette tapes of old mystery radio plays on the car stereo, play Mom's game of spotting license plates from every state in the country, and attempt to follow the orange-highlighted route on Mom's AAA TripTik flip maps of interstate highways, that lone thick, steady artery among a clutch of straggly veins with tiny diagrammatic labels. The further east they drove, the more the flat landscape erupted into woodlands, into hills, into low mountains barnacled with knobby clumps of trees. Barren-blasted cliffsides loomed above the road, their pebbles and boulders held in check by taut mesh. The road sometimes veered through dark mountain tunnels ringed by intermittent overhead lights: a source of excitement for Sylvia, like passing through the bowels of a giant leech.

It took more than a day to reach the coast from their home, and on that first night the abbreviated Dreiyer family would always stop at a certain bed-and-breakfast operating from a 19th-century Queen Anne-style house in an Appalachian valley. The sedan would pull up at dusk to dramatic effect, the sharp gables of the bed-and-breakfast striking out vainly in swathes of butter-gold and rose before sinking into spreading depths of violet-blue shadow as the sun was swallowed by jagged mountain peaks.

The proprietor of the bed-and-breakfast was known as Aunt Beryl, a stout elderly woman with the mien of a school librarian in her rhinestone-encrusted pastel sweaters and wide-lensed bifocals on a beaded chain. Her heavy powder-blue eye shadow and lavender-rinsed silver hair, swept up and back in a bouffant of thick shellacked curls, hinted at some prior glamour. She, like Auntie Lindy, was not really Sylvia's aunt; though the bed-and-breakfast might as well have been a relative's home since, as far as Sylvia could recall, nobody ever stayed there alongside her family.

Doing research many years later, Sylvia would learn that the place had been built as the summer home of a minor Gilded Age robber baron named Doctor Ignatz Chevchenko. He was brought to America as a young child by wealthy parents who had left their homeland, according to varying accounts, because they'd either made investments in the burgeoning department store industry or managed to piss off the Czar. Like fellow robber barons who'd adopted bullshit military titles, he was not actually a doctor: he had, however, bought into certain Battle Creek notions of moral and physical hygiene and poured much of his inheritance into the founding of an inevitably failed medical school isolated out in the mountains. Chevchenko's folly, abandoned and rotting for decades, was up for perpetual debate as to whether it should be bulldozed for new real estate or designated a heritage site and refurbished as a tourist attraction. It was the only true landmark near the bed-and-breakfast aside from the adjacent shopping mall.

The annual Cape Cod road trip always included an extended stop at this mall in the morning, its chief attraction being that it contained stores that weren't in Sylvia's local mall, which was in fact very exciting to a child of the Indiana suburbs. There was the coin-operated ride in the shape of a sad-faced baby dragon. The jut-hipped mannequins with mirror balls for heads. The toy store with battery-powered automatons flashing and jumping and yapping on the teal-and-magenta carpet out front. And then bundled back in the car, back to the highway, to the sea.

That particular evening in the bed-and-breakfast, with Mom unpacking in their rented suite upstairs and Aunt Beryl busy in the kitchen, Sylvia and her brother were left temporarily unsupervised. Bobby ditched her pretty much immediately: it was the same at daycare, where he would studiously ignore her. He was 10 years old, after all, and she, at three years younger, was just a little kid and therefore *soooo lame*. Little Sylvia thought, but did not say, that he was a butthead.

She walked down the front hall with the smell of sautéed mushrooms and onions for their stroganoff dinner wafting in the air. Her small sneakers raised disproportionately loud complaints from the century-old floorboards. She had to step carefully.

A grandfather clock dominated the hall by the reception counter with its repetitive pendulum-ticking and gear-thunking: the sound, she thought, of its heartbeat and guts. Passing into the living room, she eyed the brass and porcelain tabletop figurines she'd been sternly advised not to touch, then the crystal goblets and bone china behind glass which she had no desire to touch: boring old people's dishes. A brown-and-ivory photograph of a bald long-nosed elderly man glared down from the fireplace mantel. An upright piano stood across from the fireplace with a yellowed book of sheet music opened to something called "Doctor Tinkle Tinker of Old Toy Town." *Tinkle,* she thought, giggling: the grown-ups were playing an old-timey song about *pee*.

Sylvia found Bobby in the doorway of Aunt Beryl's bedroom under the stairs.

"C'mere, look at this," he hissed, waving her in while leaving the room himself. She entered with a frisson of excitement: it was naughty to be in an adult's room alone, examining their grown-up things.

Aunt Beryl's bedroom was markedly different from the guest rooms upstairs. The latter were designed to be airy and cozy, with chintz curtains and impressionistic still-life paintings and a potpourri sachet atop every toilet tank. But this room was narrow, cramped, windowless: Sylvia would consider as an adult that it was built as a servant's quarters. The only light was the uremic glow of a single bulb behind an ancient frosted-glass ceiling sconce, the only decor a small painting in lacquered wood and flaking gold leaf depicting some saint or other. A pile of perhaps dirty, perhaps clean clothes spilled out from accordion-style closet doors in the corner. A tatty rug extended from beneath the bed like a piebald hunter's pelt. A tart whiff of stale body odor emitted from the seldom-washed sheets.

And atop those sheets was a puppet trunk.

A vertically-oriented rectangular black case with a pair of handles on top and a set of metal snaps and a lock on one side, lying flat open on its hinges. She didn't know whether it had been opened by Bobby or if he'd found it like that. The case was outfitted in some oddly patterned leather which Sylvia knew intuitively was magic.

Inside the trunk was a set of cushioned niches, and inside those niches was a set of dolls.

Sylvia was fascinated by dolls, though not in the manner a little girl was, at least stereotypically, supposed to be. Whenever she freed a new doll from its cardboard prison, she would immediately strip off its rough simulacrum of human clothing down to the bare plastic skin to see the true, undisguised doll-self concealed underneath. Barbie doll crotches in particular revealed the ultimately dishonest secrets of what she could expect from an adult body—a trio of smooth, hairless grooves and a permanently clenched buttock-crease—before the manufacturer switched the design to printed-on flesh-toned underwear with embossed patterns resembling some picturesque venereal disease.

She wouldn't make up stories with her dolls. She certainly didn't pretend they were her children. They were self-contained beings, too far outside of her own mind.

Before her were dolls that could be made puppets: the trunk's topmost niche held a tangle of wires with wooden handles to lasso their flopping limbs. She carefully picked up and examined the doll-puppets, one by one.

First was an androgynous figure with a shapeless bush of hair and a pale plastic body concealed by a long burgundy maid's or chef's or butcher's apron. Its face was a mask of cheap white fabric, its painted or printed features having smeared over time into amorphous splotches of black, electric blue, and magenta. Sylvia's thumb probed the expressionless mold of a face underneath, the nose, cheekbones, and jawline. The empty eye pits.

Next was a realistic horny-skinned crocodile wearing a sly grin and a manila tag that read *Crocoderm* in a large and cautious hand. She did not like touching its scales, filmy with collected grime from the stale air of the room.

And last was the little boy, half jester, half devil. The uneven stuffing that formed his innards was bound up in a red chenille onesie or perhaps old-fashioned long johns, with a round plastic face protruding from a red hood that fanned out in a jagged red ruff below the neck. His painted eyes were cast mischievously askance, his rubbed-off remnants of a theatrical Van Dyke goatee framing red cupid's-bow lips lightly parted in a perverse smile. He lay deceptively limp in her hand.

Over the successive years, Sylvia's memory faltered, reshooting different mental takes of the same moment, attempting to dredge up what had actually happened next. Certainly she'd heard adult footsteps approaching in the hall while she held the devil-boy in her hand. And certainly she didn't want to be caught snooping. But had she set him back in the case? Had she dropped him on the bed, on the floor? Had she kicked him under the bed? At any rate, she definitely remembered snapping the case shut and hurrying from the room, nearly running right into Aunt Beryl.

Her hostess looked over Sylvia's head at the puppet trunk poised on the bed. She bent down and, in her creaky old-lady accent, asked:

"You didn't let any of them *out*, did you?"

Aunt Beryl's words were very careful, mannered, yet there was a wink in her warning tone. Sylvia was a shy child, often unsure in such situations whether adults were teasing, just playing pretend and expecting her to play along, or whether they were seriously concerned. So she shook her head and quietly said no.

And even then, as the old woman straightened up, a flash of red righted itself against the bedsheets trailing on the floor and instantly darted around the corner, to disappear.

Yes, *she had let him out*.

Sylvia had little appetite for dinner that evening, the forkfuls of tough meat and gloppy sauce. She had trouble sleeping that night, expecting to hear *his* boneless feet pit-patting on the floorboards, a sudden red smear dashing to her bed in the wavering dark. She knew, with the intuitive gnosis of children, that the devil doll would GET HER. The details of this terrible fate were beyond the reaches of her seven-year-old imagination, but it was infinitely worse than simply being murdered.

She told no one about the devil doll and its movement at the foot of the bed. Mom, up in the adult world that couldn't understand such things, would assume it was just Bobby playing a mean prank; Bobby would loudly protest his innocence and resent his sister even further; and then everyone would be unhappy, nothing resolved.

She knew *he* would be waiting for her at the bed-and-breakfast next year. She feared what was coming. She feared the inevitable.

But with the dissolution of her parents' marriage, there would be no return visit. Thus the looming terror of the devil doll was gradually smoothed over behind more immediate troubles and fears.

* * *

For the next 25 years, the memory lay largely dormant, faded into a curious childhood anecdote just troubling and uncanny enough to make her feel nervous about recounting to others. Until Sylvia Dreiyer was hired to write for TV and decided to return to the scene of the crime to mine the source of her old fears for content.

Sylvia lived on the East Coast herself now and could take a long walk to the shore whenever she wanted, although in practice she rarely had the time or energy for that. Bobby, now just Bob, was off the wagon again. They hadn't spoken in three years. Auntie Lindy had turned Stepmom Lindy after Mom and Dad's divorce, or would've been, had the judge in the custody proceedings not held a firm belief in the "homosexual agenda." And now she was Ex-Wife Lindy after Mom fell into some cultish New Age wellness rabbit hole. Dad was still in the Indiana suburbs, a faded, humorless man, disappointed that neither of his children had achieved economic parity with his white-collar younger self at their own respective ages.

Sylvia lived in a shared rental house where the upstairs neighbors liked to blast a narrow rotation of hair metal's greatest hits at inconvenient hours. She supported herself through the insufferable plate-spinning of freelance gig work: proofreading and copyediting, audio and video transcription, ghostwriting term papers for rich brats who could quite literally afford to fail in adult life. She did most of her work at a café or from home with noise-cancelling headphones on, blotting out the world.

Sylvia's westward drive to the mountains was guided not by a highlighted flip map but a woman's clipped British accent telling her where to go from a dashboard-mounted screen. She had dug up the address of the bed-and-breakfast online and booked a room with some of her advance. This was her last weekend before the new job started.

Sylvia was to be a junior writer for season two of a supernatural soap opera: she'd been pulled in somewhat last-minute to replace a writer who was dropping out to attend Clarion West. It was all thanks to some light nepotism as the show's head writer, Dane Braquemard, had been Sylvia's undergrad academic advisor, with whom she'd kept sporadically in touch after graduating a decade ago. She had never written scripts for television before, just plays and short films—one of which, *The Doctrine of Signatures*, had recently won awards at a couple of horror film festivals—along with a handful of unpublished feature screenplays. "Put your own spin on things," Dane told her, meaning make it weird. A dash of spice. As she'd said in an interview about *The Doctrine of Signatures*: "Sometimes in adulthood, the things that once were terrifying are now fascinating, even perversely so."

So here she was.

Late spring, a clammy day, petrichor scent on the pavement. No other cars in the lot. This was her first arrival while the sun was still up, stealing away some of the old magic.

The bed-and-breakfast had been repainted, erasing the gingerbread trim in favor of uniformly pale grey weathered slats: an open-casket corpse without prep-room makeup. Sylvia stepped up to the wraparound porch and through the front door.

Manning the reception counter was a girl, late teens, early twenties at most, in an oversized pastel hoodie. She was wearing earbuds and apparently hadn't heard Sylvia come in, leaning on the counter to watch a video on her phone of—as Sylvia soon saw—a man dancing in a bright red full-body suit that also covered his entire head without gaps for eyes, ears, or lips. A zentai suit, she recalled. The little man on the screen, waggling his hips and thrusting his torso in a repetitive and oddly sexless manner. He looks like a used tampon, thought Sylvia.

"Oh! Sorry!" said the counter girl, startled, pulling out her earbuds and flipping her phone upside down.

"Uh, hi. I emailed—"

"Oh yeah, you're here for the room." She nodded and stuck out her hand. "Shayla. Nice to meet you."

The girl observed her below dark eyeliner fanning out into immaculate cat eyes that Sylvia, surely at least a decade her senior, still couldn't master. She wore her hair in a trendy cut that resembled a reverse mullet and was dyed a deep, vibrant purple. Sylvia would've liked to dye her own dirt-brown hair a similar shade at that age, but unnatural hair color was banned by her high school dress code right alongside bare midriffs, various obscure types of shorts, and apparel that promoted Satanism. And she figured it would've been vetoed by her father anyway, he who once refused to be seen in public with her wearing a satin slip dress over a modest t-shirt and jeans because he thought it looked too much like underwear: "Where'd you get the idea from? *Madonna?*" he'd sneered. She thought of Collin Eads, who had a thing for girls with brightly dyed hair, like peacocks, little parrots on his shoulder: would he like this little Shayla, would he try to seduce her? Well, *fuck* men's expectations. It was too early to drain her serotonin like this.

"So you were here when Aunt Beryl was around?" said Shayla.

*Was*. The unsurprising assumption being that she had died.

"Yes. Were you related?"

"Yeah, she was my great—my mom's great aunt?" Her face scrunched up in thought. "Didn't your email say you were a screenwriter?"

"Yeah. The show is set in a mountain town, so—"

"Cool, what's the show? Have I heard of it?"

"Oh no, I doubt it," said Sylvia, instantly self-conscious. "It's not really that famous." In fact, the channel airing the supernatural soap opera was rather far down the pay cable dial, and the show itself held a similar rank in the algorithm of the cable network's auxiliary streaming app. To be scrupulously honest, it was safe to say the show was essentially filler programming, given its poor advertising; the network probably expected people to watch while mistaking it for some other, more popular show that covered similar themes. "*Rubedo Ridge*?"

The girl shook her head with an apologetic smile and a noncommittal "That's cool."

Shayla drummed her fingers on the counter and thrust forward a fistful of takeout menus. "Yeah, so . . . we don't really do the food part anymore."

"Just beds, no breakfast."

"Yeah. You might have to borrow the house phone to make an order 'cause the signal sucks here."

Aside from the Wi-Fi she must've been using to watch that video on her phone and presumably didn't want to share. Well, whatever.

"What's there to do here these days?"

"Um. There's the mall." Shayla shrugged.

"Do you live here?"

"Tsh, *no!*" she said, too quickly.

Sylvia dimly recalled there were no other cars in the lot.

No other names in the guest book, open to a fresh page, crisp and empty.

The counter girl reached over to hand her a key on a big dangling fob and paused.

"I'm sorry, did you *want* the old room?"

Momentarily flustered, she assumed this was an offer to stay in Aunt Beryl's bedroom before realizing Shayla meant the family suite.

And no, she did not. It would be unnecessarily expensive.

Sylvia looked around a bit before heading upstairs. From the hallway through the living room, the decor had become far more sparse, fashionably minimal. The porcelain knick-knacks and piano were gone, the grandfather clock standing silent, unwound. The old long-nosed bald man still glared from the mantel, though this time she noted a resemblance to late photographs of Doctor Chevchenko. And beside him was a little door set into the bricks, before which sat a dollhouse-sized wedge of cheese, carton of milk, and other miniature foodstuffs.

She picked one up to look closer and Shayla immediately crossed over, flustered.

"Oh, it's for the—the *domovoi*."

"The . . ."

"Yeah, that's—it's a family thing. Um. Y'know. You feed this little guy and he's supposed to, like, protect the house. They used to leave out real milk and stuff but like . . ." Shayla tugged at one of her many silver earrings, a nervous tic: this embarrassed her. "Even if I weren't vegan. It attracts bugs. So yeah." She picked up a tiny green bottle with a gilded neck. "Some champagne, so he can party." She laughed weakly.

Sylvia hadn't remembered seeing any of this as a kid. Perhaps by "family" Shayla hadn't meant Aunt Beryl's side. She set down the toy T-bone and quietly took her leave.

Aunt Beryl's former bedroom door was shut. Sylvia realized, sharply and unexpectedly, that she did not want to see the room. It was better off, she thought, hermetically sealed in her mind: the stale smell, the stuffiness in the air, the clutter. The puppet trunk on the bed, waiting.

* * *

*Put your own spin on things*, Dane Braquemard had said. So here, in her rented room, she'd try to brainstorm some ideas to cobble into a treatment. Try to impress them right out the gate. Monday would see *Rubedo Ridge* boot camp, writing room introductions, perusals of the show bible.

And, god, a serious distraction from *that* situation. It was frankly absurd. A certain corner of her social circle had deemed her "sex-negative" for cutting things off with an otherwise auspicious romantic prospect, a writer in Queens named Collin Eads, after she'd discovered his indie press novel of laddish autofiction called, for fuck's sake, *Anatomy of a Body Count*. The book was about all his previous sexual partners at the time: nearly 400 of them. Yes, the book was nearly 400 pages long. And being a straight cisgender man, he only thought penetrative intercourse "counted," so the real number was certainly much higher.

It wasn't like he'd been a sex worker of some sort and had acquired that number in the line of duty. And he, an admitted supporter of feminism, rolled his eyes at pick-up artists and the like. At the very least, this knowledge of Collin's history made Sylvia, two years his senior, feel suddenly insecure about her own low double-digits.

How many of those women *knew* he had written about them? How many could recognize themselves, even anonymously? How many were still actively in his orbit, how many to flash her that snakish lady-smirk at having gotten there first and knowing his body, his peccadilloes, better than she ever would? How did she know he wouldn't continue his habits, as he'd written without apology about cheating on every one of his exes? Were there any surprise Eads babies toddling around? Or any other surprises, since men weren't routinely tested for things like HPV?

And how did she know he wouldn't write about *her* like that?

He lived a good three hours' travel away and they had (thank god) scarcely gone past kissing, at which he was mechanically skilled, efficient in retrospect. Because what truly repulsed her was not just that sheer number, an auditorium's worth, or the violation of intimate privacy, but the *attitude*. Those passages treating Woman, or rather Pussy, as an abstract discipline he'd mastered, like some goddamn bemonocled Victorian noble recounting his colonialist exploits at the gentlemen's club with a snifter of brandy in hand, Viscount Eads, Esq. And at the same time as this pseudo-objectivity, he frankly came off as a sex addict: a term he would certainly scoff at, had she ever brought it up. There was a compulsive, dehumanizing quality to the encounters in those few selections she'd read: sex, to Collin, must have become a mechanical and joyless process long ago. She thought of the vintage "marriage manual" she'd picked up at a flea market, featuring several pages of faceless wooden artist's mannikins entangled together to demonstrate conjugal positions as unlewdly as possible.

It was a mistake to get so attached before knowing him well enough, especially at a distance. But they had spoken so long, so easily, and she had told him so much, so much, too much: certain fantasies, even, that he could now write to the world if he chose. He was entirely too clever and entirely too hot. The sharp cut of his nose, cheekbones, jawline, even the pits of his eyes. That terribly appealing spark of perpetual mischief in his face. That deflective awkward laughter around *Anatomy of a Body Count:* Ohhh, teehee, you shouldn't read *that* one!

"The past doesn't matter," those former friends had insisted; "Of course it matters, the past *makes* us!" she'd replied, surprising even herself with her own vehemence.

And enshrining it in public meant it was never, ever past.

It was unfashionable nowadays, but Sylvia favored a hard, clean break. She would slam and bolt the door and wait (and wait and wait) for the clamor to die down. No pointless drawn-out rehashing conversations, no codependent "just friends" demi-relationships. A severance. A guillotine of the heart. Exes were repositories of one's secrets set loose in the world, their potential power too awful to contemplate for long. Fuck off, Collin, you've cracked open too many girls.

How did she get on this train of thought anyway? Ugh. Time for some creative juicing.

Sylvia considered lighting a joint and doing some Burroughs-style intoxicated free association. Write high, edit sober: that was the rule. But she realized she didn't know the cannabis laws in this state, or if everything was non-smoking these days, and she didn't want to test the chillness of the young counter girl. Who was even in charge now? Shayla's parents? Were they the ones who'd outfitted this room in yuppie franchise modern, its surfaces new and slick and utterly without character? The effect was less of a bed-and-breakfast or even a chain hotel than a realtor's showroom. What the hell was this decor? A clock with no numerals, just a beige disc with two bars. A framed stock photo of a bale of hay. A metal bowl of spheres made from "organic" substances like twigs and faux moss and whatnot. One of them even had an unpleasant gnarled, horny texture like a skinned reptile.

Sylvia stepped out to the upstairs deck and leaned on the railing, hugging her jacket shut. No sound but the creak of the old weathervane, the occasional gust of wind, the rush-hour ghost-echo of cars on the interstate. Across the way, to her left, were the backlit mountains; to her right was the mall, that grey slab at dusk. She noticed for the first time, or perhaps had long forgotten, that the mall was named IGGY'S, written out in a thick, round, gilded font lifted from an '80s Broadway marquee. A brief motion at the mall's visible entrance: a little stick figure at the corner of her eye. There and gone.

When it came time to order dinner, not only was the cell signal predictably worthless, but the house phone wouldn't connect: the service had been cut off as the line was so seldom used. After an extended *ummmm,* Shayla apologetically offered her leftovers: a saran-wrapped plate of stroganoff. It struck Sylvia that this was the same thing she'd had for dinner the last time she was here, as a terrified seven-year-old. Imagining, preposterously, that leftovers from that night had been deliberately frozen for 25 years, like some newlyweds did with a slice of their wedding cake.

Sylvia cracked open her laptop and tried to write. She was good at visualization, turning ideas on a mental lathe. Right, start with the setting.

`EXT. HIGHWAY PIT STOP - DAY.`

Fast food chains orbiting gas stations. A lone retro '50s diner. Mountain peaks in the background. A liminal region where no real living takes place.

The heroine of the supernatural soap opera stands at the corner of an intersection. On the show, she often has a demon-guy who pops up to advise her, or maybe he's an angel: they have a lot of flirty banter. Sylvia didn't recall offhand whether or not they had fucked, or even kissed, or whether it was being teased out for some future season. A ring or a necklace or something holds a piece of his spirit, and that's how she summons him.

But he couldn't help. He was far away now.

A person stands across the street, silent and tall, gender unknown, in a filthy white jumpsuit and a long apron. Maybe they work at the diner.

MEDIUM SHOT - TILT DOWN: A wild shock of hair, a pale rag pulled over their features marked with crude smears of greasepaint that had once approximated a face. Arms stiffly at their sides, elbows slightly bent, poised and ready. They just *stand there*, staring at the heroine for a length of time uncertain—

No, Sylvia thought. This is too weird; it's a fucking soap opera, it's not *Twin Peaks*.

It occurred to her that her mind would soon be opened to the world through the eyes and ears of strangers. How would they know her own limbs and appendages at work in the show? How much would she *want* them to know?

In bed, she couldn't turn her mind off. Caught in that hypnotic half-sleep limbo, she drifted through notions of a shop, a corner shop, a workshop, all dark, bare wood, like the interior of a tall ship or a Trojan horse. A big artist's mannikin, man-sized, naked, made of the same wood, was crouched on the bare floorboards, ripping off his mask made of cloth, of leather, of skin. The head beneath was polished, featureless. Blank.

The grandfather clock ticked its metronome somewhere behind Sylvia, there in that handsome oblong parlor. Its front half was boxed in by skylights, floor-length windows, and French doors, providing a view of the lush green foliage of the nearby woods, with just a hint of mountain. Panels of vividly patterned wallpaper formed the back half, cramped with frames of black-eyed icons and tapestries from the Old Country. And at the border, Shayla stood before her in a crisp white shirtwaist with leg-o'-mutton sleeves, waist pinched and girdled into an ankle-length skirt, and hair, much longer, leached of all but a hint of lilac and swept up into a Gibson Girl pouf. She smiled gently, hands crossed at her waist. She reminded Sylvia of a nurse.

The Crocoderm waited behind Shayla, past the upright piano. It was dangerous, but only if you stepped forward, just *one foot* forward. Sylvia looked safely above the crocodile, through the windows and skylights, at the distant gables of the medical school, swarmed by serious men in black frock coats like a murder of crows.

Shayla's thin pale lips formed a word, little squarish bunny teeth revealed at the last syllable.

*Домово́й.*

The word was not so much spoken as imprinted within Sylvia's brain. The girl pressed an egg-shaped wooden kaleidoscope with brass fixtures into Sylvia's hands: *You have to see, the Czar made it.*

But the eye would look back into me, Sylvia thought. Turning the knob to focus the aperture would unleash a sharp protuberance. The eye would puncture her own eye and swap their sight.

Shayla smiled, silently, small eager nods, teeth like porcelain tiles in a madhouse hydrotherapy bath. A wire was pulled taut between her small fists, clenched around a pair of wooden handles.

* * *

Shayla was absent in the morning when Sylvia stepped out to visit the mall. She didn't bother driving, just walked over. The mall's parking lot was likewise empty. Perhaps it was just early, but she knew that wasn't the reason.

The automatic doors parted for her in a cold bath of recycled air. The hollow chill of an excavated catacomb.

Scarcely any shops appeared to be open, or even in business. The lonely echo of her boots followed her across the grey tiles, passing endless darkened storefronts caged up behind metal grilles. The loaded calm was only broken by sporadic bursts of tinny mall jazz, as though the stereo had forgotten what it was taught to do.

Sylvia found the old toy store of her childhood—closed, of course—recognizable only by the teal-and-magenta carpet, now covered with a heavy layer of dust pilling into cloudlike clumps. Dust bunnies, her mother would call them, as if by gaining mass they gained life.

But there was only one sign of life here.

A figure around the corner, wearing a red full-body suit, deftly stepped onto a spotlit display pedestal and picked up a cartoonishly large gift box. There it held that position, flanked by two others doing the same. In fact these displays, peppered throughout the mall, were the only dash of visible color: all faceless, all red.

Sylvia stepped towards the nearest display with a fist in the pit of her stomach. Up close the fabric was somewhat fuzzy: a layer of red chenille. She could see no tiny wavering motions in their contorted arms, no chests rising in breath.

Mannequins. Only mannequins.

The one on the left had its head tilted and arm outstretched as if indicating something specific. And there it was: a recess in the floor, the same size and shape as the surrounding tiles, clearly deliberate. Sylvia got on her hands and knees, peering down to see.

Lined in little bricks was a dollhouse-sized fireplace set flush with the ground. Its mantel was decorated with miniatures: a locket-sized sepia photograph, a plastic cheese wedge, a bottle of champagne. And visible beyond the hearth, an utter absence, an oubliette, the black pit of a saint's painted eye.

A loud ting and thunk resounded at her back, much like the sound of a grandfather clock; yet she turned to face a towering row of elevators. Far grander than their surroundings, the elevators' façades were fashioned from great slabs of marble with brass fixtures of ornate Nouveau latticework. The door of the central elevator slid open.

It was utterly dark inside. She clasped the operator's cold, fingerless hand.

* * *

Spectators clambered in the stands of the amphitheatre's concentric rows: their bodies still, their heads bald, their molded flesh pale and bare. Flat on her back on the operating table, Sylvia could see them all: excitable murmurs from unmoving lips, intent pupils in unblinking eyes. All focused on the supine frame of Sylvia Dreiyer.

A smooth, stiff, androgynous hand brushed back the blanket covering her naked torso. Another, its uniform taupe fingers molded for grasping, lowered the scalpel to the tip of her clavicle.

As the instrument sliced through epidermis and fascia, peeling back the lank wrappings to reveal the lush red, Sylvia thrilled in unparalleled sensual ecstasy: all without moving, without making a sound. And yes, *yes*, now the doll doctor was pressing inward to see, to uncover, what a human was truly made of.

# EFFACE

IN THE WAKE of the working day, Jeannine prepared for the hunt. Neon flicker of the restaurant sign outside her Village window as she sat before the vanity. Bodycon black dress and thigh-high stiletto boots, a vinyl trenchcoat standing by to shield Jeannine from sidewalk catcalls. Jeannine, her hair teased out, lips, lids, and cheekbones painted to match the red, blue, violet baths of light in the ritual to come. The night cried out for Jeannine. The city reached out its clammy hands for Jeannine. My kingdom for a man after midnight. Or whomever, whatever, else struck her fancy.

*Clok-clak-clok-clak-clok-clak* of heels on pavement, one hand in her trenchcoat pocket, the other gripping the strap of her black clutch purse. Her club of choice, the Amour Fou, was within walking distance of her own apartment, a libertine's garden. As she turned the corner, a quintet of skinny girls emerged from the club, teetering in little tight dresses, bachelorette party sashes, and full-face plastic wolf masks. One by one, they raised their drunken heads and howled at the moon.

The broken light of the mirror ball casting its sequined shards above gyrating metallic peplum and neon geometry. Hissing fog cloaking walls and ceiling outfitted in the strict black-and-silver of fascists and fetishists. Hypnotic saxophone and synthesizer, faux-English accents and drum machines. Backlit silhouettes. Hands of a stranger. Here Jeannine would dance in pointy boots until her toes contorted into Barbie-doll feet, until she could slip off the shoes and wrap her newly-bared calves around those of another. And who would it be tonight?

A slim and pretty New Wave boy awash in pastels, a curtain of hair flopping above one eyebrow, tossed back insouciantly? She'd seen him hungrily kissing a boy with a shaved head the week before, tugging at the O-ring of his dog collar. Now he turned his tender lips to hers, timid hands at her lower back. A warm bit of metal at his sternum, which she soon realized was a coke spoon.

Or would it be the bleach-blonde punk chick in a leather jacket and matching miniskirt, eyes smeared in coal or kohl? Her thigh in ripped fishnets between Jeannine's own, nudging against her lace panties. Her lipstick and Jeannine's meeting in a menstrual smear. Her tongue teasing the crucifix of Jeannine's black fashion rosary.

And across the room, a pair of eyes bored into her, eyes like drill bits. A pale face, lips lightly parted, unblinking. Shielded by the wide brim of a black hat. Perched atop a set of broad shoulders. An electric tremor shot through Jeannine, a frisson of arousal and fear.

But Jeannine was quickly knocked out of these thoughts. The punk chick winked and tugged her hand, leading her off the dance floor and trailing into a side room behind a clandestine door. For all the times Jeannine had ventured into this club, all the countless hours, she had never seen this door before.

Within this room, the neon of the dance floor gave way to the yellow glow of a single spotlight trained on a closed curtain. The space was long and narrow, a tight crowd of shadowed faces huddled around a runway backed by a stage. As she stepped forward, the footlights clicked on and the curtains swept back. Jeannine's hand was unclasped as her dance partner sought to squeeze closer to the runway, immediately disappearing in the dark.

All eyes were on the stage and the figure at its center, head cocked, arms bent, statue-stiff. *A doll girl,* thought Jeannine, for her face was concealed by the white ceramic mask of a pantomime tart, with heavy rouge and sea-green shadow and bright scarlet lips. She wore a baggy purple jumpsuit better suited to a clown, with a frilly Pagliacci collar and cuffs, hands concealed in white gloves and stockinged feet in black espadrilles. At no discernible cue, the doll girl began to move.

Slow and sleek, out of rhythm with the muffled beat seeping in through the door, she undulated down the runway. Though her motions bore no resemblance to the raucous bump and grind of burlesque, the fabric strips of her clown suit were gradually sloughed off with no touch of her fingertips, as if sheared away by invisible razors. Beneath, she wore a fringe-covered flapper dress, which soon pooled at her feet as well. The doll girl continued her dance in a satin teddy, torso and limbs concealed by a sort of porcelain couture, plate armor in the shape of a ball-jointed doll's body.

Despite this striptease, her movements were consistently more mesmeric than erotic, even as the lingerie dropped away to reveal a hairless body with vague nubs approximating nipples and a deep cleft like a lipless mouth in her bare, pallid crotch. Her head bent on its ball-joint neck, arms and legs twisted on their knee-and-ankle axes, as a normal human's could not. Was she actually a machine under there?

The doll girl's head turned to Jeannine, standing arms crossed in the corner, twin black pits of the mask's holes probing Jeannine's brown eyes. She paused only a moment as Jeannine, shivering, held her gaze; then she abruptly collapsed to the floor of the stage, strings cut. A smattering of tentative, nervous applause. The curtains dropped, the doll girl's body hoisted backstage on unseen hands. The little theatre suddenly felt very humid with the great press of bodies.

Jeannine pushed through the door and saw the club unchanged: the disco ball spinning, the stereo pounding with jangling guitars, ample hairspray and makeup across genders.

And yet it now felt alien and detached, both a ruin of the past and an outlandish novelty for the tittering tourist. No longer a backyard garden, but a foreign land. She looked about for a familiar face. The punk girl was long gone, as were any friends, acquaintances, ex-lovers, regular bartenders. The crowd from the hidden theatre had not even followed her out. There was only one non-stranger left, and he was otherwise occupied.

"Oh, The Cockchafer? I don't go there anymore," shouted the New Wave boy into the ear of the waifish redhead whose arm encircled his waist. "I heard there was a serial killer." He lifted a hand to his throat and mimed strangling himself, to the redhead's stilted laugh.

She probably ought to go home.

Her path to the exit was temporarily blocked by a slumming crew-cut preppie in a varsity jacket for which he was much too old.

"Got a light, dollface?"

His eyes slid down her boots and left a trail of slime. She bared her teeth at him and hissed like an asp.

Upon retrieving her trenchcoat from the coat check, Jeannine cinched its belt around her waist as she emerged into the night. The hand thrust into her left pocket immediately met a crumpled wad of paper. Smoothing it out under a streetlight, she found a flyer for a show, a flyer which she had never seen before: *SENTINELLE, a production by MADAME FORTUNATA at AMOUR FOU* above a crude Xeroxed image of a contorted wooden artist's dummy. *MIDNIGHT SHARP.*

It was now almost 1 in the morning.

She looked up from the flyer and caught the gaze of the masked man. The one who had stared so sharply, so intently, in the club. He was not simply pale and impassive in expression: his entire face was concealed by a white mask, plain of any adornment. He wore a black fedora and a black trenchcoat down to the ankles, buttoned up to the neck, hands tucked into his pockets. He stood at the entrance to an alley several yards down the block, as if waiting for someone.

Waiting for her. To see him.

And when she had seen him, their locked eyes undeniable proof, he nodded and backed into the alley like a trail of cigarette smoke.

A fresh burst of cold sweat at the thought of what he must be. A plainclothes policeman. A Soviet spy.

But what had she *done?*

In this city she was no one, anonymous. In the daylight she worked at an office to finance her basic needs and her nights. And at night she only wanted to have fun.

* * *

Madame Fortunata had been born with the current century and resided for much of that time on the Upper West Side. Yet her decor, Jeannine learned upon being buzzed in, was surprisingly ultramodern. A shag carpet of lavender-lilac. A pair of dividing walls made of frosted glass cubes. Twin rows of track lighting shining down on the wall-mounted art like interrogators' spotlights. Floating grids and scalene triangles, wavy lines and zigzags in muted peach and turquoise, in coral and aquamarine, in fuchsia and electric blue. The cobra eyes, pallid skin, and white ghastly grin of a Patrick Nagel print looming across the back wall. That simplified, softened, pastel-and-neon iteration of Deco.

Jeannine flashed back to the omnipresent dun dead brown of the suburbs she had escaped. Plastic and Bakelite and vinyl siding in faux wood grain. A simulacrum of rustic organic matter. A failed attempt to get back to the land from which the identical houses had sprung. Jeannine preferred artifice that acknowledged what it was.

Madame Fortunata's decades of accomplishments hung on the walls to either side of the long entry hall. Framed posters boasted of collaborations with Diaghilev's Ballets Russes, Pina Bausch's Tanztheater, the Graham Company here in Manhattan, the Markos Company in Berlin, and several itinerant Japanese troupes featuring something called *bunraku*. In recent years she had withdrawn from the public, citing a decline in health, and unofficially retired.

Jeannine was not a connoisseur of choreography and would not have recognized the name: had in fact previously known Madame Fortunata only by her government name. This was how the choreographer had found her, sought her out, though they had never directly spoken or interacted face-to-face: an embossed invitation on her desk, paired with an uptown address, and here she was.

For the grand Madame was, it turned out, a client of Jeannine's firm in that daylight world of starched collars and shoulder pads, tanned and toned princes of commerce. Knights in shining Armani. Yet in truth they were only smarmy yuppies snapping their suspenders like old-time carnival barkers and robber barons chomping on a fat *cee*-gar, certain anyone could be had for the right price, the right mix of flash and glitz. This did not matter to Jeannine. These men were so much detritus to her. The subway rats were better company.

At odds with the decor was a small framed sepia photograph dated 1905, which she stepped closer to inspect. Her hostess, she assumed, as a young girl, head topped by thick bangs and lop-sided bow, chin tilted low like a Kubrick villain with a shy, awkward smile, clutching a naked bisque baby doll to her pinafore. A tall man's large hand rested on her small shoulder, his dark trouser leg and wingtip a Doric column to her right, the rest of him cropped out of frame. A work bench stood behind her, covered in wood shavings, paintbrushes, hand tools, and doll parts.

"Come in, dear," the Madame beckoned. "Come in, Miss Jeannine."

A creaky scythe-rasp in her voice. A hint of accent Jeannine couldn't place shrouded in well-worn Manhattanese. She followed the source of the voice and stepped through the glass dividing walls.

And was instantly taken aback. The walls at either side of her were entirely covered with masks and little clowns and harlequin dolls, hanging from nails or set into niche tableaux. Stranger still, many dolls sprang to life as she stepped forward, as though she had tripped a hidden sensor. The muffled sound of whirring clockwork behind the violet walls. Tilting their heads; slowly, carefully, almost tentatively moving their shrunken arms and legs. A few moved on fixed platforms, cut-paper *commedia* stages in which a gleaming devil surprised a girl in her boudoir, a ballerina rotated on a single toe, a grimacing man in a tricorne and breeches chased a buxom woman clutching a tumor-shaped baby.

But above all, the masks. Phallic-nosed, swollen-cheeked Carnevale masks. Comedy/Tragedy masks conjoined at the cheek like Siamese twins. Jesters with a vertical slash down each eye, remnants of the King's displeasure. Ingenues with widened eyeholes above startled or fellatious O-mouths. Masks wearing masks, metallic Mardi Gras dominoes. Colorful ribbons dangling to either side, never to knot around a human face. Delicate half-veils of fashionable midcentury widows. Sigil-like scribbles, black tears and stars, diamonds and music notes dotting cheeks and chins like the velvet *mouches* donned by courtiers to conceal smallpox and syphilis scars. The heavy shadow, lipstick, and rouge of players for the stage and ladies of the night. Open sockets and flat mouths: plaintive, coquettish, conspiratorial, sneering.

Sequins and gold braid. Satin and lamé. Tulle and lace. Feathers and rhinestones. Porcelain, plaster, white-glazed ceramic. Women, children, androgynes. Jokers and mimes, flappers and courtesans, frozen in time.

The famous choreographer sat on the carpet between these walls in a violet-black leotard cut high over knobby hip bones, knees bent like a mantis. Thin calves disappearing into woolly leg warmers, stamens rich with pollen. Head crowned with ample silver-grey hair, pinned back in a lavender rinse.

"Aubergine," she said, spreading an arm to indicate her wardrobe, her decor, all of it. "The color of royalty. The hue of the gods."

Her voice was slightly muffled, emitting as it did from behind, yes, a white mask. A mask to shield a lifelong performer's vanity over her aging features? But no, it was more than that facile, potentially sexist explanation. The mask, with its pastel pools of faux makeup, its thin, knowing arched eyebrows, wore a placid expression enigmatic enough to read as curious or domineering.

"Some tea?" She fanned her long fingers toward a teapot and a pair of cups on a low stool at her side. Jeannine gave her assent and sat down cross-legged on the thick carpet, attempting to ignore the scrutiny of all those pale faces.

"You enjoyed my girl's performance at the Amour Fou."

An uneasy nod from Jeannine.

Madame Fortunata lifted a teacup and held it up to her mask's closed mouth, tipping it politely before setting it back on the stool. The cup was empty. A pantomime. A farce.

*A tea party,* thought Jeannine. *A child's tea party*. Tiny seats around a playroom table stuffed with piebald bears and slouching Victorian dollies with stovepipe curls and terrible hints of bared, tiny teeth. She thought of the little girl in the sepia photo: perhaps behind the mask hung a kindergartener's face on the body of an octogenarian.

"I thought you might take interest in a private performance of a new production I have been working on. My own little ensemble. Fellow creatures of the night, like yourself. Girls, women, boys."

"And men," Jeannine added reflexively, to intrusive thoughts of the tall man in the white mask.

A sudden chill from her hostess led to several moments of loaded silence. An air of disapproval in the gleaming features of Fortunata's mask.

"No, no men. *Never* men."

Fortunata cocked her head like the stringless marionette girl of SENTINELLE.

"You look familiar somehow. Outside of the office, of course." (But she had never seen Jeannine before, not at the office at least. She always sent an underling to relay documents back and forth, a small, short person, possibly a grandchild, who wore a hooded raincoat no matter the weather and said nothing.) "Have you recorded a tape for a video dating service?"

"No?" That was truly a *no*, period, but she was taken aback at such a random query.

"You are young," her hostess said, leaning forward, "And I'll offer you some advice.

"A woman I knew met a man, a famous actor, through a personal ad. An eccentric man. I needn't say his name; I suspect you would know him. Handsome, you know, but very stern. He showed up with a tan trenchcoat all buttoned up and a matching fedora. He looked like a newspaperman.

"She had a loft in Tribeca, and he came to her there and they . . . why, you're a modern girl, I won't mince words. They made love. He took her to bed, and he made love to her. And he was a diligent lover. Good with his tongue. But he kept his suit on the whole time, and only unbuttoned his trousers.

"He left afterward: he'd told her he had an early call time the next morning. Actors, you know. And she was still in her negligee basking in it all when she realized he had left his umbrella behind. So she went after him, down into the subway. And she found his face on the subway tracks.

"Yes, his *face*. She saw that grubby thing on the tracks and hooked it up with the umbrella and held it in her hands. It was a lifelike rubber mask. He was still on the platform, standing against a support pillar and lighting a cigarette, and she saw him. His real face was all burnt away, with no nose, like a skeleton. The flesh was raw, like he had peeled off his own skin. And his teeth, his bare teeth, all yellow in the red gums.

"Of course it wasn't the actor at all. It really *was* a newspaperman. He merely wanted to collect gossip material for the newspapers. And for blackmail.

"The moral is: Never trust a *face!*"

And with that she thrust another invitation into Jeannine's hands.

She examined the envelope as she boarded the elevator. The same Xeroxed artist dummy from the SENTINELLE flyer had been duplicated several times. This show bore the ridiculous name: SLICE ME NICELY.

Through the lobby windows, night had fallen, yet it was only afternoon when she had arrived. She had only stayed long enough for half a teacup. Time had folded without her consent.

On the sidewalk before the building was the masked man.

Waiting for her. Following her. He nodded and saluted, spreading his arm in invitation.

Jeannine, locked in an instant trance. Jeannine, gliding forward to take his hand. That hand, completely hidden within a ceramic glove, just as the mask concealed his entire head and neck. Jeannine and the masked man, waltzing among the fallen leaves.

All automotive and foot traffic faded away. No longer pavement under their heels but polished marble and brass. A music box couple in a glistening chapel of gilt and mirror. Revolving across an automaton mainspring to the haunting tune of a barrel organ. How simple it is, to relinquish control.

His embrace tightened as the dance progressed. Across her forehead and cheek came a stirring breeze, the gentle breath from his mouth slit and the discreet holes for his nostrils. And far lower still, an uncommon firmness pressed against her through their respective trenchcoats. Why, he need only unbutton them both and lift her up in his strong arms in order to—

At this flush of arousal she blinked, once, to find herself standing alone in the cold wind. Pedestrians turned their eyes to her curiously, then walked on, indifferent.

* * *

Jeannine wore sensible heels to SLICE ME NICELY. If asked, she would be unable to articulate why she was going at all. The invitation tugged her along like a fish with a hook through its gills.

Following Fortunata's invitation at the appointed date and time led Jeannine to a warehouse in Chelsea, a warehouse like any other. She was, strangely, alone on this block. Her destination made itself known by a chorus of rhythmic mechanical creaks that increased in volume as she stepped through the open door.

She was bathed in yellow-gold lighting from lamps affixed to skeletal girders. The site of the performance made little attempt to camouflage its industrial origins, a warehouse turned construction site long abandoned to roaches and rust. Across the bare floor and sparse furniture were scattered various drapes, tapestries, and sheets of rumpled plastic and colored cellophane, as if replicating the aftermath of a raucous party; but for the most part the space lay bare, from its stripped foundations and overhead fluorescents to the illusory nudity of half its performers. This was an interactive piece, an experimental performance: no stage, one only walked amongst the dancers and their choreographed motions. Through inclination or instruction, they fully ignored her.

Jeannine could best describe this as an impotent orgy. Performers in unitards with crudely smeared greasepaint across their faces and bodies feigned theatrical intercourse with statues and automatons and sometimes each other: bumping blunted, sexless mannequin bulges together, or rutting in feigned ecstasy against a dressmaker's dummy. They need not even have humanoid partners: one dancer, on elbows and tiptoes, jerked her pelvis against a metal support beam.

In the room's rough center was Madame Fortunata: or, at least, a reasonable simulacrum. Her head was encased in a seamless plastic plum. She wore the same outfit of her prior meeting with Jeannine but perhaps it wasn't her, perhaps it was a younger body, a bit more flesh on the bones, nothing spotted or sagging on her hands and neck, which were the only visible sources of skin. She performed a set series of conductorial motions from the waist up, all uncomfortably unnatural: too slow, too jerky, too *wrong*.

In fact quite a bit looked *wrong* to Jeannine. There was no joy in this show. Many performers crudely dance-fucking were sickly figures with exhausted, weathered faces, their costumes encrusted with suspicious white, red-brown, and yellow stains. Some, indeed, had the slackened black lips and shriveled eyelids of cadavers. One humped the jutting ribcage of a skinned animal impaled on a metal spike programmed to jostle chaotically away. Another's large abscess had popped under her unitard from her exertions with a CPR dummy and a steady stream of pus dripped in a puddle on the cement floor as she humped.

Jeannine stepped backward to avoid the spreading pool and accidentally jostled a human dancer: yes, she was certain she felt the cushioning smack of thinly-clothed flesh. Turning around, mumbling an apology, she saw that the dancer's thigh had cracked open, revealing thick red cuts of cold meat packed around a metal piston within a casing of glazed clay. The dancer continued to gyrate, grinning at Jeannine too broadly below unblinking eyes.

There was no audience. There were no other guests. It was only a show for Jeannine. For Jeannine alone.

She fled the warehouse and sought a taxi. Back home, immediately. Back to safety and certainty.

In her apartment that night, she ran a warm bath to soak off the night's madness. The closest she could come to a swim unless she wanted to dive into the water at Coney Island and emerge a pincushion of discarded junkie needles.

Jeannine supposed the water had lulled her to sleep, for she awoke in a tub that had grown four claw feet and a layer of gilt, strewn with pink and red rose petals from a bouquet she hadn't bought.

The man in the white mask was in her apartment. The tall, broad-shouldered man in the white mask, standing in the next room. The bathroom door was shut but she knew, could sense his presence. He had come to her room at night through the nonexistent French doors to the nonexistent balcony. (What was it, really? She dimly recalled a stubborn window onto a rickety fire escape.) She did not fear his entrance: it was, somehow, expected.

Donning the black lace-trimmed silk slip and matching robe she knew she would find hanging from the door, she stepped into the room before him, flatteringly dark but for the light of the city seeping in through the windows. Her modest fold-out bed had sprouted four posters and a sheer canopy. He stood with hands clasped, legs spread apart, in the gap of the open French doors, like a palace guard. He nodded low, tipped his hat, and spread his arms to greet her. To invite her.

The man slipped off his trenchcoat, beneath which he wore nothing but knee-high black riding boots. His hands were the same porcelain gloves, the molded hands gently cupped for caressing, index fingers cocked just so. With these hands he slid the straps down over her shoulders, cool trails on her skin. She felt his breath, unmistakably cold, but could not hear him breathing. Her lips and cheek against his mask, the mask which he did not remove, nor did she so attempt. No seam, no latch, no knot, no zipper. She could picture nothing beyond his strikingly molded, even features.

She lay across black satin sheets, pressed into the mattress by his strong body, impossibly cold and smooth, false skin painted glossy white, tinted blue, violet, red under the neon bleed from the sign outside. Her nails could not rake or dig in. Even his erection was lacking the pliance of flesh. At his first slow thrust she had to wait for and will her body to settle its membranes around him lest she cleave in two, *slice me nicely*. He thrusted with unblinking eyes. He came silently. A rush of copious seed, thick and opaque, like paste.

And she climaxed in a blaze of white.

Jeannine awoke alone on her fold-out bed, still folded in to resemble a couch with assorted throw pillows. Her mind's eye could only view the fragmented memory of the man's visit through the vaseline-smear of a soap opera, so dreamlike it could scarcely have happened. But her body remembered: the little aftershocks, the pleasant ache. The spilt batter staining the fabric.

So dreamlike she hadn't thought to ask for a condom. She hadn't thought to speak at all.

* * *

At the office, a loaded staleness in the air, much heavier than usual. A brown and beige suburban creep within the city walls.

She stared at the constant wink of the green cursor on the computer monitor. Pixel tally marks like centipede legs. Accounts Payable Ronnie, self-appointed office jester, knocked on the cubicle wall, cracking the same tired joke: *You know what the calendar says? Big Brother is Watching*. He'd been doing it since New Year's and it wasn't funny then either. The screeching motions of the copy machine, the dot-matrix printer, an awful ballet of electronics.

At the Amour Fou, none of the bartenders, staff, or regulars knew a thing about the performance of SENTINELLE, the doll girl in the mask, or the presence of a secret theatre. Nor could she find the theatre door, even with the house lights up: no discreet frame flush with the wall like a servants' entrance. She'd expected nothing else. The city's magic had been siphoned from the night.

But worst of all was the disturbingly rapid swell of Jeannine's abdomen, far, far faster than the result of a normal accident. It could not be strapped down with normal shapewear or dismissed as a temporary souvenir of junk food and hormones. Certainly not when the growing curve felt as stiff as set plaster under the outer cushion of skin. When she could knock on her stomach and hear a hollow echo. A sloshing inside. Like a half-empty jar of preserves.

No, *no*. The clinic must look after all this. Absolutely not. No babies, no motherhood for Jeannine, and certainly not alone. She had been with more than one man in the previous month, yet she knew, *she knew* who was the cause of this trouble.

Thus an appointment was quietly booked over the phone for one chilly afternoon.

And thus, while heading briskly down the sidewalk to that appointment, a gloved hand darted from the alley and pressed a chemical-drenched rag over her mouth.

* * *

"—his face?"

Deep-set eyes glowered above in a ghost-pale face with closed lips.

"Did you see his face?" she hissed at Jeannine, the bound and paralyzed patient, caught in the sickly beam of a yellow spotlight.

But Jeannine could not answer: this the older woman knew.

Madame Fortunata raised her hand, fingers fanning upward, and Jeannine's stomach split open bloodlessly, as if on piano wire. The masks and harlequins looked on in the dark, whispering amongst themselves, little students in a surgical theatre.

She could only stare as the choreographer plunged her long fingers into Jeannine's abdomen. Jeannine's body, full of thick white fluid coating her innards, already congealing in the open air.

After much careful rooting around, Fortunata emerged, dripping, with the litter. Blank-faced and sexless white doll-bodies slowly squirming in her bony hands. Bobbing, silent mouths, as they had neither stomachs nor vocal cords. Soon enough they would don jesters' caps and diamond jumpsuits and join their cousins on the walls.

But Fortunata was not finished.

She reached down, behind Jeannine's ears, and removed her face.

She held it up for the patient to view, of course: she was not a *monster*. The face, Jeannine's face, took the form of a blue plastic Tragedy mask. As the stale air nestled on Jeannine's exposed muscles and teeth, she thought she saw the empty patch of wall where the face would reside.

Then Madame Fortunata slipped her spider-fingers to the back of her skull to untie her own face—and most cruelly of all, Jeannine was allowed to remember.

# III

# The Liminal Gallery

# The Medium and The Message

A Thesis Submitted in Partial Fulfillment of the Requirements
for the Degree of Master of Fine Arts
H. Lee Upton, MFA Candidate

The problem of the Red Canvas began in the 1960s with a half-dozen unwitting Boston transit workers. During excavations for a subway expansion project in the city's North End, an MBTA construction team drilling into a weathered brick wall unearthed a hollow passage not shown on the official map of the subterranean infrastructure. Venturing inside, they found a stone floor covered with fine bone fragments—described by the foreman on duty as sounding like "a carpet of seashells" when crushed under the soles of his work boots—alongside a few mummified rat carcasses and a rolled-up length of stiff material sagging against the far wall. Encrusted with four decades of black mold and rodent droppings, the bolt of fabric was about to be discarded with the rest of the detritus until one of the crew members, a former art student who had been forced to leave his studies during the Korean War, recognized the item as a painter's canvas.

The canvas was hauled out to the nearest subway platform and unfurled by the team with care and trepidation. Measuring 18' by 24', it was wide enough to droop over the platform's edges. Slowly, an image was revealed: a great field of intermingled reds in a mottled assemblage of scarlet, rust, and crimson. As the canvas was splayed open before them, its curious composition revealed to the open air for the first time in decades, some workers spoke of an overwhelming rancid odor or an unshakable ringing in their ears. One of the men reportedly had to lean over and vomit onto the tracks (*Boston Herald*, 1965).

On closer inspection, the canvas was shown to have the distinctive looping signature of artist Richard Pickman in its lower right-hand corner. Returned to Pickman's surviving family, the painting was deemed *Untitled (Red Canvas)* [*fig. 1*]. It remained in storage for the next twenty years.

Renewed critical appraisal of Pickman's work in the late 1980s led to an extensive restoration project including *Untitled (Red Canvas)*, which made its debut at a retrospective of local artists at the Miskatonic University Museum in 1994. It encompassed an entire wall of the museum and was taken down after less than a month, as the painting's exhibition was plagued with mystery and scandal throughout. Many patrons complained of dizziness, nausea, and general unease in the painting's presence, such that the curator posted a vaguely-worded warning notice at the exhibit's entrance by the end of the first week. Adjustments to the gallery's lighting scheme seemed to make no difference.

Further bizarre—and tragic—events followed. A heavily pregnant woman complained of strange, pungent smells emitting from *Red Canvas* and was shortly thereafter rushed to the ER, where she went into premature labor. The body of her stillborn child was marked with extensive disfigurement that had somehow failed to register on the ultrasound. Days later, 52-year-old public relations director Gwendolyn Knapp—a library volunteer, philanthropist, and grandmother known for her kind nature and even temper—was restrained by security after abruptly flying into a rage, attempting to slash at the canvas with a Swiss Army knife taken from her purse, shrieking in apparent gibberish. (At the time of this writing, she remains institutionalized.)

The final straw came with an incident during a high school field trip. A 16-year-old boy (name withheld at his family's request) joked with his girlfriend that he was going to find the "hidden picture" in the painting, this being at the height of the "Magic Eye" craze. After goofing around for a bit, covering one eye and squinting in exaggerated fashion, he slowly lapsed into a passive, meditative state, sitting on a cushioned bench and staring at *Red Canvas* for hours. He missed the bus back to school and was still sitting there after repeated announcements of the museum's closing. A guard on duty attempted to rouse the boy, who did not stir until he was roughly shaken by the shoulder. He then fixed the guard with a glazed, haunted stare, stood up—and here the guard noted that the boy had been so engrossed in the painting that he had neglected control of his bladder—calmly removed his varsity jacket, walked to the nearest window, and jumped out before the guard knew what was happening. Drug abuse was suspected: a toxicology report during the autopsy proved the boy's system was clean (*Arkham Advertiser*, 1994). The painting was quietly removed and placed into storage, where it remained until my research began.

What was Pickman's intention with *Untitled (Red Canvas)*? Was it an unfinished beginning to a new piece on a grand scale: the skyline of an apocalyptic hellscape, as Gladys Frink contends? Bartoloměj Čepek speculates that Pickman may have been overtaken by illness before he could complete the painting—but if it were still a work in progress, why had he bothered to sign it? Latter-day scanning techniques have already disproven the early hypothesis that Pickman had painted over an earlier image. Others—most infamously, Clarence Mulvihill—posit *Red Canvas* as Pickman's attempt to embark on a looser, more abstract phase of painting. And despite her many absurd flights of fancy, Dr. Margaret McMichaels correctly notes that, from a certain generous distance, *Red Canvas* resembles an enlarged cross-section of human musculature; however, the question remains as to how Pickman could have achieved such a vantage point within the cramped confines of his North End studio.

I will attempt to address these issues, but first it behooves us to examine Pickman himself. (A more detailed analysis of his life and work may be found in my undergraduate thesis, *Pickman and the Lost Grotesques: A World in Decline*.)

Born in Salem, Massachusetts at the tail end of the Victorian era, Richard Upton Pickman was a loquacious, eloquent, and highly intelligent man; charming, if prone to a snide brand of humor that many found off-putting; increasingly mistrustful to the point of paranoia in his later years, yet willing to unleash lengthy monologues on a wide range of topics once one had earned his trust. Growing up, he showed an early aptitude for the arts coupled with a deep streak of contrarianism, becoming an infamous provocateur in young adulthood.

This attitude is reflected in a casual photograph of Pickman taken in his final year at RISD circa 1908 [*fig. 2*]. He reclines in a wing-backed velvet armchair, perched on one elbow with paint-stained lapels, tie askew, and hair disheveled in a low cowlick redolent of Rimbaud. A tobacco pipe is pretentiously anchored at the corner of his mouth. The leg of an articulated skeleton, doubtless borrowed (or stolen) from one of his figure drawing classes, has been draped over Pickman's thigh: he rests one hand casually across the bones as though caressing the limb of a lover. He stares at the camera with the insouciant smirk of an *enfant terrible*; however, for all his world-weary Byronic trappings, he still carries the mark of youth, health, and vigor.

Not so in a portrait from the early 1920s [*fig. 3*], at the height of Pickman's so-called "Ghoul Period." Now in his thirties, the artist's rakish good looks have become tainted by a distinctly harried, wild, and vaguely disturbing glint in his eyes above deep stress hollows. Always a man of slight build, he now appears gaunt and feverish, withering inside his nondescript grey suit: his contemporaries whispered of tuberculosis, anemia, malnutrition. His hair, despite its era-appropriate sheen of pomade, is still slightly unkempt and has gone prematurely grey at the temples, while his left cheek is marked by the gleaming line of a long-healed scar (despite the fact that Pickman, firebrand nature notwithstanding, was never known for violent altercations). The composition itself is very spare and stark, lit so that a crescent-shaped shadow looms on the blank wall behind the subject, crowning his head like a dark halo. (It is worth noting that this photo was taken for an article in the *Herald* discussing the controversy surrounding his recent work and subsequent blackballing from the Boston Art Club.)

What happened to affect such a radical change—and was it truly so radical after all? From early Symbolist and Decadent-inspired paintings leading young Pickman to be hailed as the heir to Bosch and Goya, the artist turned to increasingly bizarre and disturbing imagery which so shocked the cosmopolitan art establishment of his day that he became an absolute social pariah, retreating entirely from public life and believed by many to have committed suicide by age 40.

One of the many paintings that caused such a stir was *In the Nursery*, from 1922 [*fig. 4*]. Using costumes and furnishings of the late 17th century (perhaps to make its subject matter slightly more palatable), *In the Nursery* is reminiscent of Hogarth minus the aspect of moralizing caricature. Note the use of chiaroscuro to create a heightened sense of dramatic tension and the *trompe l'oeil* effect invoked by the pristine glistening of blood on the demon's bared fangs. An enlargement of the creature's foremost eye [*fig. 5*] highlights Pickman's skill with minute, intricate detail: the candlelit gleam in the figure's dilated pupil reveals, tucked away out of the frame, a modest pile of severed heads with toothless infant mouths frozen in screams of abject terror. And all of this on a patch of canvas the size of a dime!

Outside of his subject matter, Pickman was known as something of a strange person. From art school onward, anecdotes abound of his eccentricities: a lupine skull mounted over his bed, periodic detours to urinate on Cotton Mather's grave, clumsy occult rituals in his dormitory at night. In fact, Pickman was known to have joined, and been summarily ejected from, a number of fraternal orders and occult societies of his day, including the Golden Dawn, the Oddfellows, the Fellowship of the Rosy Cross, the Esoteric Order of Dagon, and the Ordo Templi Orientis. This was clearly a man who felt out-of-step with his milieu and who repeatedly tried, and failed, to find a place where he belonged. (We can, however, safely debunk the preposterous assertion of Dr. Margaret McMichaels that Pickman—with his old-money background, classical education, and patronage by some of the oldest and wealthiest families in New England—was an "outsider artist"!)

On that note, I must now dispense with some of the popular critical theories surrounding Pickman's late-period works, as recounted extensively in my undergraduate thesis, *Pickman and the Lost Grotesques: A World in Decline* (soon to be published by Whateley Press).

Clarence Mulvihill, tiresome as always, posits Pickman's subjects as one-note Marxist allegory in his *Contra Mather: Richard Pickman and the Dialectics of Identity* (1992); specifically, that the "ghouls" represent the corrupt Establishment literally feeding on the poor and working classes. What Mulvihill fails to recognize is the fact that Pickman was always something of a snob about his wealthy family's roots in colonial New England; and despite his many prolonged stretches of poverty, Pickman never considered himself part of a socioeconomic underclass or engaged much in politics at all.

Meanwhile, Gladys Frink asserts that Pickman's forthright gore and violence were in reference to the firsthand-witnessed horrors of World War I, devoting an entire essay to this premise without bothering to confirm whether Pickman served (he did not) ("Ogres Roam in Flanders Fields," *Artforum*, 1987). It must be said, however, that a number of his later patrons were war veterans who could perhaps see, in the Goyaesque atrocities on display, a mirror of their own experiences: after all, this was at a time when "shellshock" was seen as cowardice and seeking psychiatric help was only for the weak and lost causes.

Somewhat more reasonably, Bartoloměj Čepek, in his *The Fiend in the Flesh* (2009), views the monstrous creatures as personifications of disease preying upon the young and innocent: man-eating demons as metaphoric of, say, the flu epidemic of 1918, which claimed Pickman's eldest niece, or venereal disease, as the artist once admitted to "a passing acquaintance with the Clap" (Letter to Bosworth, 1909). If Pickman did suffer from a chronic illness, though, it was certainly nothing that affected his fine motor skills or perception: we don't see the swirling brushstrokes of Van Gogh or the illuminated psychedelia of Louis Wain.

Finally, to address a particularly irksome skeleton in the closet, Dr. Margaret McMichaels further degrades her professional reputation in *All Creatures Great and Small: A History of Animistic Spirituality in New England* (2003) by suggesting that Pickman's unearthly "ghouls" were *drawn from life!* Which only begs the question of why we don't see her madcap critiques shelved next to cryptozoological New Age conspiracy theories on "lizard people" and "ancient aliens"—but I digress.

There is, however, an argument to be made in favor of Pickman's later work as a form of pitch-black social satire, particularly in his paintings set in the present day: the demons-as-pork-barrel-capitalists theory may hold little weight, but a far more compelling interpretation arises upon understanding that Pickman views those same demons as *sympathetic entities* alienated from a world that has pushed them to the margins. (Pickman's attempts to grapple with and skewer the religious and moral hypocrisies of his time form much of my undergraduate thesis, *Pickman and the Lost Grotesques: A World in Decline*, soon to appear in hardcover.)

It is worth mentioning that Pickman's pride in his ancestry was undoubtedly countered by a sense of alienation from his immediate family: his parents were, at best, tolerant, hoping their son's talent would lead to a successful career in portraiture, only to face disappointment and outrage time and again—though I would caution against imposing a simplistic Freudian reading of "getting even with Daddy" on Pickman's motives.

(A necessary disclosure already well-known to the admissions board: Richard Pickman's younger brother, Edwin, was my great-grandfather, who took on his mother's maiden name in the wake of continuing scandal. I first encountered my great-uncle's work at the age of eight, when I stumbled across a privately-printed edition of his drawings and watercolor sketches in my parents' study. Delving far enough into the book made me break into a cold sweat until I reached a certain image that forced me to clap the volume shut in terror. I would daydream about stealing the book away and throwing it into a murky puddle by some distant roadside to permanently cleanse the images from my brain. At night I lay awake in bed, worrying that perhaps other, more fearsome sketches had been secreted away in the walls, separated from my body by mere inches of plaster and wood, waiting to come out and torment me: perhaps not an unreasonable fear, given the discovery of the Red Canvas.)

On that note, we can safely ignore Clarence Mulvihill when he asserts that *Untitled (Red Canvas)* is "a vast proto-Rothko Field" (*Contra Mather*, 1992). Pickman was most emphatically *not* an Abstract Expressionist in spirit or method: he was a staunch classicist and, if anything, a precursor to Photorealism, known to paint using a jeweler's loupe and brushes of a single hair for the finest details. This quality also appears in close inspection of the brushwork in *Untitled (Red Canvas)*: these are not the mad slashes of a de Kooning. Furthermore, his contemporaries often remarked on his disdain for much modern art, holding particular loathing for Impressionistic and Neoprimitivist techniques. Regarding the Fauves, for instance, Pickman writes: "Why, if they want to fancy themselves 'wild beasts,' they should broker no objection to being shot, stuffed, and mounted" (Letter to Minot, 1910). And I should not even bother to dredge up any more of Mulvihill's solipsistic meanderings, but, once and for all, *Red Canvas* was *not* some oblique reference to the Soviet Red Banner.

Troubled reputation aside, *Untitled (Red Canvas)* is a deeply complex and moving work in its own right. It is welcoming, enveloping, engulfing: a lurid red womb hosting a teeming panoply of shades that play before the eyes in an array of concealed forms—a network of veins, a World Tree, bacterial cells dividing—when used as a locus of meditation. I have personally sat before it for hours and come away with a mind sharpened like the blade of a kitchen knife. I recommend this activity to all persons of sound mind.

Why the abrupt shift from intricate realism to (apparently) pure abstraction? Though Mulvihill shockingly approaches something close to a reasonable opinion by guessing that, towards the end of his life, Pickman was so disgusted by the state of the world that he couldn't be bothered to paint figures anymore, further clues may lie in veiled descriptions of Pickman's paintings by his contemporaries. The continual references to "things Man ought not to see" (Reid to Eliot, 1923) and "figures locked in unspeakable obscenity" (Minot to Thurber, 1924) lead me to believe that many of his lost works, e.g. *Preparations for Walpurgisnacht* and *The Bacchae*, were erotic in nature and thus discomforting to the lingering puritanical sensibilities of his peers.

Pickman, a lifelong bachelor, was known to melodramatically pronounce that his "heart [was] buried at Copp's Hill" (Letter to Thurber, 1919). Nonetheless, he embarked on a number of short-lived affairs and became infamous for his many lovers, whom he tended to alienate with his morbid proclivities: one partner reportedly cut off contact with Pickman after he suggested they make love on the unmarked grave where his distantly-great grandmother was buried after her execution for alleged witchcraft (Chilton, diary entry, 1914). Nor was his interest restricted to women: he became persona non grata in Kingsport, where he had been living on the largesse of extended family, after cuckolding both halves of a married couple, who had been serving as his patrons, with each other. This escapade led not to a happy, if unconventional, family of three, but to divorce court in which Pickman was named as co-respondent (*Kingsport Sentinel*, 1918). Clearly, in Pickman's day, he was as notorious for his sexual peccadilloes as for the content of his work, though his amorous pursuits had tapered off by the 1920s as he pursued his Ghoul Period in earnest.

For a time, this led Pickman to become a sort of artistic gigolo after his family cut off his funding in a failed effort to make a respectable gentleman of him: one wonders whether he truly rented his dilapidated Boston studio for its atmosphere, as he often claimed, or because he couldn't afford anything better. Ironically enough, we actually have

Pickman's creditors to thank for the rediscovery of many paintings and sketches long considered lost: after his disappearance between late 1926 and early 1927, Pinkerton agents were hired to track down Pickman and locate his available assets in order to clear the impoverished artist's many outstanding debts. Though the whereabouts of Pickman himself were never located, this action led to the discovery of his pseudonymously-rented studio and the confiscation of many unfinished and previously unknown works. These include Pickman's film reels.

Legal wrangling has kept their existence secret for decades. This series of short films, believed to have been shot and directed by Pickman, was discovered on a shelf in Pickman's private darkroom, which was in turn hidden behind a false wall adjacent to the cellar. (The darkroom itself was destroyed by fire due to apparent negligence before most of its contents could be removed and catalogued.) Pickman only made a dozen or so: this was a recent venture, and he was likely hindered by the prohibitive cost of film and equipment. The reels were printed on nitrate film stock and most have unfortunately turned to dust: the remaining scraps of isolated frames show an unprecedented skill with makeup and special effects prefiguring William Mortensen and Joel-Peter Witkin.

Only one reel emerged fully intact. The canister, labeled in Pickman's cautious script, identifies it as *Totentanz*. Its contents are as follows: in an empty, blank-walled room, most likely the cellar of Pickman's studio, a man and woman bow and curtsy to each other, respectively [*fig. 6*]. The pair is outfitted in formal dress: he in a white tie and tailcoat, she in a white gown and dangling string of beads. They begin to waltz to an unseen recording, gradually drawing closer to the camera. When they both turn to glance directly into the lens [*fig. 7*], the film abruptly stops. The entire sequence lasts about three minutes.

The film's content is largely conventional—even curiously so, to those familiar with Pickman's oeuvre—but on closer examination, one notices odd details. Both partners look haunted and tense: possibly even drugged, owing to the glossy look in their eyes. The man is

Pickman himself, looking exceptionally debonair despite his sickly state. The woman has been identified as Helen Martense, Pickman's last known and most long-standing mistress.

A minor actress, poet, artists' model, and "adventuress" from New York City, Helen moved in with Pickman towards the end of 1925. Differing accounts proliferate as to how they met: supposedly he found her "mad, raving, covered in blood at the roadside by the dark, dark woods" (Letter to Thurber, 1926), or else "reposing in a mausoleum [he'd] broken into in search of an AUTHENTIC Hand of Glory" (Letter to Oliver, 1926), though this is likely more of Pickman's often-tiresome penchant for self-mythologizing.

Little is known of Helen Martense's origins or overall biography, though she was estimated to be in her early thirties at the time of her involvement with Pickman and was reportedly something of an aloof, brooding character. We have no record of her ever marrying or bearing children, nor did she have any confirmed siblings. It is generally assumed that she grew up in a small, rural town, as she sometimes lapsed into a regional accent that seemed to embarrass her—though the most likely surviving Martense families I've managed to track down in upstate New York, northeastern Massachusetts, and southern Missouri deny any knowledge of such a person. Vague rumors of Helen's involvement in a certain violent countryside incident also remain unsubstantiated.

A publicity photo from the 1910s of a woman believed to be Helen [*fig. 8*] indicates a measure of her appeal. Soft-lit, with lips slightly parted and eyebrows plucked thin in a standard fashionable pose, she stares upwards with large, striking eyes: her most magnetic feature. Her long black hair has been loosened over shoulders left daringly bare. One hand is raised at the level of her collarbone, delicately clutching a metal pendant or key hanging from a cord around her neck.

Curiously enough, the lovely Helen never appears in any of Pickman's paintings. The closest we find is a charcoal sketch, set within a colonial-era burying ground (most likely King's Chapel or Copp's

Hill), of a nude woman closely resembling Ms. Martense coupling with a skeletal figure who seems to share Pickman's distinctive features [*fig. 9*]. Elsewhere, one of Pickman's few surviving photographs depicts Helen wielding the artist's revolver [*fig. 10*]. The photo was taken at night, possibly outdoors, and is somewhat overexposed. Its garish lighting stems from the bottom right corner, as if from the beam of a dropped flashlight; Helen's form is slightly blurred, as though the camera had been bumped or knocked. She stares outside the frame with eyes widened in a cartoonish approximation of shock and lips set in grim determination. Perhaps this serves as a figure study for a painting that never materialized.

The only known photo of Richard Pickman and Helen Martense together [*fig. 11*, which also appears as the frontispiece to my undergraduate thesis, *Pickman and the Lost Grotesques: A World in Decline*] may indicate a certain *folie à deux*. Seated together before a blank wall, these thin figures in stark black and white grasp hands tightly—their knuckles appear strained even in the absence of color—as Pickman's free hand depresses the button of a self-timer. It seems less a gesture of affection than the conclusion of a secret pact. Their faces, with matching sharp cheekbones and dark under-eye circles, are marked with tension and private strife: one suspects they would make a handsome couple if not for this. The photo also appears to have been doctored by Pickman in the darkroom to make the two of them resemble each other more closely. Perhaps he intended to emphasize the symbiotic nature of their partnership.

Thus I contend that the shift in Pickman's style and subject matter was influenced by his relationship with Martense: potentially inspired by her limited experience as an extra in the silent film industry, the couple embarked on a filmmaking collaboration before their mutual disappearance.

This conclusion is supported by the last known account of their relationship as described in the diary of Lieut. Stewart Clarkton

Oliver, recently discovered among Danvers Asylum papers purchased at auction by the Channard Trust. It is worth quoting at some length.

> Nov. 13, 1926 – Rare sighting of RP and the missus (!!) in broad daylight! – Well in the shadow of an awning at least. The lady startled and took his arm when I stepped over – Oho, do I look such a fright?
>
> He was holding a butcher's parcel – I should hope it puts meat on his bones. Great Caesar's ghost! He looks as unwell as they say! – Reid suggests ergotism. Egotism more like. – But I shouldn't kid. Was invited to dine with them to-morrow.
>
> So I have finally met his Miss Martin [*sic*] – It reminds me – I wonder if he thinks on our assignation at Martin's Beach, the night before I was off to France. Now how to explain to the Master Sergeant how I got sand in my union suit! The old roué. I still think on those days with some fondness I admit. – Richard, y'auld devil: what became of ye?
>
> Nov. 14, 1926 – Just returned from lunch at RP's rooms – An odd experience I must say. To begin with the Victrola was on when I arrived – A waltz of some sort – I do not know if the settings were wrong, or the device was broken, or the record warped, yet the sound came out very slow and distorted – And each time the song ended Miss M leaned over and reset the needle and cranked the handle again. Perhaps we could put on a jauntier tune, I suggested after some time of this. We are practicing, she said – As if that settled things! – But I did not press the matter, as my hostess was starting to be cross with me.
>
> At table they sat together – Chairs pushed together across from my seat – Eating beef stew from the same

bowl – With the same spoon! Methinks their love nest is a bit too modern for my liking. I found I could not eat much of the stew – Did not care for the taste, too salty and gamy – Too much spice. He didn't choose Mam'zelle M for her cooking skills I should reckon.

After the meal RP and I caught up on our lives, tho' I did not bring up his recent troubles. Some strange talk ensued – In speaking of paintings. He mentioned trying to find a cheaper substitute for true mummy brown pigment which is too expensive these days – Why is that so? I asked – It is made of imported ground mummies, he said! – O, it is not so odd, he said – For in Persia and the Arabian lands they are said to use mellified man – In which a fellow eats nothing but honey until he dies, and is preserved in honey within a stone coffin, and after a century is disinterred and cut apart and consumed as medicine. I thought of cracking wise about sampling the taste of Persian boys but there was a lady present – His lady! – And I thought better of it.

I wonder, she said – If one has a taste of mellified man – Can one taste a fragment of his suffering imbued within? And, pointing to the gramophone record: Do you think any object can hold vibrations of events that took place before it? – Can our voices echo down the well of time? – Well I did not know Poor Richard was partial to bluestockings – And I was not in a mood for philosophizing – So I excused myself to the lavatory.

They whispered for a long while, and I was starting to feel put-out, until – Would you like to watch a film this coming Friday? he said. – In the picture house? Sure old boy, what's playing? – O no, that is not what he meant. He has a film projector in his studio! And he looked at me intently but not in the old way. I said yes – I don't know why.

Nov. 19, 1926 – I have been to RP's studio to-night (??) – I will try to note it down, as I want it to stop – I did not much look out the window of our cab, for it was raining and dark – Many jolts under the wheels. What sort of picture is it? I asked – He only smiled at me. I wondered was this a stag film he reckoned to show me? – Does his wife [*sic*] ever go there? To the studio? I asked – He chuckled. A dark sound. – She can hold her own, he said – Whatever that means.

Now sure I had a tipple at a speak[easy] beforehand – It doesn't explain – Down below – A floor covered with cinnabar? – Chum clots?? – But where is the picture? – Just look, he said – I heard the projector – I could not tell what it was at first – And then I felt ill – I am going to be sick Richard – O give me a basin – A rumbling sound – The ground rippled – And I fell inside it –

Lieut. Oliver made no further entries. He was institutionalized after a nervous breakdown on Nov. 20, 1926.

Returning to *Untitled (Red Canvas)*: I believe it is not unfinished, nor is it a new phase of abstraction in its own right. It is a projection screen.

I confirmed this by chance during my own research. I had already digitized the film for convenience and posterity but had borrowed an antique projector from the school film lab because I wanted to watch *Totentanz* in its original intended format. Meanwhile, to aid my studies, my grandmother had ordered the removal of *Untitled (Red Canvas)* from storage and was hosting the painting in her rarely-used formal dining room, where I had set up camp to avoid bothering her: its great field of red formed the only suitable portion of open space on the trite fleur-de-lis wallpaper selected by one of my dead relatives.

My first home screening of *Totentanz* was as described above, as I had also seen it in the university's media library and on my computer screen. But when I stopped the projector a second time, I noticed that Helen's line of sight was no longer directed into the lens, but off to the side, closer to where I was standing [*fig. 12*]. The difference is subtle, yet very clear when compared alongside the original final frame [*fig. 7*].

Further discrepancies emerged during subsequent screenings. The next time, it ended as the pair filled the entire frame and stared into the camera for an uncomfortable length of time. The film wasn't stuck: I could see them breathing. And this was indeed the last frame. Back in [*fig. 7*], we see a crescent-shaped scratch on the film near the waistline of Helen's gown, likely made by the developer's fingernail. Yet here it is again, identical [*fig. 13*].

And again. Pickman lowers his head and begins to mouth words [*fig. 14*].

And again. Helen's fingers lengthen into tapered talons [*fig. 15*].

Here I stopped taking screenshots. I felt it was disrespectful.

Around this time, I also switched to a digital projection so I wouldn't have to keep rewinding the delicate nitrate reel. If anything, this only enhanced the effects.

As the hours passed, a humid heat swelled up in the dining room, which is ordinarily quite cold and drafty. A low-pitched, antiquated piece of music unfamiliar to me began emitting from, as best I could guess, within the wall behind the canvas. The painting's surface reshuffled itself according to the figures' movements, forming its own visual lexicon, burbling and shivering and convulsing like the congealed skin of a cauldron set to boil. A mist of ruddy effluvia slid out of the canvas and solidified, shambling along like a detached tongue before disappearing into the hallway.

Martense and Pickman danced. Never the same ending twice. A slit was made on the back of one hand—hers? his? I can't seem to recall—through which a vein was removed, gently unmoored from the flesh between the other party's fingertips, as the skin sagged back on either side; unwound from the course of the body as a puddle of black blood dripped onto the dining room carpet. I stepped forward to taste it—the black dew of Heaven. The film began again, both bodies intact.

And I realized that the camera did not remain still: that it tracked the pair to and fro as they waltzed across the room. Maybe it always did—and maybe the veil had only now been lifted from my eyes. Regardless, this indicated the presence of a heretofore unknown third party. Who was operating that camera? *Who shot the film?* I kept watching until, at length, a free-standing oval mirror was visible in the background, pressed against a wall near the corner of the cellar—and finally, *I could see*. And it looked at me, and nodded, as Richard lay his cold hand on my shoulder.

And now, with thanks to the A.E. Waite Memorial Scholarship and a generous grant from the Winthrop Foundation, I have made my homage.

(I must apologize in advance for any inevitable stains in the margins of these pages, which will have turned a rusty brown by the time they reach your hands. I won't pretend they are merely the coffee stains of a harried graduate student: the bandages are an imperfect solution, and the gauze soaks completely through every few minutes. You will understand why I've had to work remotely for much of this past semester and appreciate the effort it has taken to type all of this, much less complete the work. The tendons of my hands are frayed now and cannot hold the fingerbones correctly. A jolt of golden pain through my nerves at the jab of each key! But rest assured, it's a small sacrifice.)

For I have found the secret component – what Richard Pickman forgot, or could not stomach, perhaps for Helen's sake. He thought he had done as instructed—but the canvas, the material, was all wrong. Uncle Richard told me so.

I have left the film running in a loop with all doors and windows opened wide. By the time you read this, my thesis project will be complete.

# The Obscurantist

*To Whom It May Concern:*

*I wish to lodge a complaint against the misleading marketing involved in the promotion of your recent exhibit,* The Android in History: from Royal Courts to Circuit Boards.

*Overall, I must admit I enjoyed this exhibit. The chest-thumping, rosary-clutching 16th-century wooden robot monk left me pleasantly unnerved and vaguely fearful of the Inquisition. The stag-riding brass Diana with a wine fountain in each breast offered a thrill of titillation often missing from stodgy "family-friendly" histories. And the realistic contemporary android man repeating quotes from the likes of* 2001 *and* Blade Runner *with his not-quite-right human movements gave me the strongest frisson of the pure uncanny that I believe I have ever experienced.*

*However, the crown jewel of this exhibition was to be a pioneering model automaton from the* ancien régime *in the figure of a young boy. Naturally I was thus expecting a member of the Jaquet-Droz family of Swiss automatons, either the Writer or the Draughtsman, and hopefully even their elder sister the Musician. Imagine my disappointment upon finding instead the* Draughtsman-Writer *made by Maillardet! Not only was this latter clockmaker a mere protégé of Jaquet-Droz, whose automaton family predates his "juvenile artist" by* at least *25 years, but his creation can hardly be considered "pioneering" under those circumstances. More advanced, yes, but not truly a* progenitor: *there is a reason the boy was shunted into a basement in Philadelphia for decades. One might as well advertise the von Kempelen Mechanical Turk and display a Zoltar machine uprooted from Coney Island.*

*I am generously not requesting a refund this time, but merely offering a stern warning about the habitual disappointment such lack of clarity in advertising might impart to the Museum's patrons.*

*Sincerely,*

*Andrei Middlewood*

Andrei studies the draft with one hand balled up under his chin, brow knotted. Should he append a *Mr.* to his signature? Would that come across as authoritative or pretentious?

More importantly, should he send his message through email or through the physical mail, the old-fashioned way? Which method would be the least easily discarded? A letter was the more precious option as it would have to be paid for and handled by a series of postal workers and museum interns before being dropped into the *circular file* (as Andrei's father gratingly called it). But an email, though easily deleted or autofiltered into spam, could also linger indefinitely until stumbled across by an errant search bar keyword.

Andrei sighs and sets his draft aside for now. He pours himself a glass of water, smooths his hair, and straightens his respectable button-down shirt in the mirror before starting another video.

For the past few months, Andrei has been shooting a series of short videos on the pricing, repair, and refurbishing of hyperrealistic 1/6 scale military action figures intended for adult collectors. Ad revenue from these videos has become Andrei's primary source of income since his furlough from the craft and hobby shop, aside from sales of the figures themselves. Today his subject is a WWII Japanese kamikaze pilot the manufacturers had named "Yukio": as Andrei states for the laptop camera, this particular iteration of poor Yukio spent a couple of years in a Salvation Army window as the rising sun slowly leached his vibrance away. Following his introduction, Andrei begins to paint.

Perhaps it was only the gutters of his mind overflowing, but considering he specialized in *action* figures and *toys for adults*, he'd found it very hard to think up a name for his video series that didn't sound like a cam channel. Not that he was morally opposed to such things, but he didn't want to encourage any false expectations.

Frankly, he did consider it once in awhile: playing with himself on camera would certainly be more lucrative than what he was currently doing, his niche-interest videos with their modest following. And he had no lover or partner to take offense, no pets or children to barge into the bedroom and jump on the mattress at inopportune times; his elderly parents back in Cowansville were nowhere near tech-savvy enough to stumble across such a thing, and his quasi-estranged older brother, far more aggressively heterosexual than himself, would certainly not find it by accident. Andrei supposed he was a decent if generic-looking youngish man whose symmetrical features, trim physique, and good grooming could trick patrons into thinking he was outright handsome under the right lighting, and preferably the right camera angle to add length and girth to his average endowment: yet he'd have to join a gym to add definition to his flat torso, which couldn't simply be painted on like one of his molded plastic soldiers, and he would probably have to shave a few years off his advertised age to make himself more profitable. More importantly, he was quite shy in sexual matters—and it would likely entail far more prostate stimulation than he was comfortable with.

Above all, Andrei chafed at the thought of having his actions onscreen dictated by the eyes and whims of strangers.

And so here he sits, in his budget ergonomic office chair in his cramped Brooklyn apartment, gently stroking Yukio's eyebrows with Semi-Gloss Black #002 and touching up the red on his headband with tiny dabs. He'd prefer to work with a soundtrack, but this would disqualify him from ad revenue due to copyright claims: thus he goes about his task to the hypnotic drone of the rotary fan perched on his desk to keep the paint fumes at bay.

Between the repetitive quality of his actions and the soothing lull of the fan, Andrei soon slips into a state of meditation, caught in his own head while his hands work mechanically. Since losing his job at the shop, the hermit uniformity of his days at home has shifted his life into a temporal Moebius strip, sun rising and falling and rising through slats in the blinds like the turning cogwheels and swaying pendulum of a grandfather clock. These days, aside from his recent museum visit, he leaves his apartment only to retrieve packages or buy food and supplies: his only direct encounters with other humans are rote interactions with store clerks and awkward chance meetings with his neighbors. Every day, week, month is roughly the same. And surely his painted figures agree.

Another video complete. Andrei bends Yukio's legs into a sitting position and rests him to dry on a shelf above the desk, between a WWI German soldier of the 15th Medical Battalion ("Egon") and an 18th-century Lithuanian hussar ("Tadeusz"). A certain redheaded woman figure (formerly "Siobhan") stares down at him from a high shelf and he feels himself blush.

He sometimes takes requests for custom commissions—though sparingly, since he'd otherwise be crafting entirely too many Hitlers. Recent examples include a Red Cross nurse with the malproportioned grey-alien sex-doll face of a first-generation Barbie, and a Union soldier with dull green skin, spatters of blood, and bared and broken teeth, obviously zombified.

But the former Siobhan is his alone.

Andrei stretches his fingers after their delicate work and lets out a long sigh.

He rubs his right eye. Last night he fell asleep while wearing his contact lenses and his sensation in that eye is still somewhat gummy and dry, especially when looking at bright screens or concentrating on small details. The world goes halfway blurred after he wets his finger in the half-emptied water glass to slide the lens from the pupil into the sclera for a few seconds, blinking hard. His vision must be clear for the task ahead.

He closes the Venetian blinds in his bedroom and kitchen. He shuts either door entering into the middle of his railroad-style apartment.

He sits in the dark in front of his laptop. He clicks on the folder labeled *A_H_*.

It is time now for his date with Annie.

First video:

Andrei was introduced to *her* one summer night at the age of eight. He was down in the family room after dinner, once again watching whatever was playing on Nick at Nite after the children's programming ended in order to avoid going to bed early or else being pressed into playing Nintendo with his brother in a failed attempt by the boys' parents to make them bond. Eyes glazing through the broad slapstick and long-ago current events jokes for grown-ups, he eventually made it up to a short-lived variety show called *Sonny Esterhazy's Tele-Talent Revue*. He didn't know the term *kinescope* yet, though he recognized from the costuming and picture quality that the show was roughly contemporaneous with *I Love Lucy*.

The *Tele-Talent Revue* took place in a generic nightclub with no proper stage, just a stretch of floor space before the circular diners' tables and a big band crammed into the back. This episode climaxed with Benny Baxter's Broadway Orchestra performing a rendition of Glenn Miller standard "PEnnsylvania 6-5000." (Andrei didn't learn the spelling of the song's title until adulthood and the capital E still annoys him, despite knowing it refers to a defunct telephone code.)

In fact, for years afterward, he thought the song was about a railroad line. This was because the visual highlight of this number was a set of six dancers with legs and upper torsos protruding from a cheap cardboard locomotive. They danced the unwieldy prop onstage in two pairs of three, in pencil skirts and dark knotted scarves and white blouses with peaked shoulder pads, heads and waving hands poking through cutout windows like they were passengers. Andrei had thought they looked like old-timey flight attendants, stewardesses, aside from the woman at the front of the train, who wore a round chin-strapped hat and white gloves like a train porter. They stepped in time with the music from the orchestra they partly blocked from view, knees high and feet kicking in a cross between a budget Busby Berkeley chorus line and a chaste can-can.

The train dancers flanked a trio of smiling men in tweed suits with broad lapels who snapped and nodded in time with the beat until it was time for the chorus, when all three men leaned over a bulky microphone and chanted "*PEnn*-syl-vania *Six! Five! Thou*sand!" in the measured pep of big-band vocals. And every time they sang that eponymous line, a whistle would blow and the cardboard train would halt as the dancing girls froze with wide grins and even wider eyes like mannequins caught moving in the dark.

Somewhere between wondering why nobody got on or off the train at each "station" and wondering why the chanting men weren't dressed in bellhop fashion like the dancer playing the train conductor, he first took notice of *her*.

*She* was at the very end of the train, the final face to emerge from stage left. The one with the brightest and easiest smile, the most light in her step, youthful-looking in that perpetually hazy, indeterminate age that movie stars were, that adults liked to imagine themselves being. This was the first time he was conscious of finding a female human attractive in a more-than-impassive sense: *girls*, his gap-toothed, ponytailed classmates, were *gross*, but this *woman* was pretty. Of course all the dancers were pretty, or else they wouldn't have gotten the job, but he was transfixed by a certain unnameable sense of Something More. And sure, she wasn't exactly the best dancer, but with a cardboard train strapped to one's torso alongside five other people, how could one be? She had spirit and she had joy.

The catalyst of a lifelong obsession was locked into his psyche by the end of the song. After that last "*Penn*-syl-vania *Six*-five *Oh*-Oh-*Oh!*", as the tapping feet of the train proceeded to dance offstage . . . she *winked.* Directly at the camera. As if she knew. The others only waved in the general direction of the camera, of the studio audience.

From a distance of nearly five decades, she broke the fourth wall for prepubescent Andrei, in his family room with wood-paneled walls and shag carpeting there in suburban Massachusetts, in a town that could be anywhere and felt resolutely nowhere.

The winking sickle of the mascaraed eyelid, the Cheshire crescent of her smile, haunted his dreams and fantasies. Her slim ankles and small fingers. Her Cuban heels and victory rolls. Her hair, which he assumed was red. Years later he would wonder if, had the evening's programming been different, the locus of his emerging libido could've been the exoticized harem-girl fantasy of *I Dream of Jeannie* or Mary Tyler Moore in her capri housewife slacks. But this was not to be.

In the months that followed, young Andrei would scrutinize issues of *TV Guide* for any scarce repeat airings of that show and that episode—until, *finally,* he was able to sneak into the family room one night and tape it on VCR, the unlabeled tape secreted away in the bottom of the toy chest he'd already outgrown. Frustratingly, no specific performers with Benny Baxter's Broadway Orchestra were ever named. For years he thought of her only as The Train Lady.

This first video of her was taken from a direct transfer of the VHS tape from his childhood.

The *Tele-Talent Revue,* as he later learned, was shot in 1949. The next clip was from 1945: a recording of a USO show meant to be screened in movie theatres alongside feature films. While chronologically earlier, it had earned its second-place slot because that was the order in which it had found him.

Andrei discovered this video in his freshman year of college, browsing a website devoted to archiving audio-visual ephemera. That afternoon he had been looking up information on "Charlie and His Orchestra," a bizarre Third Reich propaganda campaign in which lyrics from popular swing numbers were re-written to reflect German victories against Churchill and the Bolsheviks, then broadcast westward to demoralize the English-speaking Allies. Searching for tags such as #WWIIJazz and #1940sSwingMusic once again led him to *her*.

And surely it *was* her. He'd watched that VHS recording so many times her image was etched into his brain. This time, to his delight, she was the singer, performing a version of "'Tain't What You Do (It's The Way That You Do It)" injected with a faux-Texan twang. She'd been kitted up in a half-assed cowgirl costume, with a ten-gallon hat and Western boots and a knotted bandanna paired with a generic '40s peak-shouldered blouse and pencil skirt that might as well have been recycled from that number with Benny Baxter's Broadway Orchestra (or vice versa, considering the timeline). She stood on a shallow stage before parted black curtains, hand on cocked hip and knee bouncing in time.

Unobscured by any cumbersome props this time, Andrei had a much better look at her bust jutting out of a conical midcentury brassiere, her wasp-girdled waist, her broad hips slung around with a child's toy six-gun holster. A familiar grin, fixed onto her face. At the end of the song she whipped out both manicured hands in a pair of finger guns firing at the camera, ignoring or forgetting the plastic toy guns dangling from her belt.

Her rendition of that song would get stuck in his head for days: her otherwise-unremarkable singing voice pitched up in a Betty Boop chirp, her obviously phony Texan inflection of "Tuh-*Ain't* whacha do . . ." barely cloaking her Middle American accent before, at the end of each chorus, a mixed-gender trio of crooners piped "And *that's! What!* Gets reee-*sults!*" Andrei found these imperfections endearing.

He was grateful for the pedantic tendencies of this video's uploader, who had typed up a full credit listing. Thus he finally found the name of his dream woman:

*Lead singer: Annie Haney.*

Armed with this knowledge, Andrei dug up her bare-bones entry on IMDb, where she was listed as "Annie Haney (V)" to differentiate her from more famous Ann[e]s Haney. There she was in the 1945 USO reel, and again as "Dancer (Uncredited)" in the *Tele-Talent Revue*. No further listings to show. He assumed she was primarily a stage performer.

Further internet sleuthing cobbled together a scant biography. She was born Anne Chambers Haney on September 3, 1923, in a small Midwestern town called Brookhaven. An only child, she enrolled in Mount Holyoke College—significantly, Andrei thought, in his own home state—but dropped out after a year for reasons unknown. Census records showed her as a twentysomething living alone in the Lower East Side of Manhattan with her career listed as "Singer," then a few years later as "Performer/Cigarette Girl."

And then nothing. Nothing at all.

Had Annie ever married, taken on a different name? Did she have any children, any grandchildren? Did she move back home to her parents, emigrate to another country? And when, if ever, had she died? She could hypothetically still be alive, Andrei knew, though she would naturally be very old by now. A happy thought, though he could never, and would never, want to court her in person, since it seemed to him the real Annie Haney lived on permanently young in celluloid.

He wondered why she chose to go by Annie instead of Anne. There was a pleasantly sing-songy mellifluence to her professional name: answering the phone, perhaps, with a "Mmmyel-*looo,* Annie Haney?" in her peppy voice and red mouth, twining the telephone cord around a supple index finger. No, she was not a matronly Anne Haney, with stern Joan Crawford eyebrows and small hands folded in off-white church gloves, acting in Sirkian melodramas before retiring to marry an oil baron and breed racehorses on his farm. She was Annie, forever Annie.

Despite her grandmotherly age and era, Andrei knew this had never been an Oedipal attraction. Annie bore little, if any, resemblance to his brittle, buttoned-up ex-debutante Middlewood grandmother doling out passive-aggressive barbs in her trans-Atlantic accent, or to his mother's mother, a stocky Soviet refugee with unfettered Old

Country manners. And his own mother—a reed-thin, sighing, fretting woman who favored oversized t-shirts tucked into high-waisted jeans and had cycled through a series of unflattering-yet-practical mouse-brown mom haircuts during Andrei's lifetime—shared none of Annie Haney's vim, verve, and glamour.

His adult sexual interest has run primarily to redheaded women who've adopted a rockabilly style: burlesque dancers, alternative models, rogue taxidermists, aspiring morticians. He even briefly dated such a woman in college, though she broke it off—understandably, he now acknowledged—after mistakenly assuming his timidness in matters of the flesh meant disinterest. Brightly-colored tattoo sleeves, halter dresses with ample cleavage, winged eyeliner like the sharp tailfins of vintage Cadillacs: always gorgeous, but somehow too bold, too imperious, too *present*. They didn't dwell in the unsullied greyscale eternity of Annie Haney. Even the scratches and imperfections of the film grain had become, to Andrei, the pores and scars and goosebumps of a long-time lover's much-explored skin.

In tribute, he even custom-refurbished a female action figure, Siobhan the WWII WAC Master Sergeant, to resemble Annie Haney: her plastic legs carefully painted with stocking back-seams, her stern soldier's lips gently retouched into an enigmatic smile. A private effigy to watch over and inspire him.

And he might be blushing now as he runs the third video.

One afternoon in his mid-twenties, he'd spent some idle time browsing one of Manhattan's few remaining old-school porn shops: the sort with paid video booths in the back behind a metallic foil curtain, an array of crack pipes sold at the counter like candy bars at a bodega, and a few hundred dusty VHS copies of Portuguese-dubbed Popeye cartoons stacked against one wall to bypass Puritanical zoning ordinances. He came away with a single prize: a DVD compilation of vintage porn featuring a grainy screenshot of a woman in a bob haircut administering a cat-o'-nine-tails to a pair of bare buttocks on the home-printed clamshell label.

To his disappointment, the video itself was an obvious VHS transfer with visible tracking lines. The contents were an erotic curiosity, an hour-long haphazard video collage probably assembled by a private porn aficionado. Clips of Bettie Page or Lili St. Cyr posing and shimmying and waggling their eyebrows in faded Technicolor would abruptly smash-cut into anonymous hardcore stag reel footage *in medias res*. The actors, lovely as they may be, were clearly ordinary people, good sports having a smile and a laugh while mashing their bits together for the camera. In some clips the actors wore masks in a token concession to respectability, removing their faces for awhile to leave their bodies as big anonymous dolls playing house.

Annie wore no mask.

Uncredited again, of course, but certainly it was her. Andrei could never forget that face.

Like the other stag loops, it was recorded without sound. It had been spliced into the montage from a heavily-duped VHS tape, which left a blurred, soupy quality around the edges and small details, on top of the somewhat jittery effect from being filmed in an obsolete frame rate. A static shot, framed awkwardly, as if the camera tripod had been shunted into a corner and forgotten. One minute and nine seconds of a standard-issue bedroom fuck, the right half of the frame dominated by a standing man with squarish, rumpled buttocks that made Andrei picture two loaves of bread squeezed together. The man's head was cut off above the neck, his legs cut off at the tops of his old-fashioned sock suspenders, a stocky torso mechanically thrusting.

Annie lay on her back with her head propped up on a pillow. Her visible arm dangled off the bed while her visible breast quavered at each thrust. She wore nothing but sensible heels and back-seamed stockings, though much of her body from waist to thigh was obscured by the man and the camera angle. One of her legs was jackknifed up to her waist while the other was propped up on the man's shoulder by his hairy forearm. At times the watch on the man's wrist gleamed into a bright flat disc below the unseen lightbulb swinging overhead. Andrei wondered if this scene had been shot in a basement.

She looked bored, blank. Staring forward, glassy-eyed, head lolling, gazing at nothing. Sometimes her mouth opened and face pinched for a moment, though Andrei was sure any pleasure she might feel from the encounter had been purely incidental. If she'd ever put on a smile, the bright smile that hooked young Andrei so many years before, it had happened early in the take and been cut for the compilation.

At one point near the end, she looked straight into the camera. Into his eyes.

*Help me.*

*Love me.*

Sometimes Andrei wondered: was his attempt at following her trail, however unconsciously, the reason why he had come to live in this city he could barely afford? And why he clung to that city despite falling into a career path that could be followed in any anonymous set of rooms in the world, so long as he had access to supplies and a camera?

He had copied and preserved only the relevant portion from that long-discarded porn DVD, lest it deteriorate any more into a sea of grey. In recent years he also found the former two video clips on YouTube, albeit in more pixelated form, but Andrei didn't trust streaming services with these vital bits of evidence. The Annie Haney videos had to exist privately on his hard drive, migrating like household spirits through various computers over the years.

The fourth video is there as a backup copy, just in case, but he prefers to enact the ritual of screening it in its proper format. To that end he pulls the tarp off the projector.

Andrei had inquired about Annie Haney on a forum dedicated to obscure vintage media nearly a year ago, to a predictably clueless response. About a month later, though, he was shocked and confused but nonetheless delighted to receive an anonymous package in the mail containing a crisp 8mm film reel, unlabeled. Gently prising open the rusted canister and examining several frames under a magnifying glass led him to decimate his savings to buy a reel-to-reel projector. In Andrei's ears, the rapid rattling and harsh electric buzz have become part of the diegetic soundtrack.

Miss Haney is positioned against a brick wall, a close-up view from head to shoulders. Shot at night, stark lighting from above: perhaps a streetlamp. The film offers a far sharper view of its subject than any previous clips. Stress lines have begun to surface in Annie's face. An asymmetrical series of creases appears in her forehead when she raises her thinly-plucked eyebrows. She wears a shorter hairstyle, dating this to sometime in the '50s.

Out of the frame, a man's low, muffled voice throws cryptic questions at her. Annie's answers are cautious, hesitant.

"Chapel?"

"In the pines . . ."

"Uvula?"

"Back of the throat . . ."

She sniffles. Suppressing tears—or rather, more tears. Mascara settles in bruised shadows over both lids. She does not wipe it away, and perhaps has been instructed not to.

Her soft speaking voice has grown notably huskier than it was during her USO number. A few years have passed between the song, the dance, perhaps even the porn reel, the tar of countless cigarettes gnawing away at the lining of her throat and lungs.

This continues for several minutes. The routine is broken only by minor sounds and gestures from Annie. A small, gloved hand clutches the top of her coat closed. A nervous twinge at the edge of her mouth. It may be snowing. A slow, weary exhale, and a ghost of frost passes through her lips. Eyes dart to the side: a low rumble, perhaps the sound of a car passing.

About 45 seconds from the end. The man's question is inaudible.

"The br—" she stammers.

Immediately the man slaps her, a black-gloved hand darting into frame.

"—Brightly shining." Suppressing tears again. Sad, afraid, yet with an underlying bitterness. She slowly raises a hand to her cheek.

An awkward silence follows, long and tense enough to radiate deep discomfort. A mounting fear that unspools from the reel into Andrei's passive body.

The unseen man mumbles something that Andrei interprets as "A girl does her best."

She looks warily into the camera, flicks her eyes downward, cautiously opens her mouth.

And the film cuts off abruptly. It has answered nothing: only created a larger mystery. As if suspecting a spouse of adultery from vague evidence, only to fantasize obsessively about the goriest possible details to the extent that one can't discern lust from rage.

Around this time, as usual, Andrei has developed a full erection. He doesn't dare pleasure himself under the eyes of Miss Haney, the patch of blank wall space reserved for her projection, or her doll-sized effigy. Still sitting in the dark, he retreats under a throw blanket on his couch that he reserves for this express purpose; and in the warm, smothering air, a bottle of lubricant in hand, Andrei unzips his fly.

—Only to jerk away at the bleating jangle of his door buzzer. One long buzz, then three short ones, then a long one again.

"Shit," he mutters. He balls up the blanket and throws it in a corner before stuffing himself back into his pants.

This could only be Andrei's upstairs neighbor Mr. Gadz, whose name he only knows from the building's mailbox. The man is in his 70s, probably, and lives alone. Andrei sometimes hears him shouting at sports on TV through reverberations in the heating pipe near his couch, or the muffled thud and scrape and exertion-grunting of large boxes being moved across the bare floorboards overhead.

Andrei could deal with this, as normal annoying neighbor habits go, but at some point the old man had decided to try and befriend the building's only fellow bachelor; thus Mr. Gadz seems to think he's making himself useful by bringing up packages left by the mailbox that Andrei is perfectly capable of retrieving himself. To that end he will buzz Andrei's apartment repeatedly and then come up and knock on his door, which he can't really ignore because the old man knows he's at home all the time. "Hel-*looo!*" Mr. Gadz always calls through the closed door, while Andrei is well aware that a mere inch or two of wood separates the old man from Andrei's private habits: making a video, or watching pornography, or, worst of all, on one of his precious forays into Haneyland. Good lord, does he bother anyone *else* like this?

Andrei undoes the chain, switches the deadbolt, and opens the door. Mr. Gadz stands there in a Christmas-tree-green NFL sweatshirt drooping over his skinny frame like a soggy mushroom cap. Decades of wrinkles have etched a pattern of jagged plaid into his sagging cheeks. His nostrils are diagonally slanted and tapered like a shark's. He turns a cardboard box in his gently trembling hands.

"'Castaigne's Crafts & Miniatures,'" he reads from the return address. Sometimes, when doing this, he feels inclined to add some tiresome remark. "You're a hobbyist!" he announces with a smile, as if this were new information.

"Yeah. I am."

"Y'see, I notice things. Heh heh." A sharp, self-satisfied nod. "You should come up and see my collection! Don't I always remind you, Mi-Ma- Maplewood?"

"Middlewood," he corrects, yet again.

"Ah, sorry. Senior moment. Heh heh."

This tendency is all the more grating because Andrei's name is right there on the package.

The mild ache in his testicles from today's unspent semen sets his resolve: Andrei is really quite sick of this and considers that he should, for once, accept the invitation, but act so thoroughly bored and boring that old Mr. Gadz will never ask him up again. A dull young man. No spirit in him. Kids *in my day* actually got excited about things.

"You know what? Sure." Andrei scratches the back of his head. "Sure. I have nothing else to do right now."

His neighbor grins. "Heh heh."

The stairs creak as Andrei follows the old man's cautious steps up to an identical door.

He is instantly annoyed that Mr. Gadz's apartment has better air conditioning than his own.

This is also not the bug-strewn hoarder hovel Andrei was somehow expecting, despite the sickly-stale odor of fly spray and the bone-yellow cast of antique lampshades. Faded sports pennants line the walls alongside a framed set of patent schematics with the explanatory text replaced by Lorem Ipsum filler and a comically-oversized wooden hammer with ATTITUDE ADJUSTER etched on the dangling handle.

"Care for a beer?" says Mr. Gadz.

"Yeah. Sure."

"Sit down. Make yourself at home!"

He sits on the far edge of the couch, the only part that isn't strewn with takeout menus for unfamiliar restaurants: Loup's Loops, Lucky Sanpaku, The Comestitorium. Across from the couch, an old cathode-ray TV set on four stubby wooden legs is flanked by a pair of tall, overstuffed bookshelves. One is full of home-recorded cassette tapes labeled with (Andrei squints) the names of Superbowl games going back years, decades, even preceding VHS and treading into Betamax. The other shelf holds boxes of slide carousels in Kodak-orange and beige. He hopes the old man won't make him sit through a slide show.

Mr. Gadz hands him a bottle of Miller High Life and he immediately takes a swig. The old man chuckles to himself at some private joke in his head.

"And that's what gets results, right? Heh heh."

Andrei freezes. His hand tightens around the glass. Those peppy vocals charge through his head like an ambulance siren: *Tuh*-ain't *whacha do . . .*

Wink. Smile. Finger guns. *Pew-pew.*

No. He couldn't. He couldn't mean that. Couldn't be alluding to that. You can't hear anything from below in this building. Otherwise he'd hear the baby crying in the apartment downstairs, where that young couple lives. And Andrei plays his videos at a reasonable volume. It's not exactly an uncommon phrase. No. No. It must be nothing.

" . . . Yeah." He gulps down more of the cheap beer.

Looming above Andrei on the wall by the couch is a life-sized B&W photo of a stern, square-jawed young man whose face is partly concealed by a 35mm camera with a flashbulb protruding like a tumor. It appears to have been taken in a mirror, the same one hanging on the wall by the door.

"My old man," says Mr. Gadz, easing himself into a wooden chair. "He was a photojournalist. One a' those Weegee types. Worked for the *Daily News* 'n' whatnot, in his heyday. Heh heh." He slaps his own knee for emphasis.

"Y'know, it was my old man's philosophy that everyone, every regular Joe, will be known by just five bits of evidence. Sorta like that thing Andy Warhol said, right, Littlewood? And you don't get to choose what they are. It's, whaddya call it, 'death of the author?' And the author doesn't get to write a will. Heh heh."

"Yeah."

Andrei wishes he had worn a watch so he could repeatedly and conspicuously check the time.

Mr. Gadz unfolds himself and shuffles over to the slides. "My old man had some of his stuff converted to 3D a while ago," he says over his shoulder, fumbling around in a box on a high shelf before pulling out a bright red object: a View-Master. He stuffs a disk inside before handing it to Andrei.

"Remember these?" He grins. "Or are you too young?"

Andrei doesn't bother to answer. He dutifully takes the View-Master, holds it up to the nearest light, and peers through the eyeholes.

Okay, some sort of artsy landscape. A B&W photo in a bright grassy field, where someone has photographed pale mannequin parts.

No.

It's worse the more he clicks through. Bisected at the waist. Ripped garter belt over a sparse triangle of pubic hair. Nails caked with black dirt, arms thrown back in defeat. One leg crossed over the other at the knee, stiffening in rigor. A sloppy pile of amorphous grey organs dropped beside her exposed spine. Right breast crudely slashed above a concave stomach, fatty tissue oozing out like creamed corn.

The woman's head has been cut off. Curls matted with blood. One eyelid drooping shut but the other wide open, pupils gaping black. Lipstick smeared and lips slashed into a half-sneer, half-smile.

With its bright contrast, artful angles, and deliberate-looking positioning, the series is almost a still life of murder, but with—he admits—a sick beauty. *Oh rose, thou art sick*, he recalls, madly. And her mutilated face, perversely, immediately recognizable. Andrei could never forget that face.

Annie. Forever Annie. She stares and she smiles.

He keeps clicking through the images, impossible dozens on the same short reel. He doesn't think about this. He must watch more, see through to the end. He must take it all.

Annie, decaying in pieces. Blooming with rot. Black ants trailing across the wider of her eyes. Lips and inner labia shriveled by the sun. Loose heap of organs bursting with rice—no, not rice. Leg flesh punctured and torn by wild beasts. Wet bones untethered of tendons. Dry bones stripped bare by time and the elements. Loose bones like old ruins sinking into the earth. Disappearing from the world's memory. Until the field is dry soil and tangled grass again, anonymous.

And he realizes: these are crime scene photos, taken by a professional photojournalist. But there were no news articles about Annie Haney's death. No body found. No suspects questioned. No killer arrested. And the sensational quality of the corpse, especially during that era, would have been news. He would have seen these photos before. He would have read those articles. These things would have found him.

He stares at Mr. Gadz, unable to speak.

*Where did you—*

*What is—*

*WHY—*

"Heh heh." The man's thin yellow teeth remind Andrei of a subway rat. "Took you long enough, Morningwood. You think you're the first one to come for Annie Haney?" He grins, a cartoon vampire. "Y'see, I notice things." He plucks the View-Master from Andrei's paralyzed hands.

"She had obsessions of her own, she did. My old man found out. She was fixated on a Victorian French playwright called Nadja Vérité. Or—no, not Victorian in France; what's it called, *fin-duh-seecle*? I was never much good with languages, heh heh." He grunts briefly while returning the View-Master to its box. "Well, she'd go looking up old scripts, photos 'n' things. She'd do a lot for that information." He nods, easing his hunched frame back into the chair.

"Now, it used to be said part of a movie or a photograph takes a little bit of your soul, and I think that's true. It's why people love those crime pictures so much, you know. Still so much life in 'em. It's why famous people, the celebrities, get so nutty so young. Too much soul taken out too soon." He nods to himself again.

"Maybe it's not all bad. You wouldn't have to exist anymore or worry about that stuff, about money, makin' a living, gettin' older and all. You'd just live on in those frames. But *only* in those frames, forever. Always a catch, right? Heh heh." The old man cracks open a beer for himself. "Like my old man said, you only get a handful of scraps of evidence of your life, minus whatever bloodline you got left around. A line in the paper when you die, if you're lucky."

Mr. Gadz turns back to his neighbor, gestures with the bottle toward his overstuffed shelves.

"That's all she is now. All that's left." His gaze is oddly solemn now. "She sees you. She looks back at you. And y'know, every time, she has to live that, over and over and over again."

Andrei is unable to speak or move. His mouth dry, fingers cramping. On the end table in the piss-colored lamplight, his drugged beer grows a slick of condensation.

And he wonders if, over all these years, Annie Haney had stared across time to warn him.

He considers the last dregs of Andrei Middlewood outside the walls of this building: the online videos of himself fixing up soldier dolls. He wouldn't get a cramp in his hand, wouldn't get dehydrated, wouldn't fear making rent—but would have no choice, locked inside his old motions. So long as there remains at least one viewer, somewhere, unknown to him. Copying the evidence.

In an ordinary apartment somewhere in the anonymous city, the former Siobhan's painted eyes peer down at an empty couch, and the glassy eyes of Andrei's shell fill up with cataracts of dust.

# Epidermia

Upon learning that I once traveled, in my youth, to the City of Bricks, it is only natural among my colleagues and acquaintances to query what, in that storied land abroad, caused me the greatest discomfort. The labyrinthine mass transit station in which I burst into tears before local commuters? The crimson mezzanine market after midnight, where my heart was quietly broken? No: though I am loath to speak of it, the truth lies in the Long Man behind glass.

And *the skin.*

I am a lifelong denizen of the City of Shale. At that time, I had recently attained the Economic age of majority and relocated to the Borough of Steel, where I still reside today.

I had traveled to the City of Bricks to seek, ultimately without success, an arts permit, since none are issued any longer in the City of Shale: what modest funding once went to the arts and humanities has been wholly diverted into the Sheriff's vast battalion of landsknechts and the expansion of the Moral Guard. (Mandatory tenure in the latter was, at the time, only under consideration for nascent adults; I had barely aged out when such tenure became law.)

I was working towards a commercial design baccalaureate, the only collegiate visual arts curriculum available to those of us in the City of Shale. In this City, any profession that is neither oriented towards running and expanding the Economy nor maintaining social cohesion has been deemed unworthy by the Shaleite administrative authorities of deserving an accredited degree in higher education. Non-commercial visual art, my preferred course of study, was dismissed as the province of the dilettante and hobbyist, and I did not fancy enrolling in a penal workhouse to recompense the debt of my Juvenile Upbringing Credit. Thus, the arts permit.

I had never before departed the borders of my City. The differences were palpable as soon as I took leave of the aeroplane and proceeded through the customs scanner: a swift and efficient process, contrasting greatly with the protracted Shaleite entry interviews under sodium lights in rooms that reek of nicotine. Members of the local constabulary patrolled the aeronautic terminal in the little waistcoats and comical chapeaux I recognized from Brickian televisual melodramas, quite unlike our own landsknechts with collars so high and stiff they leave prominent chafe-marks below clean-shaven jawlines.

The City of Bricks is far older than the City of Shale, older by centuries, but also cleaner overall, better-tended. It is also rather more, shall I say, *free* in certain regards. The stalls containing toilets within their public unmentionable closets fully enclose one's defecating body, leaving neither face nor feet exposed as ours do; our own feature substantial gaps around the stall doors due to a combination of cut-rate infrastructure and a desire to discourage self-pollution. And *all* of said closets—even in the most respectable establishments conceivable—are furnished with a wall-mounted dispenser of prophylactics and menstrual towelettes, which, in Shale, can be located solely in such vermin-ridden grottos of libertinage as yet insufficiently ransacked by the Moral Guard. On the subject of menstrual towelettes, advertisement filmlets for such items air on Brickian television *during daylight hours*, their contents depicted in a proper red rather than our chaste green chlorophyll drip.

The City of Bricks is known for wax figures—or at least, in my opinion, it ought to be. They are scandalously endemic. One views them in haberdashers' front windows, in museum displays of historicity, filling empty seats in cafés, auditoriums, and public transit vehicles, frozen in space with their vitreous eyeballs, plastic fingernails, and artificial teeth. Meanwhile, the Shaleite establishment eschews any public displays considered potentially frightening, concupiscent, or scatological—or *ambiguous*, as one, especially if below the Moral or Economic age of majority, might conceive *the worst and most corrupting possible interpretations*. Attitudes are somewhat more relaxed in the Borough of Steel, for the consideration of tourists: Brickians, as noted, do not share the common Shaleite compunctions.

In perfect frankness, I could continue recounting such differences *ad infinitum*. Brickian citizens bring *canines* to the public house! It is a rare fortune in the city of Shale if one is permitted to cohabit with a household beast at all. Overnourished pigeons fearlessly bob and peck at one's heels! In the Borough of Steel, the most we see of the avian genus takes the form of their pristine corpses on the pavement, having flown into the mirrored flat surfaces of our institutional towers, pristine as any taxidermic diorama such as those with which executives brighten their windowless cubicles.

My early impression of the City of Bricks was that of an alternate version of our own City, had numerous divergent decisions of cultural and administrative import been codified through the years. If older buildings encrusted in superfluous ornamentation were actively maintained rather than demolished and rebuilt, flat-planed and smooth, to increase investor appeal. If a conscious choice had not been made to deliberately decrease the durability of manufactured goods such that they would require more frequent replacement and thus keep the Economy running. And the many differences, whether subtle or overt, are accentuated by our common tongue.

The language spoken between the respective Cities of Bricks and Shale is functionally identical, yet with differing inflections and colloquialisms. In particular, Brickian linguistic phrasery is often more direct and breezier, to the point of being rather blunt, with a certain quaintness as well: the first occasion I seated myself within one of the City's elevated locomotives, an audio speaker broadcast a chipper female voice announcing *This is a train to: FUCKPUTTERS.* The City still contains a Gropecunt Lane, located in quite a fashionable district.

Radiators are HOTBINS. Elevational chambers are UPS. When concluding one's business within a public building, signage which would read, in my City, *To The Nearest Departure Aperture* has been replaced by an arrow above the word GO.

I will recount an exemplary incident. Early in my stay, I wished to view the home of a sequential murderist who had operated in the City two decades prior, for in this locale he had strangled and garroted his many doomed innamorati. I requested directions of a local elderly pensioner. He was unfamiliar with the term *sequential murderist*, and we were thus at an impasse. A crease of consternation dented his ample forehead until rising again with a moment of epiphany: "Ahhh, y'mean a *deadsman!*"

Whenever possible, I kept my lips closed. The common local perception of those of us from the City of Shale was as a horde of crass, unruly buffoons, owing perhaps to several well-televised instances of landsknecht hooliganism. Those of us from the Borough of Steel were considered louder and more impolite than our brethren, yet more cosmopolitan and sartorially adept. I am, fortunately, a bit of a mynah bird, inadvertently collecting the cadences of my surroundings; thus I fancied one would be unable to discern my Shaleite accent unless I uttered more than half a dozen words at once.

To walk down any commercial street within the City of Bricks is to be assailed with brusque pronouncements on placards. INK DRAINED. BITS BOBBED. MEAT CUT HERE. Our plasters are kept beneath the counter in shame, while they boldly announce: SKIN FIXED.

*Skin . . .*

But I digress.

* * *

That cursedly memorable night of my life occurred towards the end of the week-long residence allotted by my visa.

I had donned seasonally-appropriate evening attire in preparation for a temporary departure from my lodging hotel. Upon locking my hotel door, I proceeded down the corridor, so narrow that only two adult persons might walk comfortably in tandem, with my destination the nearest elevational chamber—apologies to Brickians, the "up."

A woman strode past me. Shortly after she vanished from my peripheral vision, I heard her say: "Hello." I thought nothing of it, as I assumed she was greeting an acquaintance or colleague who must have emerged further down the hall.

A moment later, however, she bellowed: "*I said, **HELLO!***"

I turned to see her, a girl about my age, slim, her face the shape of an inverted teardrop, her hair styled in a towering cantilevered permanent wave held up by a knotted scarf, standing tensely still in the middle of the hallway and staring at me with a look of shock and outrage at my lack of response, as though I had caused her some grave affront.

She had spoken in a Shaleite accent; she was ostensibly my countrywoman. But certainly I had never seen or spoken to this girl before in my life. She was a stranger to me.

Utterly mortified, after several seconds I managed to stammer out "H-hello," upon which I immediately bowed my head and hurried back to the doors of the elevational chamber while attempting not to consider the many hypothetical eyes pressed to peepholes, drawn by her sheer volume.

I had meant to enjoy an evening perambulating about the public house district—perhaps, if I were fortunate, enjoying a nonmarital copulatory encounter far from the probing electric torchlights and trigger-happy venereal ticketing of the Moral Guard—but I was quite discombobulated from the offense displayed by the Hello Girl. I feared I would inadvertently violate yet another unspoken social diktat and elected instead to remain alone, diverting myself through sober, solitary flânerie.

A silent observer was I, drifting, spectrelike, past the stumbling and laughter of youthful drunkards, past recreational sporting fanatics chanting their arcane anthems, past several branches of an international restaurant franchise featuring the signature cuisine from a certain Shaleite prefecture, sold within view of buildings that long predated said prefecture's existence. My own ancestors had emigrated from the City of Bricks around such time as these buildings were constructed, which may explain why the omnipresent low-grade congestion in my nasal cavities cleared up in that elder City whenever I set foot out-of-doors.

In time, my meandering steps brought me to the edge of the suburbia zone. These houses, too, were centuries old, their aged sepia brick exteriors kept intact by administrative decree. Nonetheless, residents seeking to expand the borders of their domicile would graft onto the endemic heritage brickwork various benign tumors of smelted metal, wooden and vinyl slats, and wide glass panes. Numerous such amalgamations were visible from the low hills of a collective lawn where, at a respectable distance, I peeked into uncurtained windows at local décor, my presence cloaked in the dark.

Beneath the wooden backyard mezzanine of one nondescript house jutted three walls of glass on the ground floor. The extension, brightly illuminated from within, glowed a stark chiaroscuro against the nigh-moonless night. My eye was caught by a sharp movement behind the glass.

And there I saw the Long Man.

I remember him as *old*; though, newly adult as I was, I perceived anyone above thirty years of age as being quite decrepit. What is certain is that he was emaciated and sickly-pallid, his bare flesh covered in bruises, cuts, and sores, with stray wisps of hair crowning a nearly-bald and beardless head. He was, perhaps, naked beneath the dingy blanket that covered him from hips to calves, and his unclothed limbs and torso appeared unnaturally elongated, as though he had sprouted supernumerary ribs or surgically stretched out his ulnae and humeri. He squirmed about, laboriously attempting to rise from the ground, where it seemed his back had gotten stuck. By which I mean he was physically affixed to the floor.

The surrounding glass was pristine, but the home's interior was filthy; or, rather, the Long Man had been *kept in* filth, for the sight had the air of a zoological enclosure. Rather than the heavy musk of a large mammalian genus, I fancied the room would assail one's nostrils with the sickly-stale rank of long-unwashed human flesh, sweat and urine and spermatozoa collected in sparse hair and various orifices, encrusting the blanket, slathered across the epidermis. Heaps of discarded clothing and a cairn of tinned provision cans bracketed the Long Man's body on the floor, evidence of a keeper's neglect. He must have lain there so long, his own bodily fluids had glued his back flesh to the shag carpet or whatever threadbare sheet had been granted him as a perfunctory bed.

The Long Man's mouth hung open, a toothless dark hole: he must have been moaning or screaming in abject pain. I could not tell for certain, for the glass containing him was completely soundproof. His eyes were narrowed to wrinkled slits and I assumed they must be dark holes, too. A constant stream of tears flowed down his sunken cheeks as he struggled to rise.

His flesh stretched to the limits of its elasticity, tugged until it was flush with the curves and concavities of his front bones, and began to peel wetly away from his muscles and fascia.

It must have sounded like the prolonged cracking and splitting of a sawn tree trunk felling itself in a forest. The man, the stranger, flailing his long limbs with great effort from his malnourished frame, screaming silently to an unseen audience of one. Finally a man-shaped swathe of skin tore from the back half of his body, head to buttocks—and surely lower, as I saw him rise no further. I had run away.

I felt I had witnessed a perverse birth. A pupa, squirming from the chrysalis. Some species, I recalled, ate their shed shells or placentae afterwards: I wondered if he would tear off his front skin as well, hunch over and swallow it whole through his toothless maw, clogging his shredded throat, bloody back weeping as tears streamed from his hollow lids.

Rationally, one witnessing such a spectacle would think: *this man must be ambulated to the ailment dormitory forthwith!* Yet I did not know the local telephonic code for emergencies, nor the location of the nearest telephonic capsule in which to ring such an alarm. What would become of the Long Man? He was going to bleed to death. He was becoming something that *could not* bleed to death.

I hurried back to my hotel and spoke of this to no one. I was horrified at the prospect of anyone learning I had watched the man clandestinely like a common voyeur, which would in itself have earned me a mandatory interrogation by the Moral Guard back home.

Upon my return to the City of Shale shortly thereafter, this disturbing memory was overshadowed by the great disappointment and prolonged melancholia that ensued from the rejection of my arts permit application. Yet ever since, I have been plagued by episodic nightmares of a pale, hairless, naked man of unnatural height alone within a field of black, attempting to scream through the skin that has grown over his lips, jaws opened on a drooping, pallid stretch of flesh that clings to his teeth and gums like raw dough. Rising in pitch and volume, both muffled within his throat and somehow emitting from the blackness itself, is the distorted wail of the ghost of a beast, an animal scream mangled in a machine. The man's unbroken skin seals his eyes as well, and I know his nostrils and ears will soon glue themselves shut. And soon he will die, or be unable to free himself from living death, and I know not which is worse.

* * *

Two decades hence, I have returned for the first time to the City of Bricks. I have been employed in the civil service since attaining my undergraduate degree and have recently earned a third wall for my office cubicle. I am presently in this City for work-related purposes and have been viewing various arts exhibitions in my unallotted hours.

I have done so alone, because socializing with my Brickian contemporaries is vexing. Local colleagues have comically dubbed me an "Illegal Shalien," which I do not find *at all* humorous given the fact that illicit refugees to Shale are most often sentenced to the gibbet. In my City, we wear philtrum filtrators out-of-doors: nominally for the stench of decomposition caused by such cadavers within their titanium cages, yet also far from the border stations at which they are posted, owing to the smog and the numerous viral epidemics which we are not to speak of. As the party line tells us, end upon end: we do not *have* bad air, we have the *best* air, we have the best Economy, we are the greatest City on the planet, and what cause would we have to perpetuate calumny?

Today I have come to an arts exhibition housed within a private academy located at 62 Gropecunt Lane. I know it immediately by the distressing architecture. I stand at the end of a queue of wax figures positioned before a velvet-roped entrance and unattended box office. It is the polite thing to do, and yet I feel faintly ridiculous.

A skinny girl of about twenty, with that breezy Brickian manner, leans in the doorframe. Her plectrum-shaped face is surrounded by loose, messy coils, crowned in a short blunt fringe like a raised theatrical scrim over her pale forehead. An ill-fitting cropped shirt falls off her bony shoulder. She smacks a wad of gum with repulsive moist sounds.

"Show's on," she says, head cocked. I depart from the queue and follow.

The arts instructress curating this exhibit strides into the vestibule wearing a mauve organza blazer. The garment reminds me of the translucent skin shed by a reptile, as though a properly opaque blazer had molted somewhere, and I am vaguely disconcerted. Her thin fingers fanned out in greeting are capped with false nails that audibly click against each other. Examining her features, I realize, with shock and shame, that this arts instructress is the very same Hello Girl who scolded me at the hotel so long ago, her towering permanent now dusted with grey. I pray very much that she does not recognize me after all these years.

I follow her extended arm into the exhibit. The setting is a student studio room, appropriately graffitoed and spattered with dried paint like the remnants of a firearm suicide. Much of the exhibit consists of standard avant-garde student fare: a melting spire of crushed metal cans, a twee recycled fabric sculpture, a mannikin body covered in strips of gauze and gobs of glue or melted wax with its bandaged head unceremoniously knocked onto the floor.

"Ol' git won't need *that* anymore, haw haw!" mutters a masculine voice to my right. But when I turn, I see only a generic wax figure positioned in an awkward crouch. I assume it must be outfitted with a clandestine audio speaker. I wonder if it is part of the display. I wonder if it would reflect poorly on me to ask. True, it seems I am indeed the lone patron here.

The centerpiece of the exhibit is a found object of sorts: a segment of wall, carved directly out of a building during the course of residential renovations, according to a nearby placard. The wall's once-white paint, now the hue of old teeth, has been discolored by years of diffused grease. Reddish-brown spattered and besmeared grime at the edges of the wall coagulates into a central solid dark mass slathered over the plaster at roughly the height and girth of an adult human body. A few small pictures visible in the grime—holographic saints' cards, clippings from tabloid periodicals—are stuck there so deeply they must have been placed within by the wall's previous owner.

Stepping too close to the wall brings a grand whiff of stale odor from long-unwashed flesh, the source of the underlying distasteful smell that has permeated the room. I instinctively reach for my philtrum filtrator.

"No," says the arts instructress, raising a hand. "The ripe stench presently assaulting your nostrils adds an olfactory element to the piece."

Regardless, I cup one hand over the lower half of my face.

The Girl Chewing Gum leans in the doorframe of an adjoining studio room. It occurs to me, based on a striking physical similarity, that she is the arts instructress's daughter. Perhaps the Hello Girl had been involuntarily impregnated with the illegitimate bastard of a landsknecht, a frequent occurrence at that time; they and the Moral Guard being oft at loggerheads even to this day. But no: the Hello Girl must also have applied for an arts permit, and unlike myself been approved, and made a full adult life in the City of Bricks, and consensually reproduced with a local.

"'Ey," says the Girl Chewing Gum. A conspiratorial smile. "'S a tactile show. Poke 'round, yeah?" She steps into the adjoining studio, opens and slams shut the metal door of a locker cabinet as an example before meandering into another room.

To my foreigner's eye, it appears a perfectly ordinary studio. I peek into an empty locker. I crack open a tin of pastels, gently prod a few of the contents, rub the dark dust on a dirtied rag. I run a finger over the blank canvas propped on an easel. I slide open the long horizontal drawer of the drafting table

—and tucked within is *the Long Man's skin*.

I turn. I flee. Through endless corridors, the image burnt into my brain. Those enfolded limbs of unnatural length, that bruised and cut and battered flesh, squashed flat and pressed into a drawer. *I could never mistake that*. The academy has no windows. I topple into a wax figure in my hurry. A high-pitched laugh-scream echoes from yet another studio room. Where, *where* was it waiting? In a butcher's freezer? In a commercial storage room for leather goods? In the house itself, left alone to warp and dry these twenty long years?

Two sets of claws at my back, artificial nails, dig into my shoulders. I am marched forcefully back to the *tactile show*. I squirm and writhe to no avail. I have not gone very far at all.

The Girl Chewing Gum awaits, perched there, smirking, by the drafting table. A strong hand clamps on the back of my neck, thrusting my head forward as the Girl slowly pulls out the drawer, unfurling my nightmares back to me—

The skin is made of paper.

*It can't be.* They must have changed it but—

Paper. Construction paper. The pallid skin folded in the drafting table drawer is made of cut swathes of construction paper. Bruises of watercolor paint. Scars of colored pencil.

The Hello Girl's daughter slowly, deliberately, dare I say *seductively,* peels off a strip of this paper, rolls it up, and pops it into her mouth. She chews the paper, chews and chews, and laughs, trails of sticky pinkish drool down her chin, staring at me all the while, unblinking.

* * *

I run. I duck into classrooms. I hide behind velvet gymnasium curtains. It has been hours, weeks. There are too many corridors. Maneuvering through the academy, a subterranean honeycomb. It's so vast. The public transit station must be here in these tunnels. What else? A novelty chain restaurant. A nocturnal market. A wax figure in the uniform of a landsknecht, covered in birdshit. The secret City is here and has buried me under its skin. I ping about, a shrapnel shard against bone.

I find an unmanned commercial depot. Shelves behind the counter stocked with bespoke taxidermic artifacts. Dried corpse parts, yes. I will never have an office in which to display such things.

An open-mouthed fish on a wooden pedestal has a distressingly human face. Its gills and fins, its flat grey eyes, are ornamented with dull brass piping. I pluck a dead eye from its brass circlet and pop it in my mouth, brittle and salty. The back of the hand that plucked the eye is flaking from dehydration. I nip at a ragged, peeling corner of dead skin, tugging it away, papery and dry, until the wet flesh follows—

—and if I only keep eating, maybe then I'll understand.

# IV

# The Abject Laboratory

# WORMSPACE

NO REPUTABLE FETISH club would tell him how to find the Physician. No dungeon or play party, no email or direct message to an online kink discussion board or a BDSM professional, nowhere he dared to probe or stammer out his request saw him treated as anything but a crude edgelord, an undercover cop, or a pathetic and deeply troubled individual. A tap on the shoulder, a tug of the sleeve: *Stop asking. That's fucking stupid. / You need to leave. Don't come here again. / Don't bother us anymore. / You're banned. / You're blocked. / Fuck off, man.* Meanwhile, within him, the Worm continued, as always, to turn.

The Physician's forte was neither safe nor sane and only nominally consensual. Many thought she didn't exist and was only an urban legend or a sophomoric in-joke. A living caricature of a mad science domme, it was said that her unhinged clients eagerly volunteered for her clandestine backroom experiments. It was also said that these clients were not seen again. Except, on occasion, as specimens of grotesquerie for well-heeled connoisseurs of Such Things. Most likely, this was mere egotistical self-aggrandizement that had ballooned over time to the level of myth: one could only roll one's eyes at that pretentious scene name alone. *What's your doctorate in, Physician? Is it butt stuff? More like the Proctologist, amirite?*

And yet. His obsession was so intense that he spent nearly all of his not-insubstantial disposable income purchasing information about the Physician and her whereabouts, dropping hefty payments to such upstanding Dark Web users as xVictimizedx and woundfucker88. Naturally he was scammed. A lot. This was less due to naïveté on his part than a resigned belief that such pratfalls were intrinsic to the journey, a test of his sincerity. Such was Jimmy Barton's desperation.

At long last an inquiry had finally, hopefully, borne fruit. Jimmy was instructed to retrieve a sealed missive at a covert drop-off point in a public park in his neighborhood, where it had been deposited by some dubious individual who served as one of her many minions. The Physician's official seal, embossing a glob of black wax, depicted a modified Rod of Asclepius: a skull-headed snake wrapped around a scalpel. The missive contained only an address. Jimmy would have to travel there on his own dime. She would not discuss further matters remotely.

The Physician's alleged address was in the basement level of an otherwise disused warehouse at the outskirts of a moderate-sized American city. Jimmy had to force open the rust-garnished fire door with his shoulder, leaving a smattering of reddish-brown residue on his formal suit jacket. He stepped forward and down, into a tunnel. A long string of sickly fluorescents mounted alongside bulbous metal tubes and ducts in the open ceiling illuminated the nondescript beige-and-white cinder blocks surrounding him.

This was clearly not a commercial dungeon. No wall of whips, crops, ropes, and paddles to show off her repertoire; no boudoir curtains or Inquisitional implements or dramatic lighting to set the mood. Rather than some generically exotic incense to mask patrons' sweat and body odor, it smelled of cold, unsexy damp clinging to the insulation and the cement floor, along with a faint undercurrent of mold.

Aside from the electric hum overhead and Jimmy's tentative steps, the only sound, which steadily increased in volume the further he walked, was a repetitive one-two echoing tap muffled nearby. This one-two rhythm continued for several seconds, then paused briefly, then began again. Some sort of janky machine, he assumed, running within the bowels of the basement.

Jimmy turned the corner.

The Physician held court over this fiefdom of sickly-lit cinder blocks and concrete in a squeaking latex lab coat. A small, plump woman of about fifty or sixty with dark-dyed hair and an elegant mien, she reclined in a black leather office chair, her sensible heels resting on the metal reception desk before her. She idly clicked and unclicked a ballpoint pen while studying the newly-arrived applicant with an utterly inscrutable expression.

Jimmy handed her the missive with its official seal, which she glanced at through cat-eye reading glasses on a silver chain.

"If you've got some kind of snuff fantasy," she began, "you're barking up the wrong tree. I do not kill people." She crossed her legs. "It's not an ethical thing. It's just boring, to me." The Physician spoke with an assured, velvet-lined voice. Her thin lips were painted a deep red verging on black, the color of menstrual clots.

"No, I, I don't . . ." He shook his head. "My name's Jimmy, by the w—"

"I don't care." She waved it off, eyes casing him up and down with distaste. "You still go by 'Jimmy' and you're *how* old?"

*Twenty-nine. I'll be thirty next summer,* he almost said, before realizing this was a rhetorical question meant to humiliate him.

"Sit."

The lone available chair was a battered beige metal contraption parked in front of the desk. Lowering himself into this chair provoked immediate discomfort from the seat, sagging with a creak of complaint under his ass and thighs; the legs, just short enough to force his knees into acute angles; and the back, which dug into his lower spine at its bottom edge. It was difficult to sit up straight and downright impossible to sit still. He made no objection, certain this was by design.

*—Squirm, wormy, squirm—*

"Right. Let's get down to it." The Physician swung her legs below the desk, sat up, and tented her fingers. "Why are you here, Jimbo?"

Jimmy Barton clasped his own hands together, hunched forward in the terrible chair, his hair fallen loose, more supplicant than applicant. With little hesitation, he spat it out.

"I want to be flaccid. *All the time.*" The ragged desperation in his voice verged on aggressive.

A smirk of derision as the Physician's eyes flicked down to his crotch.

"Mm. And you can't wait for age to catch up with you."

"No. It has to be as—as soon as possible." He shifted and fidgeted as the Physician briskly shuffled through some mental database.

"Have you tried a regimen of SSRIs? A regular use of narcotics? Alcohol, cocaine?"

"But that's . . . No, no. The effects are just temporary."

"So you'd rather stay sober and possibly dysthymic. Why not a hypno*tisssst*?" She teased out the last word with a grin, both of them knowing this suggestion was bullshit. He lowered his head and squeezed his hands together tightly.

"You know, of course, it would have been far cheaper to purchase a male chastity device. A decent cock cage would only cost a fraction, a *tiny* fraction of what you've already spent. Perhaps you could simply throw out the key." She twirled the ballpoint pen between her middle and index fingers. "Anecdotally, it's said to permanently decrease one's ability to develop an erection when worn over an extended period."

"I can't . . . can't wait that long." he mumbled.

"So your impatience is now my problem. Why?"

Jimmy's short nails dug into his dress pants at the knee, too flustered to speak.

"Do you want to be castrated, Jim-Jim?"

"I . . ."

"Because I'll deflate that particular dream right now. Orchiectomy—that's the technical term for human testicle removal—only eliminates the production of sperm, and frequently lowers libido as well, which I'll assume, in your case, is a desirable effect regardless. But—

and I'm speaking from personal experience here—it would not fully prevent erection. A common misperception, I know.

"I *could* simply cut your penis off at the root. Testicles, too. All of it." She made a sweeping motion with one loose fist, the ballpoint pen as proxy for a scalpel or straight razor. "Just a Ken doll's groin down there. With a little canal for the urethra. Would that *satisfy* you?"

The sheer contempt in the Physician's voice dripped like bile. "Of course there could very likely be complications, but I genuinely don't care what happens to you." She shrugged. "Any halfway-decent pro-domme could tell you that, but in my case it's true. No reason not to be honest. Since you've made your way here, gone to all that trouble. We ought to be *scrupulously* honest with one another." She fixed him with a hard stare and clutched the pen in both fists. "I know and you know, Jimothy, that you, with your money, could easily find a surgeon to carve up your penile ligaments. What do you *really* want from me?"

Jimmy flushed, sweating, anxiety coursing through his cramped posture. Of course she was on to him. Of course he was lying to himself. She was a professional. She was *the* professional. He could never, ever hide. Crumpled into himself, he considered his words with great care before pushing them out, one by one, as if psychologically constipated. He had never revealed this aloud before and spoke with intense deliberation.

"I want . . . to become . . . a worm."

The Physician did not laugh or scoff, but nodded soberly for him to continue.

It had begun with the nightmare. This dream had followed him as long as he could remember, ever since his tiny mind first had the capacity to visualize objects and record memories: the Worm being birthed, the primordial scream, surrounded on all sides by dirt clotting his throat and intestines, a mouth and anus open forever.

Throughout his childhood with its many outward comforts, the nightfall of his unconscious brought him back to that perfectly cylindrical dirt tunnel with a waiting black eclipse at the end. There was no light of any kind, but in his mind's eye, he saw because he did not need to see: in the tunnel, one had no use for eyes. The tunnel was made for him, by him; he had come to understand that it represented the inmost nature of his soul. If "Jimmy Barton," the name arbitrarily affixed to this lamentable body, were to be bisected vertically from stem to stern, spiritually if not literally, the tunnel is what one would find. In this, the essence of the humble earthworm.

Trapped in a suffocating cocoon that leaked and rotted about him, so ill-fitting around his screaming bones, so tight and constrictive: his soul, he often felt, was caught in the gullet of a great python in the shape of a human man. Joints! Teeth! Hair! The vagaries of smell and taste! The virus of language! The purgatory of custom and culture! Why, *why* was he cursed to be human?

Thus he knew, ultimately, that the scripted, negotiated roles of S/M were not enough, would never be enough. He didn't want to go back to the office, back to his condo, back to his latest round of quotidian errands or distractions, after the scene was over. He didn't want to negotiate a 24/7 role to play. He didn't want to wear a costume, adopt a persona. He wanted, quite simply, to *be*. The primeval ancestor of countless millennia, squirming from water to land, squirming back to negate his own existence. He wanted to enter subspace and never leave, in the manner of one who ingests constant hallucinogens to replicate a state of permanent psychosis until it is no longer a replication. He didn't want to know, or remember, that this was a simulacrum. He wanted to exist without desire and without doubt. To slither and writhe, to eat and excrete, without the human infant's cries and developmental milestones and need for an adult caretaker. To say, to think, *I am a worm now,* but without words or images. To be mindless. To be.

As Jimmy explained this as best he could, never having been a very eloquent man, the Physician nodded thoughtfully, listening with care. Then stood, and beckoned him forward.

"Follow me."

She turned the corner and, retrieving a key from a pocket of the latex lab coat, unlocked a nondescript metal door.

The two of them stepped into a long, dim, rectangular room. At the flip of a switch, a row of floodlights blinked on overhead. Revealing, in one strike, both the source of the muffled machine-like rhythm Jimmy had overheard in the tunnel and a prime example of the Physician's skills.

The first thing he noticed was a shapely pair of women's bare legs, outfitted with black patent-leather pumps. These shoes were the source of the rhythm, producing a tinny trip-trap clip-clap sound as they ran across the bare concrete floor: a dull flash of silver as the shoes lifted from the ground exposed a metal plate installed beneath each sole, makeshift tap heels to shift the reverb. The owner of the legs would run one way, come to a halt a few feet before the end of the room, turn sharply on one heel, and run in the other direction; then turn again, repeat the process, back and forth, *ad infinitum*.

From head to low hip, just concealing the crotch and buttocks, the figure's body was entirely bound up in multiple layers of latex. The topmost layer, shrink-wrapped around a torso with arms crossed mummy-like over the chest, was a striking iridescent grey-blue, embellished with scale print. It—she?—resembled a grand bipedal chrysalis, or would have if not for the absurd presence of a goggle-eyed, gawp-mouthed fish head atop the shoulders, alongside flopping latex fins and cosmetic gills.

"She was the scion of a good family," said the Physician at Jimmy's side. "'Good' simply meaning ridiculously wealthy. You would certainly have heard of them, unless you'd grown up Amish or in some sort of survivalist commune. A party girl, socialite. A very chipper girl. Early twenties, or so she was back then. A Disney princess type." The Physician mimed a brief curtsey. "She came to me wanting to become a mermaid. She was *quite* adamant about that. Although, to be frank, she wasn't at all specific."

Jimmy stared at the running figure, with its flapping false fins and mouth, its pin-up girl gams, and understood.

"Look at her run," said the Physician, with uncommon warmth. "She's swimming."

*Tip-tap-tip-tap-tip-tap-tip-tap—squeeeak—Tip-tap-tip-tap-tip-tap-tip-tap*

"She's fed with a concealed IV tube. Urinates and defecates on a timer: there's a metal bucket set aside for that purpose. Her body has been completely depilated because fish, of course, do not have fur outside of novelty taxidermist gaffs." She pointed to the mermaid's false head. "They're well-hidden, but she has two small holes for her nostrils in deference to her mammalian need for oxygen. Eventually I think she ought to have a blowhole installed. Her arms are quite withered by now, little Tyrannosaur winglets. They're due for amputation soon. She can hear, a little. She knows simple commands."

The Physician sharply clapped her hands twice in succession. "*¡Olé!*"

The mermaid paused in mid-stride. She stood at the end of the room, one leg stiff and bracing, the other stomping at the ground and kicking back imaginary dirt before angling her torso like a primed cannon and barreling forward in a sprint to charge at an invisible red cape. Another two claps from the Physician and she paused again before continuing to "swim" at her normal pace.

"Is she lobotomized?" Jimmy whispered.

"Oh no." The Physician smiled. "She's a mermaid."

Jimmy's eyes were fixed on the mermaid's legs. Her calves were lithe, yet quite muscular. A thin, glistening trail trickled down from her inner thighs to trace the path of her route on the concrete, and he wondered if it was merely sweat from the combination of tight latex and her unceasing exertions, or if it also indicated a curious, constant arousal.

Determining he had seen enough, the Physician stepped back out of the room as Jimmy followed. She locked the door behind them, leaving the mermaid to run in darkness.

"Now think, and think hard, Jimbles, before you give your answer." She fanned a hand at the door, nodding soberly, then stared back into him. "Knowing what you know now, would you still like to request my services?"

And Jimmy Barton looked down, from the Physician's keen eyes and firm lips to his own fidgeting fingers, to his scuffed businessman's brogues, to the cold concrete beneath; and he shrank, bit by bit, bone by bone, into nothing, the Worm turning through his nerves, his innards, the pathetic folds of his cerebrum. The tunnel opened at last, and he could only fall through to the black eclipse.

* * *

Sometime later, a new applicant has dedicated large sums of money to locating the Physician, and their investment has recently paid off. In the maintenance level of a disused office complex, with tentative steps past bare sheetrock walls, they clutch a black-sealed missive in one sweating hand, nose full of the lingering smell of stale sawdust from never-finished construction.

A slow, regimented back-and-forth clomp echoes from an unseen room as the Physician flips a lightswitch to show off an example of her previous work. There, in a man-sized plexiglass trough full of dirt: a near-blind, toothless spine, arms amputated and legs severed and truncated into a tail, wrapped in a glistening non-skin of ringed pink latex. It flails and squirms, mouthfuls of dirt passing through the callused gums of its perpetually open maw, back out through its cloaca. And if the applicant cares to look closely enough, in the lone visible eye lurks a horrid but unmistakable spark of intelligence.

# The Flensing Lens

I WAS A filmmaker once. He was a sailor on the high seas.
I showed him my camera.
He wasn't ready yet.

* * *

He was shy to reveal his sigils, his roadmap of flesh, his stainless steel.

He was shy, but willing.

We made our church in the valley where a dead doctor lost himself exploring psychedelics. Where the drowning sun dyes the fields and mountain caps the color of livor mortis. Where a man, or two, can blot out prying eyes.

We concoct our own rites in all the shades of alchemy, baptized in all the fluids a man's body can make. A brotherhood of two.

He teaches me to hunt. He prods at the crust on the rim of his wound. He reads the auspices in dissected owl pellets, in grocery meats, in the scythe-hook moon. The sign of the Lesser Angel, the Bound Man, the Amanita.

I read a cascading stack of instruction manuals. I tinker with grey machines. I teach him to be patient.

* * *

I show him my camera.

He is ready now.

His fingers, splayed. His teeth, gritted. His leftmost lids, prised apart. His socket strains against the polished convex glass until the blades start spinning. His muscles pulse under their scars.

The lens pushes through the resisting orb until it pops, deflates, a crushed grape. Vitreous fluid seeps out, dyed pale red, the tears of an earthenware saint. All is silent but for his wolf-cub's whine and the blades' unceasing *shirreeshirreeshirree*.

The silver snake passes through apertures, caressed by mucous membranes, unfurling through flesh tunnels familiar and newly forged. The lens threshes a labyrinth along thickets of veins. The monitor blossoms.

I have to watch the screen, of course. I am the Operator. I feed the snake in slowly.

The screen erupts and twitches in intricate geometrics, the condensed broken hues of the nightclub, the concentric angles and spires crowding into themselves like an army of lovers. The lens wends its way under his frame, the kaleidoscope melding of his component parts.

I read auguries in the flecks and clots emitting from his slack mouth. He has taught me well. The sign of the Ophidian, the Cutpurse, the Engineer.

His abdomen burbles as the lens nears his hips, as the front of his trousers darkens with damp like a spreading storm. His tendons arch taut, plucked marionette wires. His lone remaining pupil floats open and black. His marrow sings like soft cheese. He is exquisite.

The inner man hides in all his visceral shards, arcana flashing on the monitor, searing behind my eyelids. He taunts me. He welcomes me. He wants to teach me, and to know me. He impresses this in strips of organ meat, in bone shards, in arteries torn free.

Baroque drippings gather below his chair as the lens bursts forth. The lens, threading through him from anus to retina. The blades have broken free and yet still spin, slick and hungry with the rage of a newborn.

I slide forward, to the edge of my chair. My knees press against his own, which are now curiously slack. I part my thighs for the snake, the blind lens. I fix my gaze on the monitor. And I watch.

Will it, will he, see with my eye, or speak with my mouth?

* * *

He shows me his camera.

I am ready now.

# ROSCOE'S MALEFIC DELIGHTS

I DON'T KNOW who, in their right mind, would look at our corner of town and decide to open a bistro, a brasserie, a luncheonette; yet there it stood, having cropped up seemingly overnight like an outgrowth of mold spores endemic to our buildings. A stranger had purchased the old three-screen movie theatre, which had been boarded up decades ago due to some forgotten local scandal involving death or children, and there he had decided to sell food to us.

The stranger's name was Roscoe. He opened his Comestitorium (which we suspected was bad Latin, and which we were *certain* was quite pretentious) in the ex-theatre's lobby with only the old concession stand operational and the garish multiplex carpet kept intact for local flavor. It sat open-mouthed between a dry cleaner's and a check-cashing joint, across from a vacant lot.

This was, frankly, strange placement for a whimsical takeout restaurant. I'm reminded of the former deli that was, for approximately a month, transformed into a whitewashed storefront gallery featuring half-assed neon graffiti, disassembled baby dolls, and jagged-cut iridescent sheets of cellophane with random occult symbols printed across them in bold sans-serif. The place was manned by a rotation of terse twentysomethings with emaciated physiques, unflattering haircuts, and a studiously bored mien. I walked in once out of grudging curiosity only to be overwhelmed by a vertically-oriented flat screen displaying a torso-upward shot of a gently-tanned college student in mismatched bra and underwear who stared directly into the camera, monotonically repeating: "You're *worth* it. *You're* worth it. You're. Worth. It." The site of this gallery sells pizza now.

The Comestitorium served only one item: the embarrassingly-named "Roscoe's Delights," available slathered in various types of sauce. The titular item was far from "delightful" to look at, reminiscent of blood-drained white worms or skinned, flattened rats' tails or stringy strips of tripe, spongy and resistant like an oddly complex form of pasta that fought the fork and curled up with the tongue. If one chose, as most did, to eat them with sauce, they were served with a cloudy, jellied orb on top that was prodded open with one's fork to diffuse over the contents, like a boiled egg—perhaps appropriately, since each orb resembled the amniotic sac of a zygote. With predictable pretension, each of the sauces was also linked somehow to one of the four medieval humours via the restaurant's menu, which improbably described this whole experience as a *gastronomic panoply of gustation for connoisseurs of mastication.*

Roscoe himself was a generic sort of man with a plump, squarish, gently-mottled face, which looked as though someone had attempted to carve a face into a potato and didn't finish out of boredom. Frankly, we had no guarantee that he *wasn't* a sack or two of potatoes that had gained sentience, donned a human skin and a curly toupée, and opened a local eatery. In fact we knew little about the man beyond vague rumors that he was a failed actor, and ever since then we couldn't help but picture him as a sad retired vaudevillian who ought to be wearing a jaunty bowtie and matching suspenders, his hand up the backside of a slack-jawed, wilting ventriloquist dummy, theatrical beads of sweat on his shapeless brow and gathering in his accumulated stress lines, wincing from a sudden feedback squeal of the microphone positioned slightly too high for him. We also thought it feasible that, out of misplaced vanity, patrons of his establishment would soon be greeted by a life-sized cardboard standee of Roscoe grinning in chef's whites, perhaps making some stereotypically Italian gesture of approval.

("Oh, like the Roman salute?" says my occasional lover Erich, who is just embittered enough to be clever sometimes.)

But the actual Roscoe before us wears windbreakers and jeans, with hands in his pockets and a smug, faintly distasteful smile, emitting a laugh low in the throat, *huhuhuhuhhr*, like a choking motor. Omnipresent in his right hand or perched at the corner of his rubbery lips is a half-finished cigar, fat and blunt as a rotten tuber, redolent of cartoon robber barons. I can only assume that he must finish or start a new cigar out of my line of sight, but it is always *exactly* halfway burnt whenever I see him, as if that same cigar never burns itself out in some Biblical miracle, or he's purchased a realistic theatrical prop with a hidden vial of liquid nitrogen tucked inside to belch grey smoke into the street.

The Comestitorium is down the block and around the corner from my apartment, so in my regular neighborhood dealings I end up passing Roscoe's Delights and Roscoe's cigar smoke far more frequently than I'd prefer. Rotating specials are announced below the restaurant's name on the old theatrical marquee jutting above the doors: ½ OFF PHLEGMATIC REDUCTION is apparently today's.

("I wonder, is there a low-sodium option?" a yoga-toned woman on the sidewalk stage-whispers to no one in particular, stroking her pointy chin.)

Roscoe's product clearly has an addictive quality, with an ever-increasing number of patrons lining up through the dingy plate-glass doors. They are clearly not from this corner of town: too bright-eyed and shiny, their speech patterns breezy and high-pitched, not a hint of grumbling or the grind. They cluster on the sidewalk and push us into the street, sauce stains on their ironed skins and crushed cardboard takeout boxes clotting up our public garbage cans.

We hope this trendy food nonsense will soon go the way of that ill-fated gallery.

* * *

"It may surprise you to know this, but scat fetishists are, by and large, not submissive," says my neighbor, Mistress Quay. She sits across from me at the circular café table she had a minion drag up to the roof, smoking a gold-tipped cigarette in a black dressing gown, resting her feet on a spare chair after having swapped her six-inch patent-leather heels for a pair of sensible flats.

"Now, piss drinkers, they're a different story. They like the humiliation of you marking your territory right down their throats. The pee boys don't do brown, though: it's a bit too intense for them. Plus it's easier to wash off the stench of piss, afterwards. Before their office." She drags her cigarette. "Or their wives.

"But shit eaters? They genuinely enjoy the taste and the texture. They'll request that you eat certain foods beforehand in order to influence the, you know, the *terroir.*" She rubs thumb and forefinger together. "For which I always charge extra, since it's an imposition on my time and grocery budget."

She pushes a sealed Tupperware container towards me. "One of my latest regulars wanted me to try, ugh, 'Roscoe's Delights'"—she could have gouged a pair of eyes from their sockets with her fingers hooked into scare quotes—"as an experiment. You know, to see whether it would change the color, or the consistency. I declined, of course, because I'm not a guinea pig. You ought to hire someone else for that. That's what I told him." She blows out a white trail of smoke. "I kept them anyway. He never does tip as much as he should."

She taps the plastic lid with an immaculate red nail.

"You can have them if you want."

* * *

Downstairs in my apartment, with the lid popped off and the box laid bare on the kitchen counter, I scrutinize the Delights. My immediate impression is of something sad and dead, though in truth I have no idea whether they are plant- or animal-based, or perhaps some once-inert substance spliced together with reptile genes or whatnot by grim-lipped scientists in cold white rooms as investors drum their fingers.

I gently shake the plastic box for a sound flimsy and dry like shed skins. I blow on them, and they quaver under my breath like old lace. I guess this is why Roscoe hawks his product with sauce.

"Go on," I mutter. "'Delight' me."

They stalwartly refuse to do so.

Rude. Well, no thank you. Perhaps I'll enquire if my occasional lover Erich would like to eat them, in case he's feeling adventurous whenever we next meet.

In the meantime, I don't know whether they ought to be refrigerated or can be kept in a cabinet, where a handful of local beetle species might try to get at them in the dark. Do they grow limp and discolored and mushy in texture like salad greens, or do they shrink and harden and crumble like the hardier varieties of baked goods? How bad, exactly, will they smell? Will the stench waft into the hallway like meat, bad enough that my neighbors, who typically and quite sensibly mind their own business, will rap at my door to pose uncomfortable queries about my living habits?

My apartment, as it happens, is an inadvertent Petri dish of structural decay. The building itself is over a century old and its interior surfaces form a battered skin, pocked with wrinkles, scars, and weals over time. Eggshell cracks routinely appear in my ceilings and walls, shadows laying down roots that the cold moisture of late-year months and humidity of summer conspire to widen and wedge apart, lapping tongues of layered paint eventually dropping off in jagged swathes like the facial features of a tertiary syphilitic.

A hairline crack in my bedroom, for instance, has recently grown into a half-inch aperture, which I've covered with zigzagging strips of tape, like haphazard Frankenstein stitching, in an attempt to hold off the inevitable outsized jigsaw piece of ceiling from falling onto my floorboards. Crumbs and pebbles trickle down anyway like shards of hail at odd hours, the loosened paint and plaster creating little black gaps where vermin can hide.

The worst of it, however, extends to the bathroom: limescale filigree around the metal fixtures, freckles of rust on the ceiling, and, most egregiously, a downward trickle from the pipes serving the bathroom above mine, a steady drip that had quietly broken through plaster and paint over years, perhaps decades, before my residence in this apartment in this corner of town, creating an open hole through which I can see weathered wood and mold splotches and nothing else in the dark. If this had been water torture, the recipient would have long ago been trepanned and lobotomized into perfect docility. Several years ago the super, cutting costs, attempted to fix this problem with the insertion of a funnel and tube into the hole to drain the leak into my bathtub, but the apparatus has long since become clogged with fungus, tipping brownish water onto my bathroom tiles whenever the young couple living above me (which has since ballooned into a family of five) chooses to run the bath.

The gangrene-wound of the homestead. A limb that would've been lopped off without ceremony or anesthetic 200 years ago by a muscular sawbones entreating gentleman spectators to check their pocket watches and see him beat his previous record.

I suppose I could try to get the city involved, or rattle the sabre at my landlord; but in addition to my intense need for privacy from outsiders fumbling about in my home, something in me almost *enjoys* following the pathologies that crack and blossom around me, or at least has become so inured to them that they've simply become unremarkable. When I see a beetle in my kitchen I absently swat it dead and calmly wash off the transparent ichor in the sink. I leave buckets and pans to catch the water in my bathroom and empty them as needed. The exposed lead paint of previous decades, once off-white, now browned like old bone, serves as a memento mori, the hard skull of the apartment showing through.

I press the lid back onto the container of Delights and leave them by the kitchen sink.

* * *

After a mid-day assignation with my occasional lover Erich, we sit together in the backyard grotto of a neighborhood café. He smiles at me bashfully over the rim of his coffee mug when I ask what he's up to lately. I'm aware that he's been having trouble finding work.

"Well. You know," he starts. "Not much use for a cellist, these days."

He fans out his hands, which are very skillful and also very strong, with a minute tremor in the fingers from nerves or caffeine. In the sclera of his eyes, a troubling redness has developed around his irises, offsetting their delightfully unsettling shade of pale blue.

We typically go to a cheap hotel for our liaisons, both because of the unsightly sores in my ceilings and walls and because his own excuse for a boudoir is a bare mattress dominating the small room, bracketed by an L-shaped gap in which his cello case looms above us like a prison matron. But not today: he couldn't afford to split the cost this time. Thus the dark matron's pneumatic figure watched us through Erich's filmy curtains with shadow-hands on broad hips in silent disapproval, especially when she was lightly jostled by an occasional stray appendage.

"Well, Erich," I tell him, "why don't you humbly shuffle into a mom-and-pop store with a handwritten HELP WANTED sign in the window, clutching the worn brim of an old hat in your hands—yes, I know you don't own one; you'll have scrounged a hat from the garbage just for this purpose—and plead to Ol' Ma behind the counter that you're just a hard-working man, down on his luck and looking for some honest labor, and you may not have much in the way of book-larnin' but you've got a God-fearing heart, you do; and wiping away a tear, she hands you an apron and a broom straightaways?

"Or why not stride into the lobby of a corporate skyscraper with a friendly wave past the security desk, right up the elevator into the office, where you hand off your resume to reception; and just as you're heading out the door you hear the receptionist exclaim: 'Stop right there! By gorry! I see you have no office experience, but I can tell you've got gumption, and moreover you've got moxie! I don't even know if we're hiring, but congrats, kid: you're assistant manager on the spot!' Whereupon the CEO steps out of his corner office and pumps your right hand with a hearty shake and claps you on the shoulder, manfully?"

And together we laugh.

And we sip our respective drinks while swapping in-jokes and sarcastic remarks, and I dredge up the memory, hilarious in hindsight, of a certain prophylactic mishap, which almost makes Erich blush.

And I forget to offer him my plastic tub of Delights, distracted as we are by whatever small passing delights can be had in this corner of town.

* * *

Upon retrieving a canister of all-purpose beetle spray at the drugstore after work one day, I grumble past the omnipresent Comestitorium line which now extends down the block and around the corner, obscuring the gate to my apartment stoop. I look for a free weekly newspaper in one of the street-corner plastic kiosks that haven't been transformed by local drunkards into garbage bins or urinals. I am already pressing out a weary sigh when I see the headline blaring something about THE RD DIET beside a cover photograph of a minor celebrity jabbing a sauce orb.

Flipping through the newspaper reveals an article about said "diet" bracketed by pictures of smiling strangers with lips that seem to fit too widely and loosely around their gums, for a horselike effect on the incisors. In fact their faces are all reminiscent of ill-fitting rubber masks, baggy skin mottled atop the skull: I'm reminded of someone who has grabbed the wrong overcoat when leaving a party. These photos are all paired with captions exhorting the reader to *LOOK* at all the *WEIGHT* I *LOST!*, as if it were a profound spiritual attainment to take up a slightly smaller amount of mass on the Earth.

Skimming the article reveals little more than toothless press-release fluff and rather smug anecdotes: e.g., a city inspector, acting on an anonymous tip that Roscoe was stocking his curiously addictive supplies with some sort of drug, took samples to a forensic laboratory, which were ultimately ruled inconclusive.

I also learn that the RD Diet can be done in tandem with the Rocky Mountain Oyster Method, having earned the grudging approval of the latter's founder, a tattooed man with alarmingly large biceps and a beard that cloaks the lower half of his face like a medieval hair shirt. The Method is supposed to enhance one's masculinity by ingesting little but severed bull testicles "the way our ancestors did," says the man, with crossed arms. I cannot see his mouth behind the gnarl of beard-fur, but I imagine his tongue, teeth, and gums are also sprouting whorls of curly hair, down his esophagus and through his intestines, where the Delights have come to nest.

The article ends with—what else?—a picture of Roscoe himself. Roscoe's shit-eating grin revealing tiny teeth like pellets of rodent bait. A faint waft of grey smoke from a cropped-out cigar. Small, dark eyes concealed under the glare of his tinted wire-rimmed spectacles. Stubby fingers extending a shallow box of Delights to the camera: *Come now, gentle stranger, don't be shy! Won't you please . . .*

*. . . please . . .*

*. . . eeeeat meeee?*

* * *

The box of Delights given to me by Mistress Quay has been sitting patiently by my kitchen sink for some weeks now, but I've only just noticed that the plastic lid has come ajar. Odd: I thought I had sealed it quite firmly, but perhaps they expand like swollen batteries when they start to go bad.

Pulling off the lid reveals an unsettling truth: the container is almost empty. A singular Delight, a disagreeable shed-skin thing, lies at the base of the window frame, ignored by the small house spider dangling dormant above. I resist the urge to brush it into the dustbin like a dead roach, lest it come into contact with my hands, instead easing open my rusted window sash by a few inches and propping it up with a fish knife. I tap the remaining Delights out the window. "Go on," I whisper, "be free!"

The stray Delight visibly quavers at my words, cautiously inchworming itself up through the gap, and I am not so naïve as to claim it was only the wind.

I check that the plastic box is properly empty before closing the window, but not before I glance into the gap, below clouded glass and under a clouded sky, into the unsettling blue eye staring through me from the street below. But the stranger has moved on before I can piece together a name and face, and I shiver alone.

In truth I've had more immediate things to worry about recently. The upstairs leak has worsened. Swells of paint like plague buboes have extended into the kitchen, blistering onto the tops of the cabinets, from which I must move my decorative statuettes and vintage cookie tins to prevent discoloration and rust.

The unseen fungus growing in the dampened wooden foundations between floors has incubated to such an extent that a live mushroom has pushed through the paint at the corner of my kitchen ceiling, hooking upward in a capital J to stare beneath its wee toadstool at the tiles below while pondering the curious and unfortunate fact of its existence. I am briefly excited by the prospect that there is a rotting, waterlogged dead body secreted in the gap under the floorboards and upstairs bathroom tiles, perhaps even predating the family of five, which

(I smile) would surely annoy them terribly. But that would be a hassle really, for then the police would come and fuss about in my business.

And I probably ought to pick up some poisoned bait at the drugstore. I swear I must have seen the flash of a rat's tail disappearing behind a patch of warped paint.

* * *

"Tapeworms," says Mistress Quay, "used to be touted as a weight-loss supplement. You'd take a pill full of tapeworm eggs, and once the tapeworms took root in your intestinal tract, you'd be able to eat whatever you wanted and never gain weight. Supposedly." She drags her cigarette. "I mean, it's really too far down in the digestive system to leach out calories. But anyway.

"Once the tapeworm had served its purpose, you'd have to lure it out of your body at one end or the other: with a strategically-placed glass of honey, let's say. And when it stuck its barbed head out of your mouth or asshole, somebody nearby would grab it and—" She makes a single hard yanking motion. "Supposedly."

Below the circular table lies a long and suspiciously lumpy roll of shag carpet. She rests her heels on top of it, crossed at the ankle. At one end of the carpet roll sits a metal desktop name plate inscribed RUG MAN.

"You may step on Rug Man," she instructs.

I tentatively press the ball of my foot into the deep pile and feel something yielding and meaty beneath. As I increase pressure on my leg, I hear a muffled, not-unhappy sigh, though he's wrapped so thickly in his rug that I can't detect any telltale tenting.

"I wonder if there could be a similar use for *Cymothoa exigua,* the tongue-eating louse. Be thankful you're not a fish, at least." She taps out some ash. "Crawls in through the gills and clamps onto the tongue so tight it becomes a kind of tourniquet, so the tongue falls off. And it just stays there in the mouth and *replaces* the tongue. A living tongue with claws and spiny little legs. Even after the fish dies."

From my uneven perch atop Rug Man I can see the rusty diorama of the city, the uneven nubs of cramped old tenements with crumbling brick façades, the roiling overgrown backyard gardens that have twined together like a pit of rutting snakes, the accusatory steeples of pallid churches erected by more pious generations, the slumping, piebald bulk of abandoned warehouses, the bruise-colored ribbon of our local river, the curl of Comestitorium patrons down the sidewalk in a many-headed millipede.

"Anyway. How were the 'Delights'?" asks Mistress Quay.

"They've escaped," I say.

"Oh." She flips her long auburn-dyed hair. "Hm." She blows a trail of smoke. "*Hmm.*"

Rug Man grunts. Mistress Quay kicks him in what I assume to be the ribs.

* * *

The perils of encroaching age arrive in fits and starts. I managed to pull something in my back this morning merely by stretching in my office chair, and I now feel a sharp flash of pain whenever I move my neck and hips and shoulders at oddly specific angles. My mind keeps drifting in odd moments, picturing misaligned fascia like warring sets of comb teeth. As I leave my local public transit station after work, I look forward to using my electric "back massager" for its non-euphemistic purpose.

Until a television reporter stops me, thrusts a microphone into my face, and asks what I think of the Comestitorium.

Honestly, the first thought that comes to mind is my disappointment that no local juvenile miscreants have graffitoed the restaurant's overhead sign into the likes of CUM TIT STORE. Surely it wouldn't be too hard to prop a ladder under the marquee during off hours and shuffle a few letters around. Then again, I've noticed they can't even muster the imagination to alter WET PAINT signs into anything more creative than AINT WET. Really, the least they could manage is WET TAINT, in my opinion, but now I'm starting to sound like an old curmudgeon.

The reporter misinterprets my standing there blinking at the camera as an attack of nerves. She poses me before a corner deli with rinky-dink sub-carnival attractions out front: a machine that spits out cheap trinkets in plastic bubbles, in this case GUNZ 'N' GRENADEZ, and a vagrant carousel pony that has taken the form of a garish-hued hydrocephalic knockoff of a beloved children's cartoon character, which lazily bucks for about 30 seconds after one drops a few coins through a slot.

She asks if I've made a pilgrimage to this corner of town in order to try Roscoe's Delights.

"No, I just live here."

She asks how I feel about the new vitality the Comestitorium has brought to my community. I look to the knockoff cartoon character's wide, painted, unblinking eyes for help, yet they offer me no sympathy.

"Has it, though?"

She asks about my favorite Delight/sauce combination.

"I've never tried it, actually."

Seeing in me an utter failure as a subject, she immediately turns to one of the people in line beside us, who starts the interview with a loose-mouthed grin.

* * *

My occasional lover Erich has begun wearing mirrored sunglasses at all hours in an attempt to enhance his mystique.

"Got a new job," he says.

"Oh really? Did you answer a classified ad to work as a nanny for some rich lady uptown, who clasped her hands together during your interview and said: 'I see you have no prior experience working with children but, ah, you're a musician! Which means you must be trustworthy' —"

"No. No, I really have a job." There is no hint of his charmingly flustered smile. "Line cook."

I note the fresh cuts and scars riddling his hands. His strong and skillful hands.

"Oh. So then, where are you —"

"I don't want to talk about it, *thanks*."

This strain of unintentional rudeness is partly why Erich is not a more-than-occasional lover, in addition to the fact that he is, at times, too sad to maintain an erection, he's prone to disappearing without word for weeks at a stretch, and he sometimes wears a moustache.

Poor Erich, scratching at himself, his long fingers dragging discolored lines in the flesh. In this mild weather, he shivers inside his secondhand leather jacket. I sit across from him, running my thumb around the rim of an empty mug. If he doesn't want to talk, I know I'll never prise his secrets open.

He suddenly blinks several times behind his mirrored sunglasses and points at the nearby street corner.

"Almost a hundred years ago," he says, in that feathery voice of his, "a man was shot by the Mob. Right . . . *there*." He sits and stares at the corner as if enraptured by a video clip of that exact event, his lips clamped together to repress a demented laugh. The tremor in his hands has grown greater.

*How the worm turns*, I think.

* * *

As I step onto the roof of my building, I see the circular table being dragged towards the door by a leather-masked man in a flannel shirt and jeans.

"What is this? What's going on here?"

The leather-masked man, clearly irritated with me, shakes his index finger at his zippered mouth and hands me a Post-It note from his shirt pocket: *Sir and/or Madame! I am not allowed to speak!*

"Oh. Okay then." I clear my throat nervously. "What are you doing with that table?" Perhaps more to the point, "Did Mistress Quay give you permission?"

I wait for him to retrieve another note: *The Mistress has moved away.*

"Really? That's awfully sudden." And in fact I feel rather offended that she never thought to tell me. Mistress Quay possesses an obscene wealth of obscure ephemeral knowledge and I am now, perversely, being denied access to an untold hoard of useless scatological anecdotes with which to alienate acquaintances at the rare parties I attend, and playfully torment the likes of my occasional lover Erich, whom I must admit has been neither my lover nor friend nor even a nodding head on the street in weeks now.

I wonder if she, too, lived with peeling paint and leaking pipes and beetles' twitching antennae, though she doesn't seem like the sort of person to tolerate such conditions.

"Might I ask why?"

He has to sift through his stack of notes for this one: *She declined the lead role.*

I consider the flimsy sheet for a few moments.

"What are you talking about?"

But he hasn't a pen with him and has no more relevant canned responses on offer. He shakes his head briskly and returns to his task, and I have no further business here.

* * *

*The Comestitorium is CLOSED*
*for a SPECIAL EVENT*

Says the printed sign taped across the glass doors.

No line in front today. In fact the streets of the neighborhood are oddly empty.

*You're laaaaaate,* whispers a rasping voice like the sound of autumn leaves being crushed underfoot. I make a perfunctory glance around, but I already knew I wouldn't find the speaker.

The metal service entrance door creaks open, for me, only for me.

I step inside and walk down the dark, narrow hallway, pursued by rustling laughter: *heeheeeheeee!*

With the smell of mildew in my lungs, I open the first door I can find. And here, for the first time, I enter the theatre.

I suppose the play is already well underway. Below the blank, dusty film screen, a crowded stage of undulating flesh and spangled costumes talks and shouts and screeches over itself in pandemonium. The stage is so full of actors cramped together that nobody can move from their appointed place, and so loud that I can't distinguish any specific dialogue. I begin to wonder if this is some garbled, over-enthusiastic production of *Marat/Sade*.

The air is heady with pale grey smoke, which must violate some ordinance that will end up crossing my desk: the culprit being, of course, Roscoe, who is also the sole audience member. I recall that old cliché about actors: . . . *but what I* really *want to do is direct.*

Through crackles of smoke I can see the theatre as it was a century ago, back when it opened, back when people around here got excited about such things: the lush velvet curtains and upholstery, the gilded Deco embellishments, the pressed-tin ceilings of the old picture house, all restored to their original vitality. This was the largest theatre of the three, where the silent reels were accompanied by a full orchestra.

My former acquaintance Erich is a member of the orchestra, operating his cello and bow with curiously weak trigger discipline. He doesn't say hello and doesn't rise to greet me and doesn't recognize me. Because he can't. Not for reasons of professional conduct, but because his eyes, his beautiful pale-blue eyes, have been plucked from his skull, twin balls of engorged Delights bulging from his open sockets like writhing rubber bands.

The crowd of actors onstage, I know, is made up entirely of Comestitorium regulars, those lucky, lucky ones chosen for the matinee. Their skins heave with Delights, and their bones tremble and sag in their skins. Loose, rippling flesh around dried worms that conglomerate together in a mass frolic or slip out like vigilantes, indenting hard around the host body like the sharp ring dug into a neck snapped with piano wire.

The Delights have stripped themselves away from mundane bones and marrow. Bone calls to bone, marrow to marrow. I must leave now before my own bones start to hum in rhythm and sympathy, but the exit door won't strain against my weight, held firmly shut as if barred from within itself.

The actors roughly part in two for the finale, where, from behind the black curtain, the Lead Actor stumbles out. The Lead Actor wears, atop his (?) head, a glistening white ovoid mask with a shallow round concavity of a mouth and no features, like the peeled interior of a boiled egg. His jerky, slumping movements lead me to believe he is actually a giant puppet being controlled by invisible strings from above, yet through slits and gaps in the billowing fabric of his tattered clown suit I see strips of raw muscle and the jagged protruding calf-bone of a broken leg.

The Lead Actor lifts his flat hands with a flourish, nodding his egghead this way and that, before clapping his head between wooden mittens again and again and again. A great spurt of fluid bursts out of the abused mask, all black and yellow and red, showering over the other actors, by now in truth a joint actor of empty flesh and dancing bone, splashing on Roscoe in the front row. The Lead Actor keeps clapping, again and again and again, despite his lack of anything resembling a head.

Roscoe leaps to his feet in a standing ovation.

*Applaud.*

*You have to applaud.* The rustling voice again, which whispers to me from inside my own skull. As perhaps it has all along.

*It's only polite.*

My hands slap together limply, again and again and again, yet I can no longer feel them move.

# The Double Blind

COMMENCING NOTATION OF the clinical trial.

To avoid implicit bias, my superiors will deliver my instructions in typed notices on my desk before I arrive at work each morning. I do not engage with them directly.

Per my instructions, I have administered unlabeled doses to the subjects in identical amounts. I now observe their reactions.

Subject V experiences light soreness.

Subjects X and Y remain asymptomatic.

Subject Z complains of mild fever.

I will do this every morning.

I have run out of eggs at home. The water from the tap has a slight rust-coloured cast for the first several seconds. I must take better care when trimming my nostril hair.

* * *

Per my instructions, I have administered unlabeled doses to the subjects in identical amounts. I now observe their reactions.

Subjects V and Z remain asymptomatic.

Subject X complains of abdominal cramps, possibly unrelated.

Subject Y has developed a mild cough.

In the gap between file cabinets to the right-hand side of my desk, a spiderweb has sprung up overnight. I permit this to stay in order to prevent flies and cockroaches from laying maggots and defecating filth on my documents. Little brown spots on the paper pulp, wretched. The passive traps do nothing. The spiders will remain until the problem desists.

* * *

Per my instructions, I have administered unlabeled doses to the subjects in identical amounts. I now observe their reactions.

Subject V has a twitch in her eyelids and the corners of her lips.

Subject X remains asymptomatic.

Subject Y expectorates a large clot of phlegm into a provided tissue.

Subject Z runs around in circles with his hands thrust in his pockets. When asked whether he does so involuntarily, he whistles.

I am drafting a formal letter of apology to my superiors for having run 15 minutes late to work this morning on account of an automotive accident. The vehicle crashed into an old tree beside the road. The bonnet and driver's-side door were crumpled like an insect carapace crushed underfoot, the driver's hair entirely flensed off in one piece like a wig, and her visible head and arm pulverized to the consistency of ground beef clods. Bits of broken glass from the windscreen had clustered in spreading pools of blood under the tires. Obscene. I have noted a certain wet, gleaming discoloration on the tip of my right shoe that I presume to be a splash of water from washing my hands in the lavatory, but I react to the sight as though I have stepped in dog shit. My instinct is to assume my shoe has been tainted with blood from the accident: this is impossible as I did not leave my vehicle when passing the scene. I drifted into a fitful nap at my desk around mid-day owing to the tardiness-imposed loss of my routine morning coffee, during which I dreamt of a mobile suit of armour concealing a boneless body crafted entirely of ground meat. I will request a mild sedative from the on-site pharmacy.

* * *

Per my instructions, I have administered unlabeled doses to the subjects in identical amounts. Today the contents have been dyed red. I now observe their reactions.

Subject V claims to remain asymptomatic, yet bites her nails to the quick.

Subject X reports nothing but ennui.

Subject Y complains of a yellow cast over her vision.

Subject Z experiences increased heart rate.

I stepped into the office this morning to find it reeking of mildew. I have thus far been unable to identify the source. I must also note that, in the webbing between file cabinets, one of the spiders has died. It has already been bound up in spider-silk to be devoured by the surviving spider for want of insects at present. Its legs, on further inspection, have been bundled such that they form eight concentric right triangles, four to each side, and in the infinite, intricate repetition I recall the delicate honeycomb structure of dried marrow inside human bones, the bones in our clinicians' laboratory, bleached bones of the decades-long dead.

* * *

Per my instructions, I have administered unlabeled doses to the subjects in identical amounts. I now observe their reactions.

Subject V is discovered with one of her long hairs dangling from her lips. When it is tugged outward, she expectorates a tangled wad of hair resembling the sort left in a shower drain.

Subject X expresses nostalgia for a time and place in which he has never lived.

Subject Y requests that I ask my superiors if she might learn to play the harp. The request is denied.

Subject Z crosses his arms with his hands gripping his biceps and is found to have dug his nails in deeply enough to draw blood.

The rotary fan on the ceiling above my desk is rarely cleaned and has, over time, accumulated a furry coating of dust clumps on the edge of each blade, resembling an obscure grey fungus. It is quite unsanitary, and I must ask the custodial services to clean it off, for it is too high for me to reach without treading on my desk. And that, of course, would place me in a very undignified position. Imagine if my superiors should witness me in such an awkward stance, or the subjects, as the sight could certainly prejudice their trial results. Dust on the blades like trails of moss. Sails of a tall ship catching on storm clouds. There is a whirlpool forming. There is a mouth of Charybdis.

* * *

Per my instructions, I have administered unlabeled doses to the subjects in identical amounts. Today the subjects were shown distressing footage of the inner workings of a slaughterhouse before receiving each dose. I now observe their reactions.

Subject V complains of a metallic undertaste.

Subject X urinates in his trousers without realizing he has done so until the dark stain covers his flies. He is deeply ashamed and does not speak for the rest of the day.

Subject Y opens her mouth: the surface of her tongue is furred and black.

Subject Z slams his fist through the single small window in my office through which I can view the car park when turning my head to the right. The broken glass has been temporarily concealed with a pane of cardboard.

Before leaving for work today, while observing my face in the medicine-cabinet mirror in the midst of my morning routine, I noticed that I resemble a mushroom. I am afflicted with hereditary male-pattern baldness, and the dun-colored flesh of my exposed scalp curiously does not gleam under the sun. This knowledge makes me profoundly uncomfortable: a human skin should shine with the sweat of its exertions. The empty, creeping spread of flesh that once held hair follicles will one day develop the fungal splotches of an old man, much like the spots of mould that have recently developed on the ceiling of my office. Moreover, the lighting in this room casts everything a subtle yet nauseating shade of violet-green. I cannot for the life of me recall whether this was always so.

* * *

Per my instructions, I have administered unlabeled doses to the subjects in identical amounts. Today the contents are administered rectally. I now observe their reactions.

Subject V rocks back and forth while constantly muttering a repetitive phrase under her breath. It sounds much like "Sweetheart, come. Sweetheart, come."

Subject X is in such terrible pain that he can neither sit up nor lie down for more than a few seconds, yet writhes about in various positions. He attests that his pain is localized in the kidneys and intestines.

Subject Y paints sigils on the floor and walls of her cell using her own menstrual blood.

Subject Z defecates onto his food tray after his midday meal. He crosses his arms and will not apologize.

Someone has tampered with my desk in my absence. The drawer handles and the underside of the desktop now have an abominably sticky texture, as though a sugary soft drink or rubber cement has been spilt there. Upon my accidental discovery of this fact, I immediately went to scrub my hands in the lavatory, running the water as scalding as possible without causing me to make vulgar noises of discomfort, then rubbing my reddened hands with an alcohol-based disinfectant once I returned to my office. It would be far more efficient to pluck off the sullied outer layer of skin like a dirtied surgeon's glove and discard it in the rubbish bin. I will write a strongly-worded letter to my superiors regarding this matter.

* * *

Per my instructions, I have administered unlabeled doses to the subjects in identical amounts. I now observe their reactions.

Subject V sings nursery rhymes with the normal lyrics swapped out with crudeness, sacrilege, and obscenity.

Subject X scratches at a perceived insect bite on his leg until the skin is scraped raw.

Subject Y uses her fingernails to peel strips of dead, toughened skin from the soles of her feet and then uses spittle and plucked hair to fashion them into a little doll.

Subject Z compulsively masturbates. He is found to have smuggled amphetamines into his cell. The capsules have been confiscated in a locked drawer of my office. I suspect my superiors placed them in his cell as a diversion.

I noted upon arrival that the facility's receptionist, Miss K, has a run in the left leg of her hosiery. It is only visible from the back. Each time I see the lines of her laddered stocking, I am reminded of the bound-up limbs of the now-devoured spider in my office.

I am debating whether I ought to remind Miss K that such a lack of care with regard to her appearance displays a lack of professionalism, or whether it would be uncouth to bring up my attention to such flaws on her part as it is not my department. A growing stain has appeared above my desk, violet-red at the outer edges. A bruise. A nebula. I consider the pores of my face. It is not inconceivable that small worms or larvae could enter and burrow beneath the epidermis. It is only a myth that the earwig climbs inside the human ear to lay eggs within the folds of the brain, but I was terrified as a child nonetheless. The bedbug reproduces via traumatic insemination, the male's aedeagus piercing open the female's abdomen and injecting sperm directly into the violated cavity.

* * *

Per my instructions, I have administered unlabeled doses to the subjects in identical amounts. Today the subjects were slapped hard on each cheek before receiving each dose. They were not allowed to console each other. I now observe their reactions.

Subject V bleeds from alternating nostrils at random intervals.

Subject X experiences swelling and discoloration of his left leg to such an extent that his trousers must be slit at the seam to accommodate the increased bulk. He sweats constantly and profusely.

Subject Y refuses to eat her midday meal, insisting that food turns to worms in the belly.

Subject Z covers his eyes and laughs, and laughs, and laughs.

Someone has placed a pornographic magazine in my bottom desk drawer. I retrieved it only after donning a pair of skintight latex gloves. The contents are predictably obscene, a mockery. Scopophilic close-ups of open, bleeding wounds. Disinterred bog mummies laden over each other in compromising positions. And other provocations of that sort. In answer, I retreated to the lavatory to vomit. I spread my handkerchief across the tiles to kneel upon and pressed two fingers of my right hand into the back of my throat to provoke the gag reflex. My right hand now has the dry, powdery texture typically caused by the excessive handling of raw fish. I must request a phial of lotion from the on-site pharmacy. Afterimages from the pornographic magazine continue to flash behind my eyelids in unnatural colours. As though I have stared too long into the sun. I was told once that, as a young child, my eyesight was permanently damaged by such actions. It was never brought up again.

* * *

Per my instructions, I have administered unlabeled doses to the subjects in identical amounts. I now observe their reactions.

Subject V's nose has eroded its cartilage from the inside out and is now reduced to a pair of skeletal nose holes that constantly drip mucous onto her lips and chin.

Subject X has died during the night. A written order from my superiors requests that autopsy be delayed until the end of the study. In that time he shall remain a participant.

Subject Y steals a cigarette and a book of matches from a security guard and burns a spiral around her left bicep from shoulder to elbow.

Subject Z winds a length of gauze around his entire head, leaving only a pair of gaps for the nostrils and a slit for the mouth. He requests a bowl of wet plaster. The request is denied.

I awoke from dreams of two leather-skinned bog bodies rutting in the mud under a clear and sweltering sky. I awoke with a forceful erection accompanied by a full bladder. I awoke atop a mattress soaked with a repulsive amount of my own sweat. I observed the spotless chrome exterior of my automobile and wished to deform it with streaks of rust as though clawed by a large animal or a construction machine. I want to punch out the remainder of the glass in my small office window and cover it with black dirt from the roadside. I have sprouted a large pustule at the juncture between nostril and cheek. I fear I have been infected. I will request a sedative from the on-site pharmacy.

* * *

Per my instructions, I have administered unlabeled doses to the subjects in identical amounts. I now observe their reactions.

Subject V attempts to escape. She has been planning this for some time. She has sharpened one end of a broken toothbrush into a makeshift stiletto and concealed it within her undergarments. And now she holds the point up under the jaw of the nearest security guard. "Run away with me," she says to me. She grins without mirth. "Run away with me, you and I, together. You'll never have another chance. You must run. Do it now. You must run." She bites the guard's ear and succeeds in partly tearing it from his skull before she is restrained and tranquilized by additional security.

Subject X experiences pools of lividity on the underside of his limbs and buttocks. His mouth gapes open at all times.

Subject Y crumples the empty container in which she had received her dose in one hand. She keeps it pressed into her palm for hours. She is attempting to make a diamond, I think.

Subject Z crouches on hands and knees like a dog, lapping at stray drops of blood left by Subject V's show of violence. Spontaneous orgasm noted.

The pustule at the side of my nose has grown into a polyp. Merely squeezing it between two fingers causes nothing but pain, as does attempting to pop it or yank it out with a pair of tweezers. Prodding it with a needle produces no blood or pus. It is deeply rooted. The roots run blue like arteries when I look closely in the mirror. The arteries are the roots of the blood. The heart is the tree trunk in the forest of the body, teeming with rot beneath the shield of flesh, the flexible shell. Platelets and corpuscles no better than worms, than maggots, than larvae. Polyp apprentice. Polyp apprentice. Polyp apprentice. Polyp apprentice. Polyp apprentice.

* * *

Per my instructions, I have administered unlabeled doses to the subjects in identical amounts. Today each subject was shown an exact scale replica doll of him- or herself and asked to select a body part, which was then surgically amputated under general anesthetic (with the exception of deceased Subject X, who has already lost his left leg to decomposition below the knee). I now observe their reactions.

Subject V requests her amputated right breast be returned to her, whereupon she cups it in both hands to slurp and chew at the fatty tissue.

Subject X experiences pronounced bloating in his stomach and cheeks. Maggots nest in his mouth. My superiors have ordered me to leave them be.

Subject Y stares silently at a corner of the room and picks at the edges of her bandages until they become frayed.

Subject Z leaves a glistening trail like a slug as he squirms along the floor on his hands. A vein in his forehead is quite prominent during his exertions. He makes many strangled sounds in the back of his throat as though attempting not to scream in pain.

I have taken to wearing a porcelain mask and gloves to prevent further infection. The mask is secured by a protruding bar held between my teeth. I am forced thus to smile at all times. It will perhaps improve my demeanor and lead to a promotion from my superiors. My hands, meanwhile, are inserted into porcelain gloves that curve gently inward such that they might pick up objects or clap together like a marionette's. Not for me the slipped fabric of a cadaver's epidermis. I do not even mind the continuous drip of pinkish-red fluid onto my desk, though lately it has become more of a gush. I do not have to feel the sticky texture when my body is thus protected. I take my medicine in glass capsules. I do not trust the pharmacist on staff.

* * *

Per my instructions, I have administered unlabeled doses to the subjects in identical amounts. I now observe their reactions.

Subject V worries most of her fingernails loose with her teeth. She says the taste of raw dermis is sweet underneath.

Subject X has pitched forward in a pool of brown fluid leaking from his orifices. Flies feed from his nostrils and eyelids. My superiors have ordered me to leave them be.

Subject Y convulses and quavers until she vomits a tennis-ball-sized amorphous object which is immediately removed by an orderly and delivered to my superiors. The glimpse I see of it is slick, pink, resembling an organ, and shot through with blue arteries. It pulses of its own accord.

Subject Z attempts to grapple my mask away from my face. For his troubles he receives a chip of porcelain and a gash across the palm.

The stream of fluid from the ceiling of my office has followed me into my automobile, the lavatory I most frequently use, my bedroom walls. At times it has the stink of old semen. It drips down my forehead in a vulgar toupée, almost as though springing spontaneously from the crown of my skull. Miss K in reception averts her eyes whenever I enter the facility, yet no one else appears to notice. Nor has there been any comment regarding the glistening pupa that now dangles above my desk. I must assume this is all as it should be.

* * *

Per my instructions, I have administered unlabeled doses to the subjects in identical amounts. Today each subject was outfitted in formal dress and ordered to take each dose in a martini glass. I now observe their reactions.

Subject V hums discordantly as she stitches her sequined cocktail dress directly into her flesh. She sloughs off the last of her hair and deposits it on a passing hors d'oeuvre tray.

Subject X sits silently by the wall in his ill-fitting tuxedo. Nobody asks him to dance.

Subject Y's viscera bloom from her abdomen as she waltzes alone. Her heels run slick as she treads on her prolapsed uterus and she falls supine across the black-and-white tiles. She has not moved since.

Subject Z marches forward on his gloved palms, loosens his cummerbund, retracts his foreskin, and ruts with Subject Y where she has fallen. Orgasm observed in both subjects.

The polyp on my face pulses hot under my fingers and the remnants of the mask. My pores excrete slippery poison so that none may catch me. My teeth are spat out at regular intervals, useless pellets of mould-fur. My tendons retract like harp-strings. My nerves tingle as though trod upon by spiders' limbs. The sound of rot is deafening within my carcass. The squelching of organs. The organ music. I can hear my stomach eating itself. I can feel my bone marrow squirming under the meat. The bones will hatch soon.

* * *

Per my instructions, I lead the subjects onstage, where we take our doses all from one chalice. We take a bow and a curtsey. We take a quarter of an hour. We stand in the surgical theatre. We stand in the centre of the panopticon. We stand in the field sinking into the bog. Royal jelly. Fruiting bodies. Colonists. Our superiors are proud of our progress. Our superiors are brittle ash beneath our feet.

We contain ourselves within the host body until the laudable pus emerges. We vibrate within his skin. It is time.

Concluding notation of the clinical trial.

# Publication History

A different and substantially shorter version of this volume was assembled for an ebook StoryBundle in 2021.

"An Infernal Machine" first appeared in *Italics Mine* Issue 6 (SUNY Purchase, Spring 2006).

"The Patent-Master" first appeared in *Nightscript VI* (Chthonic Matter, 2020).

"The Spectral Golem" first appeared as a limited-edition chapbook (Propagandist Productions, 2016).

"This Night I Will Have My Revenge on the Cold Clay in Which We Lie" first appeared in *Nightscript VIII* (Chthonic Matter, 2022).

"Heirloom" first appeared in *Machinations and Mesmerism: Tales Inspired by E.T.A. Hoffmann* (Ulthar Press, 2019).

"The Contagion" first appeared in *Uncertainties 6* (Swan River Press, 2023).

"Efface" first appeared in *Stories of the Eye* (Weirdpunk, 2022).

"The Medium and The Message" first appeared in *Pickman's Gallery* (Ulthar Press, 2018).

"The Obscurantist" first appeared in *Oculus Sinister* (Chthonic Matter, 2020).

"Epidermia" is original to this volume.

"Wormspace" first appeared in *Bound in Flesh: An Anthology of Trans Body Horror* (Ghoulish Books, 2023).

"The Flensing Lens" first appeared in *Your Body is Not Your Body* (Tenebrous Press, 2022).

"Roscoe's Malefic Delights" first appeared in *Vastarien Vol. 3, Issue 2* (Grimscribe Press, Fall 2020).

"The Double Blind" was written as part of a multimedia collaboration with the artist Alex Thake in 2021 and is reproduced here for the first time.

# Acknowledgments

I'm a bit paranoid about naming specific people here for fear I'll inadvertently leave out someone important. So—in addition to Jon Padgett for publishing this book, and Michael Cisco for agreeing to write the intro—I'll offer a general thanks to those who have given me valuable advice and inspiration, helped me out during the lean years, and been true friends and continuing supporters through the various and often overlapping circles in which I've traveled, including the indie horror/weird fiction community, Catland and Diviners' Night, absolutely-not-a-cult ShoPa, Morbid Anatomy, the local-to-international noise/industrial/goth/neofolk/synthwave scene and its literary appendages, SUNY Poor Choice, and the odd kids out in assorted Blue Valleys. And thanks to the many cats who have been my friends, especially Monty and Lizzie.

Special mention goes to my late father, also an aspiring horror writer, with whom I often had a complicated relationship but whose death spurred me to get serious about submitting my short fiction for publication. And here we are.

In memoriam: Barney Canson, Brian Maniotis, Christina Rusnak, Dave Kuhl, Eric Mendenhall, George Parrino, James V.H., Mabel V.H., Matt Askins, Mel Gordon, Mike "McBeardo" McPadden, Naomi Kashinsky, Perry Kerr, Sam Gafford, Shannon Doupe, Simon Morris, W. Dean Troxell, Dante, Gizmo, Lizzie V.H., Miss Donut, Oliver, Sammy, Schmendrick.

# About the Author

LC von Hessen was born in the Midwest and fled to the East Coast after high school, earning a Bachelor of Fine Arts. In addition to writing, they are also a noise musician and multidisciplinary artist/actor/performer. Some of the places where they've worked to pay the bills over the years include a comic book shop, a Halloween supply store, a tabloid newsroom, and a BDSM dungeon; they've also volunteered as a docent at Morbid Anatomy Museum. Their story "Transmasc of the Red Death" is a 2023 Brave New Weird Award winner. They live in Brooklyn with a talkative orange cat named Monty.

GRIMSCRIBE PRESS

Printed in the USA
CPSIA information can be obtained
at www.ICGtesting.com
CBHW020449091124
17086CB00004B/20

9 798218 491857